# CONFLICT

*The perilous adventures of a young Saxon boy in 1066*

## GRAHAM TEMBY

*Best wishes,*

*Graham Temby*

Graham Temby

*For Harry and Charlotte*

# INTRODUCTION

This novel contains much of the facts of the happenings around the Norman Conquest of England. Many of the characters, places and events are real. There is a good deal of the tale that illustrates Saxon life during this period.

Many of the main characters and their home in 'Brockford' are fictional. However, their lifestyle would be instantly recognised by Saxons of the past who read this book.

The story is narrated by John Aelricson, an old man who recalls the happenings in his youth around the Norman Conquest of 1066.

John's narrative takes us through the rebellion against Earl Tostig Godwinson of Northumbria, brother of Harold.

We then move on to the Battle of Stamford Bridge, when English forces fought and defeated the armies of Harald Hardrada of Norway and the disgraced and exiled Tostig.

From there, John and his father, Aelric, march with Harold to the battle of Hastings in 1066, against William of Normandy.

John finally makes his way home to become the head of the family, and to care for his mother, grandfather, aunt and siblings.

We leave them at the Christmas celebrations of 1066, though, of course, the terror of the Norman Conquest was far from over!

# PART ONE

# CHAPTER ONE

Oh, if only we had known! But in those days, it was unthinkable. It would never happen. It *could* never happen. But the events I will re-count for you *did* happen in my childhood; *and they don't make a happy story!*

Now I am an old and feeble man, and have long hours to sit and think and remember. Sometimes, I cannot remember yesterday, but the events of my childhood are etched deep upon my memory, and will never fade. I wish they would. I would do anything for my mind to forget the horrors of that time. I still dream of that era. I see the broken bodies of men upon the ground in heaps. I see pale heads, drained of blood, impaled upon spikes. I see small children riven in two by swords and axes. I see men with their eye sockets empty, clawing their way, sightlessly, from the killing fields. As I now sit with my robes tight around me, shivering in winter's chill, I often wish that I was beneath the ground, in my cold grave, but the fates conspire to keep me alive; I know not why.

A spring day had dawned bright and warm for the time of year. *A fine day - a fair breeze,* I thought. The winter snow and rains had, at last, begun to release their icy grip from the land. Now there was much work to be done. I had already helped my younger sister to drive the geese to the pasture by the river, where she watched over them whilst threading daisy chains. She was a pretty young thing, I recall, with locks of golden hair cascading over her shoulders. She was always happy in those days, as were we all. At least it always seemed that way, but then we were children and life always seems cheerful when you are young. It is as we grow older, to adults, that life's troubles and tribulations become more apparent to us.

I had then shooed the swine to the woodland on the hillside, where my father and other men from the village were busy cutting wood. My father was a churl, and farmed two hides of land. He was a tall man, with broad shoulders and arms hard as the trunks of the beech trees. He had retained his youthful looks, and his long, fair hair wafted around his face like the corn in a breeze. His bushy moustache wrapped around his upper lip, in Saxon style. His blue eyes seemed to be constantly mirthful. But he was a serious man when it came to a day's work! It was said of him that he could do the work of two men. We rarely went short of food, unless the cruelty of the weather played a part. Yes, all-in-all, they were good days.

Some churls, like my father, were tolerably comfortable, though we all laboured and suffered hard under the crushing taxes imposed upon us by our despised earl, Tostig of Northumbria. Other churls were very poor, but at least they were free men. Below them was a class of slaves; thralls we called them. Their lives were very grueling. (There weren't many left then, as slavery was very much on the decline in our times.) Often, slaves were freed, as they became expensive to keep. They must, after all, be fed and clothed, and many people freed their slaves for reasons of cost, often when they became too old or infirm to be of much use, which I always thought was horribly cruel! To be honest, at this time, most of the thralls were kept by the church. It acted, I suppose, as a protection to the very poorest of our society, and cared for them in their old age and infirmity, which is how it should be.

Some churls held their own land, but many, like my father, leased their land from the thegn (thane). The rent we paid on the land was mostly in kind. My parents, and we children, would work the thegn's land for part of the week, and we must also give him a share of the crops we harvested.

Old Joseph the forester was also there, in the woodland on that day. His hut stood in a woodland edge clearing, where he looked down upon the village. Tom Mouse was there too. Joseph and Tom were cottars. Many cottars were freed slaves, and worked the estates in exchange for a small-holding, often on the wildest and poorest land. The land of Joseph and Tom was on that poor land, on the edge of the woodland and upland, where the trees take over from the scrubland. They often had little to keep their body and soul alive. How their families suffered in the hard times, though we all did our best to help where we could.

I sat there a while, on the edge of the woodland, idly dreaming, and gazing down upon our village, lying undisturbed and serene below me in the morning sun. In my childhood, our little village had always been a peaceful place. The spring sun seemed to be reflected from the damp and glistening straw thatch of the roofs that morning; particularly from the houses that were newly thatched and still bright; and it glinted and glittered from the waters of our river as the ripples broke the surface into a million jewels. Grey smoke rose lazily from the roof vents and thinned and disappeared into the air. My mother and the other women were cooking the day's food – no doubt, pottage.

The village was built on the slopes of the wide, sweeping valley of our river. Its waters slow and languid in summer, but wild and brown with peat after a storm, as it twisted its way through the myriad vales of the Northumbrian hills and down through our own valley to its meeting with the sea on the eastern coast. It was full of trout to be had, with patience. There were fat ducks to be taken too. We caught them in nets, and, as I sat there, deep within my own thoughts, I salivated at the thought of their greasy flesh when my mother spitted them to roast over the fire, or ground down their flesh and made it into sausage or pies; the meat would keep for longer that way.

The old village had first been built on a low mound, a little way from the riverbank, to avoid flooding, and where defence was better. In time, as the kingdom became more stable, the villagers had drifted further down into the valley plain, where the land would provide better crops, so that the people would eat better and live longer.

I often gazed over those hills, brown and green for much of the year, but swathed in purple when the heather was in bloom. I wondered what was over those hilltops. I had never actually been out of our own valley, except to the small village over the hill, behind the woodland, and to our monastery. I had heard stories, of course, of strange lands and glittering cities. My father and grandfather told me tales that they had heard. The monks at the monastery told us more; even about cities like Rome, to which one of the brothers had actually been. I loved listening also, to the tinkers who passed through. They always had wonderful tales to tell, of cities where buildings are made from solid gold — or so they told us. It seemed such a big world, and yet I had seen so little of it. Would I ever see it? Probably not. Few did. If only I had known.

I looked down on each of our houses, which were grouped inside a stout stockade, the better to keep out thieves and wolves! I recall, at that time, when I was but a boy, our house seemed large to me. It was, I think, twenty of my father's paces long by 8 or 9 paces wide. I believe he once told me that it had taken more than sixteen large oak trees to raise it for us. It had to be a large house, as we were many under that roof. I still had two old grandparents living then, along with an aunt; my father's sister. There were also five of us children for my mother and father to feed and clothe. Quite a brood!

Oh, how I remember the fire, laid upon the earth floor, surrounded by large river stones, in the middle of the house, casting its welcome heat on a cold winter's day, and filling the roof with smoke, twisting and turning in its attempts to escape, all the while curing the meat and fish hanging there, to make it fit to eat in the weeks to come. It cast a wonderful light of dancing shapes and shadows on the walls. It was a welcome foil to the cold sneaking in through cracks and under the doors and the shuttered widows.

Rich people used candles for extra light, but they were far too expensive for the rest of us. Instead we made rush lights, which were just rushes dipped in animal fat. Oh, how I remember the long winter nights, huddled around that fire, listening to the stories of old, told by my grandfather. He told such wonderful tales of times gone by. Some recounted our history, and others of legends and sagas. How many were true and how many grew with the telling I never knew, but I listened in raptures to his tales. By the time I was well-grown, I knew what followed each element and could recite them as I now tell you this tale.

I remember, too, the industry of my mother and aunt on those long nights. Spinning and weaving the yarn for our clothing, whilst they also listened to the tales with such attention that you would think they had never heard them before.

Behind our houses stood the folds for our sheep, byres for the cows, sties for the pigs, huts for the chickens, and granaries where my parents stored the season's corn, hoping and praying that it would see us through another year till the next harvest. There were the village workshops for making pots, ironwork, and weaving baskets, and huts for the storage of the equipment we needed to live our lives.

By the river was the mill. Its great wheel gently turned by a small stream, diverted off from the main river's flow by a short palisade of logs and earth. Here, Peter the miller ground our corn to make the meal for my mother to bake flatbread over the fire. Oh, how good that smelled, and how good it tasted when still warm! I will never forget my mother's bread.

Outside our village I gazed over our fields as the wind rippled the first spring growth of grass. It was here, not far from our stockade, that Cerdic, the thegn, lived in his own compound. Cerdic owned ten hides of lands near our village and a further five hides at the village over the hill. He also held two hides near to the monastery, along the banks of the river, as was fitting to his status. He was not the richest man in Northumbria, but nor was he the poorest. His hall was a much bigger home than ours. It needed to be to hold his household and his family. It had a kitchen and places for work and crafts. It was defended by a bank and ditch. In the bank was a gate with a bell. At the side stood our church; the only stone building in the village, and of which we were very proud. Our thegn was a kindly man, who was never more happy than when hunting the beasts of the countryside with his followers. Kind he was, and I oft' recall him giving gifts of extra food to the men of the village for good work done. All in all, life was hard and simple, but we fared bearably well.

The land was beginning to dry now, and to warm in the sun. Work would begin soon in those fields, to plough and harrow the land and plant this year's crops of oats and barley.

But now I am rambling, so I will continue my terrible tale. After a while of staring down upon my home, I dragged my mind back to the present, rose to my feet, and entered the woodland to see that the swine were safe and well, and how my father was faring with his wood cutting. I always loved the woodland. I loved listening to the sounds of the whispering forest, as the wind carried the secrets of the magical woodland folk through the trees. Now the buds were breaking and the trees were beginning to be clothed in a cloak of brightest, palest green; a sign of renewal and re-growth. I gathered a bundle of firewood as I weaved my way in and out of the trees – I had wasted enough time in dreaming that morning already! In a clearing, the men were seated on a large log of oak, taking a short rest from their labour. They drank ale from clay pots, and chatted amongst themselves of the work to be done, now that the year had turned. The oxen stood patiently; ready to haul the timber out of the forest and down the hill, into the village. A light steam seemed to rise like smoke in the cool air, from their sweating flanks. I joined the men on their seat and my father passed me the jug of ale. I drank gratefully of its sweet liquor and listened as they chatted.

In the trees, I pricked up my ears to the warbling of a robin. Have you heard it? It is a highly-pitched warble that moves slowly and then faster and then slowly again. It has a sharp, ringing tone to it. I always felt that it sounded a little sad and wistful. Its warning note is always a sharp 'tic', a little like the distant fall of the smith's hammer on his anvil. And then there is the thin 'tsee, tsee, tsee' sound they often make. But it was just one of many spring birdsongs that could be heard tinkling through the trees, for anyone with ears to hear.

"The plum and apple trees must be pruned soon – the buds already begin to open on the trees," Joseph said. He was wrapped in a ragged old cloak, and his woolen breeches and shirt had been mended so often that there was almost more mend than shirt.

My father nodded his agreement. "If we are to have good fruits in the autumn, we must be canny about how we prune. Sharpen your knives well, and cut off the shoots so that the tree does not grow too quickly, but makes its fruit buds instead."

Suddenly, a piercing shriek burst upon the air and we were all jolted from our thoughts. My father dropped the jug of ale, spilling its sweet contents to soak away into the decomposing leaves upon the floor, leapt to his feet and ran instinctively toward the river-meadow where my sister was tending the geese. We all followed in his wake, but could never hope to keep pace with him.

Upon emerging from the wood and onto the meadow, we could see the cause of my sister's shrieks. A great wolf was standing, staring at the geese, licking his lips, spittle drooling from his jaws, considering whether the young goose-girl standing like a statue before him was of any threat to him. His back was arched in preparation for action. His ears erect and head lowered. There was no doubt in my mind that he was preparing for an attack. My sister stood, silent and transfixed, the blood drained from her cheeks, her eyes never straying from the large and powerful predator before her. My skin crawled at the sight. My stomach seemed to leap into my mouth.

My father had burst from the woodland and now hared across the field towards the stand-off. The wolf had not seen him at this point and was still standing with rapt attention on our geese. It looked from geese to girl and from girl to geese. Slowly, hackles rising, it stalked forward, stiff-legged, towards my sister and the birds. It knew now that my sister was no threat, and it could take whatever it liked – geese or girl. Its head was lowered in concentration. A few steps and then stop. A few more. Stop. My sister stood statue-still, her own eyes locked upon the great, grey beast. It began to lope towards her. She shrieked again! The geese, at first still, staring and alert to the danger, now fled in all directions - they could not fly to safety with their wings clipped. And then my father shouted.

As if awoken from a dream, the wolf was suddenly aware of the rapidly approaching presence of a large churl. It leapt into the air and turned to face him. Indecision was apparent on its face. Fight or flight? What was it to be?

At first, I thought that it had favoured fight as its hackles rose again and it crouched to leap. What would my father do? To risk serious injury so early in the year, when so much needed to be done, could be disastrous in the extreme, but no man alive would fail to defend his young daughter and his geese from the deadly marauder. Time appeared to stand almost still and it seemed to me, in my own mind, that my father moved in a strange, slowed pace as he continued to bear down upon the animal.

In another heartbeat, the wolf turned and made a dash for the forest. Discretion being the better part of valor! My father's steps still didn't slow until he had swept up my sister into his great arms and held her close to him. An expression of relief flooded his face. My sister whimpered, more in relief than in fear now. Joseph, Tom and I diverted our paths, and ran to round up the birds from their scattered flight, whilst the wolf disappeared, tail between his legs, back into the cover of the woodland.

"John, stay with the geese," my father said, "whilst I take your sister back to the village. She has seen enough for one day." I nodded assent, but wondered what I would do, should the wolf and his pack return. I had not thought to bring my horn with me, to alert the villagers to danger.

Joseph, having seen my uncertainty, spoke. "Tom and I will be in the near forest, should you need aid," he said, quietly. I smiled back at him and nodded my gratitude.

"All will be well," added Tom Mouse, as they tramped back to continue their day's work. I watched as my father and sister made their way to the village, and Joseph and Tom disappeared into the forest. I must turn my attention to the geese now. The swine would need to care for themselves for the time being. Our boar would be a good match for a lone wolf.

# CHAPTER TWO

In the evening, the family gathered around the fire. Rush lights were lit and my mother served up our meal of a vegetable pottage stew. I ate it ravenously, as I usually did. Growing boys can never be filled! I recall my mother frowning at me as I ate, and my conscious efforts to slow my gobbling. She always said that the food would do me more good if I ate it slowly, and she was probably right. After the meal was done, we sat, drinking weak ale around the blaze. The women were spinning and my father sat, staring, seemingly lost in thought. Was he reproaching himself for leaving my sister alone with the geese? Was he imagining what might have been?

My grandfather broke the silence. "Should I tell you a tale?" he asked, of nobody in particular.

"Yes, please, Ealda Faeder, (grandfather)," we children said. We always enjoyed his tales, no matter how many times we heard them.

"Then I will tell you of the 'Saint who hated women'," he replied. My mother glanced across at him and frowned. She obviously knew the story, and disapproved. My grandfather began: "Well now, old St Cuthbert was well known in his time for a love of the birds and beasts, but a woeful dislike for women. I have heard, from my father and his father before him, that this came about in his time as a hermit, living in the hills of Northumbria.

It seems the daughter of a Pictish king became with child, and blamed Cuthbert as its sire." My mother glanced across at him again with a frown, but my grandfather continued: "Well, he was appalled at the thought of it, and prayed to God to prove his innocence in the matter. So, the ground, it opened up and swallowed the princess into its depths." We all gasped. "Now the king, anxious about his daughter, forgave Cuthbert and begged his mercy to bring back the girl.

"Cuthbert, he agreed, on the condition that no woman should ever approach him again. So the old king laid down a decree that no woman should enter any churches of Cuthbert.

"Now, Cuthbert became the Holy Bishop of Lindis-farne, up on the Northumbrian coast. Twice a day, the tide do ebb, and that leaves a land bridge to the mainland. People say that this was given by Cuthbert to the people, to allow them to reach his church at the Priory on Sundays, without getting their feet wet." *Just the men, or the women too? I thought he didn't like women,* I mused, but I let it go.

"When Cuthbert died, the monks moved his body, for fear of the Norsemen. When they looked into the coffin, the saint was as fresh as they day they laid him in it! A miracle, they say! And that's the story, so I've always believed."

We sat there, around the fire, watching the smoke curling up to the roof like wraiths, considering his words. Could the ground really open up and swallow a girl, and then give her back? Could a man be dead and not decay? It was beyond my mind to get a grip of it. I had never actually seen a dead man at that point! But I had once promised myself that someday I would be a great warrior! *More likely in my dreams*, I thought.

My father broke the silence that followed. "The fresh grass is springing well. It is time for the sheep and cows to be turned out. Some of our cows are skin and bone, so they can hardly totter out of the byres. And we have almost run out of winter feed for them now. They are eating holly. They must go out tomorrow. The grass is juicy and young. They shall soon grow fat again."

I knew that I would be helping with the cows, and the following day, after a night of dreaming about the earth opening and swallowing me, and dead men, I arose early to get to my work.

We went out into the compound and I blew my horn and called to the beasts. The cows came swaying out of the byres and made their way to the gate. They knew the time had come for them to go back to the fields. I would stay with them on the common land through the day to guard against the reappearance of the wolf and his pack. Not a thought I relished! But should they return, this time I could blow my horn and I knew that help would be swift to come from the fields. And we did have the village bull with us as some defence. Oh, he was a cunning old beast! And he could be wicked with his horns! But I usually could handle him, unless the flies irritated him, and then we must all take care to avoid his temper. I have seen him chase villagers across the common land, and tree them in the forest edge! Ho, ho, he was a demon at times!

Of course, I knew that I must have the cattle all safely back to the village before the sun went down, otherwise I would be scolded by my father for putting them at risk.

Old Brother Samuel, the shepherd, already had his

sheep up on the common land that day. Old Samuel was a monk in the monastery near to our village, and they used part of the common land for their animals. I loved old Sam, as we called him. He was a wise old bird, and often told us the stories of our religion. He would make us whistle-pipes from reeds and teach us to play tunes on them.

As the morning passed and the beasts grazed, we moved closer to one another along the line of the common, until we could both meet without leaving our charges too far behind us. Sam greeted me in his usual way. "God's peace be with you, John," he said.

"And also with you, Brother Samuel," I replied. "Is all well?"

"Aye, all is well with the brothers," he replied, "but we have other news, from the Reeve. I will come to the village tonight, to Cerdic's hall, with more of my senior brothers, whilst Brother Matthew is bringing in the sheep, to speak with the men." I knew better than to press him further.

As the afternoon wore on, I wondered more and more what the news from the Reeve might be. It must be of great importance if the senior brothers were to bring the news and talk to the men at the thegn's house. When the sun began to drift downward in the sky, toward the line of trees on the hill, I quickly led the cattle back from the common to their byre. They were not at all pleased to be leaving the grazing, but the thought of a warm byre and a milking for those who had already calved was enough to persuade them to follow me. Upon our arrival, I left the cattle in the care of my mother, aunt and sisters, who would quickly produce a good supply of milk for us, and went to find my father.

I found him deep in conversation with Benjamin the Smith. "Father," I called, as I neared, "I have news from Brother Samuel."

The two men turned. I could see a look of seriousness across their faces, where more usually, a smile would be found. "We know of the meeting," my father replied. "It is to be at Cerdic's hall, after sunset."

I was a little deflated. I had hoped to the first bearer of the news, as news didn't come often. "What is it to be about, Father?" I questioned.

"We know no detail," my father replied, "though it is certain to be important news."

After we had eaten our meal of pottage stew and fresh bread, all the men – and I was proud to be included amongst them for the first time – made their way to the home of Cerdic the thegn. We crowded into his hall, alongside his own followers and servants. I looked around me at the great hall. It was so much bigger and better appointed than ours, with a long table at one end and lesser tables and benches around the sides. Along the walls, hung the shields and weapons of Cerdic and his men. Some even had swords with which to fight, whilst most ordinary men relied upon spears and axes. I was always impressed by Cerdic's hall. The only finer place I had seen was the monastery along the valley.

At the top table, sat Cerdic, finishing a meal with a good sheep's cheese and bread. He was a slight man, but deceptively powerful, with greying hair and a full beard. His eyes were strong, but not unkind. His grey hair hung down across his shoulders, and his beard was neatly clipped. He was dressed, as ever, in a fine woolen shirt, with a leather waistcoat over. His woolen trousers were tucked into high boots.

We all assembled in the middle of the hall, between the aisles of tables. I tried to get close to the crackling log fire which was aflame in the very centre. The huddle crowded behind us, until the hall was almost half full. The men muttered amongst themselves.

After a short while, the door opened and three monks entered. I could see Brother Mark, Brother Daniel and, of course, Brother Samuel. The mutter of conversation became quiet as the monks made their way to the top table. Cerdic greeted his guests, and servants poured pots of mead to quench their thirst. A quiet conversation ensued between monks and thegn, but none of us could ascertain what was being said. At length, Cerdic the thegn arose from his seat and addressed us. The hall fell silent.

"Good and free men of Brockford," he began. "Our brothers from the monastery are here to address us on the situation in our kingdom. There is much news, and I pray thee listen to these messengers of the Reeve."

Cerdic resumed his seat and Brother Mark rose. "My sons," he began. "May God's goodness be upon you."

"And also upon you," we chorused.

"I am come to bring you news, which we have received from the messenger of the Reeve. You will know well enough of the disturbance in our lands over the past years."

"In the year of our Lord, 1063, Earl Harold Godwinson went to Rhyddian, the land of Griffin. There he burned Griffin's ships and all rigging, and put his army to flight. From there, he travelled about Wales, where a truce was called with the people there. But Tostig Godwinson, his brother, advanced with an army, over land, and he plundered the country."

A groan went up from the men at the name of Tostig. He had always been little liked in these parts, despite being Earl of Northumbria at that time. *Is this to be boring?* I asked myself.

Brother Mark continued, as the hubbub died down. "But, in the harvest months of that year, King Griffin was

slain by his own men, because of the war he had waged
with Harold. His head was brought to Harold, who sent it
forthwith to King Edward. At this, King Edward entrusted
that land to his two brothers, Blethgent and Rigwatle, after
they swore oaths to be faithful to him, and to the earl.
*Imagine receiving a man's head!* I couldn't.

The men all nodded, as they had heard this news
before. But what was to come?

"In the Lord's year of 1065, before Lammas, Earl Harold
ordered his men to build at Portskeweth in Wales. He had
thought to bring King Edward there, for the hunting. But
all was not to go well. When it was all but ready, came
Caradoc, the son of Griffin, whose head had been taken,
with all of the men he could find. They slew almost every
man and boy who was building there; and they seized the
materials stored nearby. This was done on the mass-day of
St. Bartholomew, and why this wickedness, we do not know,
except in revenge."

There were further gasps and murmurs from the men in
the hall at this news. We knew nothing of this.

"We now hear of rebellion," broke in Cerdic. "There is
much talk of growing dissatisfaction and unrest across our
own region. It seems that many thegns talk of uprising
against Tostig. We are told that they are to meet in York, in
the autumn, when the crops are in, with the aim to banish
Tostig from our lands. What think you of that?" *Rebellion!
What would this mean for us?* I thought.

A disquiet grew within the crowd, and heartbeats quick-
ened at the news. Could it be true? A revolt? What did the
men of our village think to that? I was too young, perhaps,
to have much of an opinion, and looked to my father for
guidance in such matters.

After much mutter and chatter amongst the assembled
throng, Cerdic banged on his table with the knife, with

which he had eaten. "The gossip of women is of no use. We
need to discuss what we think and what we should do."

Gather round, and let me tell you a little of Tostig, as I
know it:

Now Tostig was but the third son of Earl Godwin. His
mother was Gytha, daughter of Thorgils Sprakaleg. In the
year 1051, he had married Judith, the daughter of Count
Baldwin IV of Flanders, half-sister of Baldwin V of Flanders. She was the aunt of Matilda of Flanders, who married
William of Normandy. He was, in 1051, banished from
England, returning by force in 1052. Three years later, he
became our earl, upon the death of Earl Siward.

And what an earl he was to become! Lord knows! Could
we have wished for a worse?

The blessed saviour knows, he was never a good earl to
us, and only governed here with great difficulty. He never
was popular with the ruling classes either. He was heavy-
handed, it is said, by any who stood against him, or dared
question him. Men said that he himself had murdered
several members of our leading families. Indeed, it is said
that some little while ago, he had ordered the killing of
Gamal, son of Orm, and Ulf, son of Dolfin, even though he
had granted them safe passage to visit him. Oh, how he
oppressed our people under his heavy yoke!

Benjamin the Smith was first to rise. "I say that it is a good
thing," he pronounced. "I say that we join this rebellion,
and drive Earl Tostig back to Wessex!" A great murmuring
arose again from the crowd. One or two men looked unsure

and concerned by the magnitude of what was being said. *Could my father be a part of this rebellion?*

My father rose to his feet. "I will speak," he called, and the hall became quiet again. My father was well respected by the men of the village, and its surroundings and all would listen to his viewpoint.

"Earl Tostig has never been a good and considerate earl to his people of Northumbria. We have never fared well under his rule. He has never been strong in resisting the raids of the Scots – he is too gracious to their king." Further stirrings and mutterings from the crowd. "He has turned to his mercenary housecarls to defend the region, and to make war in Wales which has cost us all dearly in taxes. Tostig is not one of us. He is a West Saxon. I too say we join this rebellion, and be rid of him!" *My question is answered. My father will go to join in the rebellion. What will this mean for us, his family? How will we cope?*

A lusty cry went up from the assembled throng. "Aye, let us be rid of him." Though some, I remember, looked worried. One such was Anders, a boy some years older than myself. *I understand his worry,* I thought, *for he must go if the men go. What will he see? What will he do? Will he return?* Though I had not thought him a coward...

Cerdic hammered once again on his table. "I see how it is," he said. "I needed to know that my people would support any action I took, and I am satisfied that it is so. I will provide any man who will go with me with a 'heriot' of war-gear. With help from 'friends', I shall provide a leather-helm – (a helmet of leather.) Each man will also receive a spear and a shield. Many of you will also have axes that can be used. Swords and mail, I cannot provide."

A roar went up. "To York!"

All men took their leave, save for Cerdic's own men, and we made our way back to the village. "I fear to tell your mother the news, John," my father said, as we approached our home.

"But you will still go, father?" I said.

"No, John, *We* will go," he replied.

"I am to go, father?" I asked, astonished by the idea. *How will Mother take this?*

"My son, you are becoming a man now, and you must begin to take on a man's responsibilities. You will be able to help ... we may need all the help we can get," he added, quietly. My chest swelled with pride! I was to go with the men, the warriors! I was already a warrior in my own mind, before we reached the stockade!

But I reflected on my thoughts concerning Anders now! Was I a coward? Would I go when the time came? What would I see ...? Would I return?

We entered our home, and my mother looked up from her work. I could see by the look in her eyes that she had been worrying about what was to be said. My aunt and grandfather also raised their heads to greet us. "What news?" asked my mother, softly, the tone of her voice making it clear that she dreaded to hear it.

"We go with Cerdic, to York," my father told her. "There is to be an up-rising against Tostig and his men."

My mother dropped her work and stared at us. "But why must *you* go, Aelric?" she questioned, though she knew the answer.

"We must go," my father replied. "We cannot cower in our village like mice, when other men go to do our work. What would any man say about us?" He paused, unwilling to say what must be said next. "And John will come with us," he said.

My mother leapt to her feet. "No!" she cried. "I will not have my son go too."

"Maude, our son is becoming a man. He must take his

place with the men. He will be of help to us, and I will ensure that he is kept from danger," he said, soothingly.

Tears sprang from my mother's eyes and she sank to her knees. She knew that my father was decided, and that there was nothing she could say that would make it otherwise. My father turned to my grandfather and aunt. "We will not leave until the autumn, when most of the work on the hides will be done. We will all work hard until then. After that, the work of the land must fall to you," he said. "I will entrust the farming into your care." My grandfather was old now, but I could see his pride in his son, and also in himself, that my father would assign the care our land to him. My elderly grandmother, no longer in good health, simply stared at us. I was unsure as to whether she fully understood the implications of what had just happened.

My aunt now stood from her task. "It is not my place to say it, but go with my blessing, Aelric," she said. "We will work twice as hard to ensure that the hides are farmed and in good stead when you return." She glanced across at my mother, and then averted her eyes again to her work.

And so it was that I was to go with my father, the thegn and other men who could be spared from the village, to York, to rebel against Tostig and his lackeys. I was a warrior. There was little sleep for me that night!

# CHAPTER THREE

Now, as our story progresses, and so that you understand what happens afterward, I must tell you of other happenings in our land. This part of the tale concerns a great man. His name was Harold Godwinson. You have already heard the name.

Harold was the son of Godwin, as his name indicates. Godwin was the powerful Earl of Wessex. Harold's mother was Danish. Her name was Gytha Thorkelsdóttir, and her brother Ulf Jarl was the son-in-law of King Sweyn I of Denmark. His son was to become King Sweyn II of Denmark. A powerful family, you will think, and you would be right!

Godwin and Gytha had further offspring. Harold had brothers: Sweyn, Tostig, our hated earl, Gyrth and Leofwine, and also a sister, Edith of Wessex. Edith became the Queen Consort of England by her marriage to Edward the Confessor. Now, how much more powerful?

As a result of his sister's marriage to King Edward, Harold, Godwin's second son, became the Earl of East Anglia in the year of our Lord 1045, I think it was. But

Godwin's plans for the family dynasty were not to happen as he had planned. He had hoped that Edith would bear a son, who would become king after Edward, but it was not to be so. Oh, how Edith tried to win over her husband, with all the wiles a woman can use. But Edward had taken a religious vow of celibacy and it soon became clear to all that the pair would not produce the longed-for heir to the throne, and the station in life that Godwin had schemed for his family. One must wonder why the old king married at all!

But for a moment, we must turn our attention to Harold's brother, Sweyn. Now Sweyn was a man who 'desired female company', shall we say. But one night, his world collapsed around him, due to his urges in that direction.

Sweyn was seated in his hall, enjoying the last morsels of a fine repast, when there was noise and confusion in the courtyard. Sweyn's men looked from one to another and one of his housecarls arose to investigate. At that very moment, there came shouting and the doors burst open with a clatter, and a group of housecarls of the king entered, roughly pushing aside Sweyn's men-at-arms. It was obvious to all in the hall that their mission was not a friendly one, and Sweyn's housecarls rose as one and drew their weapons. Both sides eyed each other warily, and some of Sweyn's men advanced upon the intruders. But Sweyn held up a hand. "Let us hear the purpose of this intrusion, before we resort to arms," he commanded, and the housecarls reluctantly sheathed their weapons, but, nonetheless, held the hilts of their swords tightly.

"My Lord Sweyn," began the senior of the intruding housecarls, the King demands that you attend him."

"To what purpose?" Sweyn replied, eyeing the men before him guardedly. *What had the king to do with him? What was afoot?* "Though, of course, should the king have need of me, I will gladly obey."

"You are charged with a grievous offence, my Lord," the housecarl told him.

"Am I permitted to know what that offence might be?" Sweyn replied. His men muttered and looked to their master.

"I cannot say," the housecarl said. All the time, Sweyn's housecarls eyed the others warily, and looked from one to another for guidance as to what they might do.

Sweyn thought for a moment. He must get word to Harold of this state of affairs. But he could not defy a command of the king. He turned to one of his faithful retainers. "Go to Harold, quickly," he ordered. "Tell him what happens here." Then he turned back his attention to the king's housecarls. "I will, of course accompany you, to lay my defence for whatever I have done to the king. I am not aware of any offence I or any of my men have committed."

The housecarl nodded and turned to leave. Sweyn grabbed his cloak, fastened it around himself with a great brooch, and followed him, attended by a cluster of his own men.

"You will need no men-at-arms, my Lord," said the housecarl. "Your safety is guaranteed."

Sweyn turned to his men and nodded. "Prepare for my return," he said, airily, "I am sure this misunderstanding will be resolved soon." But the look he gave to his men left them in no doubt that they should prepare for trouble.

Sweyn travelled the distance to the king's hall, where he was greeted with an icy coldness by those at court. The doors to the king's chamber opened and he was announced, as he entered his heart sank. In the corner, seated with another holy woman was the Abbess of Leominister. Sweyn now began to understand what had raised the ire of the king. He bowed low to the monarch. Edward regarded him for a moment, and then addressed him in front of the assembled court.

"You know the Abbess of Leominster?" Edward asked, though, of course, he knew the answer. *No 'Lord Sweyn'*, the nobleman noticed.

Sweyn raised himself to his full height, not wanting to show anything but a confident side to the assembled throng. "I know the holy lady," he replied, and bowed to the Abbess, who turned away from his gaze.

"How well do you know her?" Edward probed – the meaning a little obvious, so that sniggers ran around some of the younger members of court. Edward turned to the crowd, and it immediately fell silent.

"I ... know her quite well," Sweyn replied, trying to be matter-of-fact about the process, as if his friendship with the lady was simply that – a friendship. There was further sniggering from the assembled court. Sweyn tried to ignore it, though Edward again threw a glance at his followers, and silence followed.

"I have heard testimony," continued Edward, "that you have much greater and closer knowledge of the Abbess than you would have us believe. That you have, in fact, led the lady astray from God's path, which she has chosen for her life. That you have intimate knowledge of the lady."

Sweyn stood, beads of sweat appeared upon his fore-head and began to run down into his beard. *What do I do now? Keep calm.* His linen shirt began to cling to his back. He lowered his head in deference to the king, and soft words came from him. "I must confess, Sire, to a mutual 'affection' between myself and the lady Abbess. I am sure, Sire, that my desire for tenderness was echoed by hers, and that our ... regard for each other was born of a fondness between us." *How did that sound?*

The king rose from his seat and the court held its collective breath. "No man can condone what you have done," said the king. The Abbess wept quiet tears in the corner, consoled by the nun attending her. "You will be exiled to Flanders and there you will await my pleasure!" Edward announced, to gasps. Sweyn looked up, startled. His hand automatically went to the hilt of his sword, but, of course, it wasn't there, having been surrendered to guards before he entered the king's chamber. The men-at-arms of the court fingered their sword hilts too; surely Sweyn would not have unsheathed his sword before the king, had he still had it? It was unthinkable.

Sweyn moved back and bowed to the king again. "I will obey your commands, Sire," he said, knowing that he had no other choice other than one that would lead to his demise, and he would much prefer to hold on to his head.

As he was led from the hall, Harold, his brother, strode towards it. He had heard of the happenings, and had been told of the charges before his sibling, and of the king's judgement. As the two men met, their eyes locked. Harold showed a look of disgust at what Sweyn had done, and the besmirching of the family name and honour. "Go to Flanders and wait there!" he snarled, and marched on toward the king's hall.

Well, Sweyn was taken forthwith to the port and placed upon a boat, attended by a number of the king's housecarls. They would see that he actually arrived in Flanders.

Harold entered the king's hall and knelt before his sovereign. Inside he was seething at the position his brother had placed the family in, but hoped to placate his brother-in-law and retrieve something of the situation. His sister, Edith, now appeared at her husband's side. Her concern was apparent, for the fate of her brother, Sweyn, and her family.

The king signalled to Harold to rise and spoke to his earl. "My Lord Harold," he said, "you will have heard tonight's happenings, here, within this hall, and of the happenings during encounters with your brother and the Abbess." At this, the Abbess lowered her head again, and shook as she wept.

"I know of it, Sire," Harold returned. "And I am sad for it. My brother shames his family. How can we make amends for his actions?"

"Lord Harold," answered Edward, "I have decided that Sweyn's earldoms of Hereford, Gloucester and Oxford should be divided between you and your cousin, Beorn. I trust that you will rule over them wisely and justly. This is my command."

Harold's heart leapt in his chest! Hereford, Gloucester and Oxford – between himself and Beorn! This was indeed an honour he had not expected in the circumstances, and went some way to restoring the family's honour. It also widened Harold's sphere of influence, and would do his pocket no harm either.

"Your command will be obeyed, Sire," Harold stated. "I thank you for the belief you put in me. Beorn and myself will ensure that the areas you mention are ruled well, and are ready to do the King's bidding at all times."

Edward nodded and resumed his seat. Harold bowed low and left the hall, after a nod and a reassuring smile for his sister. Things were not as bad as he had feared – indeed, the night's happenings could conclude well for his own ambitions, if not for his brother! But his brother's problems were his own doing! Harold, at least, had profited by it!

# CHAPTER FOUR

During that spring and summer, we knew that we must strive hard to farm the hides, so that when the autumn and winter seasons came around, most of the work would be done, and food would be plentiful for the bad times. I would take out the cattle each morning; my father the swine to the forest, to grunt joyfully as they snuffled through the dead leaves and crunched up the roots my brother dug for them from the forest floor.

One day, after the Sabbath, dawned grey as a trout's belly. We were up in the half-gloom of dawn, readying ourselves for a day in the fields.

Two of the older village boys had charge of the sheep. They took with them two dogs, who knew how to keep sheep in order. When the animals strayed too far, the boys would shout "Go seek, go seek," and the dogs would run out, in large arcs, to get behind the animals. Then a call of, "Come home, come home!" would be heard, and the dogs would slowly and skilfully bring the sheep back within guarding distance. I never tired of watching the dogs work the flock. In the pens, behind the houses, some of the ewes had new-born lambs by now. They would stay there for a few days, before the men would allow the mothers and lambs back to the fields.

Some of the men and boys were setting up hurdles on the field that would be pasture this year, so that the cattle and some of the sheep could be run upon it. Their dung would provide the goodness in the soil for next year's crops. The cattle would go in first, as they would rip at the longer grasses with their lengthy tongues. The sheep would follow, as they nibbled the short grasses, moving around, strangely I always thought, upon their knees, as if monks at prayer.

My sisters would take out the geese, but never strayed too far from the village, though we saw no more wolves for some good time, barring a few wandering over the hills, in the distance. Most of the girls' time was spent helping my mother and aunt around the house – it was important that they learned to carry out the tasks which would, someday, be theirs in their own households. My mother would never let it be said that her daughters were not capable of 'holding the keys' and running a household!

My father, myself and the other men needed to plant up much of the crops we would grow this season. The barley and rye had been planted during the winter, and all eyes were upon those strips that were beginning to sprout fresh and green against the brown earth. Now it was the turn of peas, cabbage, parsnips and carrots to be planted. The seeds had been carefully gathered last year, and stored away to keep out the mice!

We were good farmers, I have to say. We shared the tools and worked side-by-side to claim the land and to grow our crops.

We all toiled together to till the ground. The fields were

divided up into strips, and each of us had our own strips, so that each man had strips in the good land and on the poor land. The strips were around 5 paces wide, though the length depended upon the lie of the land. Some of our fields were longer and wider than others. But each strip would be about one furlong in length. (My father told me that a furlong was around 1/8 of a mile.) The word 'furlong' comes from one 'furrow-long'. The men said that it was the longest length that a team of oxen could plough without having to be rested.

The scratch-plough was pulled by our oxen. We shared the beasts between ourselves and the thegn. We could never dream of owning our own team. The plough would dig a furrow in the land, into which the seed was sown. It was always my job to goad the four oxen, whilst my father man-handled the plough. We had set off along the strip a number of times now, turning each time at the headland. Tom Mouse followed in my father's footsteps, dropping a seed at intervals and brushing the soil back over to cover it with a foot. As he went, he sang a verse from a ploughing song we all knew.

*"Prithee lend your jocund voices for to listen we're agreed;*
*Come sing of songs the choicest of the life we ploughboys lead,*
*There are none that live so merry as the ploughboy does in spring,*
*When he hears the sweet birds whistle and the nightingales to sing"*

And then my father would join in:

*With my hump along! Jump along! Here drives my lad along*
*Pretty, Sparkle, Berry, Good luck, Speedwell, Cherry,*
*We are the boys that can follow the plough, oh,*
*We are the boys that can follow the plough.*

Some of the smaller children were with us in the fields, long sticks and slings in their hands and young dogs at their feet, dissuading the birds from stealing some of the seeds being cast into the earth. Every seed represented future food to us!

At the end of one furrow, just as we turned oxen and plough, a galloping rider came into sight, from down the valley. At length, we could see that it was one of the brothers. He turned into the thegn's compound and disappeared into the hall. "Why such haste?" my father asked. It was not usual to see the brothers ride the horse. In general, they walked, unless the distance was great.

Time passed, and my mother appeared in the field, carrying a basket. We all knew its contents. As with all growing boys, I had become more impatient for it as the morning wore on. From that basket, she brought pies, bread and cheese and a large pot of ale for us to enjoy. We sat there, upon the side of the field and ate and supped, savouring the creamy taste of my mother's sheep's cheese and the fresh bread that she baked so well. We watched across the field to the thegn's house. The men discussed what errand should bring a monk at speed to relate news.

"Do you think the plot of rebellion is uncovered?" asked Luke, another big and rangy churl, like my father. A look of concern was etched upon his weather-worn features.

"It is to be hoped not, or we shall all suffer for it," my father replied, staring into the distance in deep thought.

We were about to begin work again, pies, the cheese, bread and ale having been hungrily despatched, when there was movement from the hall. Cerdic, the thegn, and the brother emerged from the large gate and began to approach us across the fields. We all stopped and watched their progress, wondering what they had to bring; wondering if our lives were to change for ever, or even to end horribly within the foreseeable future.

Thegn and monk approached us, troubled looks upon their faces. We stood, our breath coming in short gasps or not at all.

Cerdic, dressed in linen breeches and a leather jerkin, looked us all over, eyes brown as a hunting fox, and then looked at my father in the eye. "The Earl will visit the monastery and my hall within days," he announced, his voice showing concern.

"Tostig comes here?" Luke asked. "Do you think he knows of matters afoot?"

"We cannot be sure, but the brothers think not. The prior feels that it is but a stop on a journey from Bamburgh and Yeavering to York."

"Yeavering?" asked Tom.

"Aye, so it seems," Cerdic replied. "Edwin's old palace."

My father turned to the men. "All must be as normal," he said. "We must present the front of obedient and law-abiding villagers. We must appear happy with our lot."

The thegn nodded his agreement. "I will greet him cordially," he said. "He will dine with me at the hall. But we must be on our guard."

I looked around, at the faces of the men, now crowded around to listen. Anxious looks were etched there, and each looked to the others for their reaction. I noticed Anders, as I have related, a youth of around 16, shifting uneasily from one foot to another. His face was wary and he glanced around him, eyes taking in everything and ears listening to each and every conversation. For sure, he was greatly frightened by the events. I was somewhat surprised that a sturdy young lad like him would be so cowardly and afraid. He had never shown it before, but, once people are placed into a real situation, then who knows how they will react? Indeed,

I now wondered whether I really wanted to be a warrior or not! All of a sudden, it became less appealing!

As the thegn and brother departed, no doubt to talk further on what was to happen, we resumed our labours. We planted our vegetables. Other men, upon another strip, planted woad and madder, to make dye for the cloth the women wove from the wool of our sheep.

As the sun dipped toward the western horizon, we made our way back to the village to clean our tools and eat my mother's pottage.

"Do you think Anders is fine and well?" I asked my father. "He looked most worried when we spoke with the thegn. His eyes darted here and there, and he looked very nervous. I think he might be afraid." *I couldn't mock him for that. I too am nervous or what lies ahead.*

"I am sure he will be fine," my father replied. "He will be as worried and on edge as the rest of us, when the Earl pays us a visit." *Perhaps, but I felt his face betrayed more than worry.*

After a meal and a jug of ale, the family settled down to our evening's work. My father sharpened tools. My mother and aunt wove wool and my grandfather took out his small harp and plucked at the strings.

At length, as full darkness began to envelop the land, my father arose and left our hall. I watched him go and wondered what his task might be. Of course, he could simply be making his way to the latrine, but the concerned look upon his face made me wonder. I quietly followed him out of the door; no one seeming to notice my departure.

My father was striding toward the now-closed gate. When he reached it, he slipped behind the pig pen that stood there. I stood behind our hall, still as a kestrel's shadow, and watched to see what would happen.

We both stood for some short while, I trying not to

breathe heavily, and hoping that my mother would not come and call out for me, and then I noticed a movement out of my right eye. I turned, slowly, to see Anders carefully stealing across our village. He dodged from building to building, always keeping to the shadows, away from the bright moonlight.

Anders made his way to the gate and gently lifted the wooden latch that kept it closed. He glanced warily around him at every slight noise. As he pulled the gate open, my father stepped from the shadows.

"And where would you be headed on such a night, Anders?" he asked. The youth spun to face my father, a look of fear spreading upon his face.

"I, I ... was going to ... check upon the ... fields," he spluttered. "I was sure I heard a strange noise."

"Strange that you should hear it from inside your hut," my father replied, "since I heard nothing from out here in the open air."

"I was sure I heard it," he insisted.

"You heard nothing," came another voice from the shadows. "I too saw your face this afternoon. I too was suspicious of your actions." Luke emerged into the moonlight and strode toward the boy. "You thought to leave and pass on a message to the followers of Tostig, so that they came to the village prepared. But to whom would you speak?"

"I would speak to no one!" Anders replied, his voice quavering with fear.

Luke approached him and took each of his large and prominent ears in his great hands. He stared into the face of the quaking youth with hard eyes and repeated his question. "To whom would you speak?" He slowly twisted his hands until the youth cried out in pain. "I do not intend to hurt you," Luke said, firmly, "but I have not yet ruled it out!"

"To Aethelred, my cousin, in the next village. He is for Tostig, and hopes, one day to find his favour and serve him. And I too!"

By now, others had heard the commotion, and a small crowd had gathered. Anders' mother and father were among them. "What are you doing with my boy?" his mother cried.

"Tell her!" demanded Luke, and, hesitating, Anders poured forth his story to the astonished throng. His mother fell to her knees and covered her face with her scarf. His father simply stared at him, tears running down his face. "We cannot live here longer," he said, slowly. "We will leave for my brother's village in the morn."

"You will not!" said my father. "You will stay here until Tostig is gone. The boy is not to venture out from your home and the village boundary. If we see him abroad ..." His meaning was clear. "You will leave in the winter months, when all is settled one way or another. You will take everything that is yours. Then you may throw yourselves on the mercy of your brother." Anders' mother fell into a dead-faint at this, and the women carried her gently back to their hut. Anders' father took the boy and followed them. *How they must feel,* I thought!

As we walked back to our hall, I asked my father, "Why do Anders' uncle and cousins live over the hill, in the next village?"

"His uncle," my father replied, "had a strong and violent disagreement with his own father. He left to go to live in his wife's village."

"How his family must feel!" I said.

"As it says in the old poem, 'The Fates of Man'," my father replied,

" *'a man and a woman bring a child into the world, and dress him and train him and teach him'* but after all the care they take to, *'guide his footsteps',* no parent can tell what a child will do when he becomes grown in his own right. They were never a good family. Now they must go." And with that, the matter was settled.

# CHAPTER FIVE

Oh, what trouble now brewed in our land! In 1044, Edward the Confessor had brought one of his French clerics, Robert, the Abbot of Jumieges to his court in London. In 1050, Robert of Jumieges became Edward's Archbishop of Canterbury.

This appointment was badly thought out. The convent of the Metropolitan Church had already elected a kinsman of Earl Godwin to the post, and that brought great bitterness to the heart of Godwin and his kin, and all Englishmen. Those in the church, we are told, lamented the decision greatly.

Almost as soon as Robert had arrived in England, he began to make certain accusations against Godwin, Earl of Wessex. These included the rumour that Godwin had murdered the king's brother, Elfred. His task, clearly, was to set the king against his father-in-law and to bring about the demise of Earl Godwin; by now his enemy.

There were, too, disputes over land – a border dispute between Godwin and the new Primate of England served to make the dispute between the two men more bitter and rancorous than ever.

Oh, how the Primate plotted and planned Godwin's downfall!

As you may know, Edward had spent many years in Normandy, in exile from England. When he took the throne in 1042, he leant upon his former allies and hosts for support. Many of his courtiers, soldiers and clerics were Normans. This, of course, led to a strong interest in English politics by the Norman French; the end product of which we know only too well!

Now, in the year of 1051, a company of Normans, in the service of Count Eustace of Boulogne, were in Dover. A group of men arrived at a tavern and seated themselves at the long benches at one side. The landlord shuffled over to the group, who were laughing at some joke that one had related to them. "...and then she said. 'Forgive me, my Lord.' Ha, ha, ha!"

"What can I do for you, sirs?" asked the landlord, his eyes twinkling, already imagining the money he might make on this night from such a group. The Normans asked for food and drink and these were duly delivered by a young serving girl. One of the Normans tried to grab the wench, but she pulled away from him and glowered at the man. The Normans simply laughed at her annoyance. The landlord approached again. "That will be two shillings for the food and ale, sirs," he announced. "Will you pay now, or at the end of the night?"

"Pay?" asked one. "Why would we pay? We are Normans. You are Saxons, so naturally merely servants."

The landlord looked at them, unsure as to what to do or say. "But I cannot house and feed you for naught, sirs," he said.

"You must, for we will not pay for such revolting food

and ale as this," the Norman replied. "We are Normans. We don't pay for Saxon garbage."

The landlord shuffled off, at a loss as to what to do.

A group of Saxon men had been listening to the conversation. One grasped the landlord's arm as he passed. "They will pay when the time comes, landlord," he said, "or they will have us to reckon with." The landlord nodded his thanks. An hour later, the Normans had drunk a quantity of ales and wines at the quay-side inn, and were quite drunk and not in full control of themselves. At the side of the tavern, they laughed and sang. But then, one of their number made a dreadful error.

"Hey, ho, but these Saxons are a strange breed. They are not as clean as they might be, and one can always tell when they approach by the stink!"

"Aye," replied one of his friends, "It is not recommended to approach too close to them, in fear of what you might contract!"

The alehouse fell silent. Saxon men enjoying a jug of ale turned to face them. The look upon their faces displayed their inner feelings. Still they restrained themselves and simply stared at the Normans.

"I wonder if their women are worth the risk?" asked one.

"No!" replied another. "You are better off with a comely Norman wench," his friend replied.

"The young maid in the corner is of fine face."

"Tis not the face you need to be fearful of!" replied another. Raucous laughter filled the inn.

A large Saxon, his gingery hair and beard beginning to be tinged with grey, turned upon his heel. He was thick-set, but without a spare ounce of fat upon him. Slowly, he paced toward the bench they were occupying and stood over them. He looked through ice-blue eyes at the Normans. "I think you have said enough," he said. "'T' would be better were you to mind your language, sirs, and have more concern for your hosts."

One Norman looked up at the interloper. His was not a face to meet on a dark night. His jaw was angular; his mouth wide and cruel.

"Who are you, to tell a Norman what he might and might not say? We and our kind are in your land, as honoured guests, at the behest of your king! You will treat us as such."

The big Saxon glowered at him. "My Lord," he said, a little mockingly, "I simply ask that you show common courtesy to myself and my countrymen, and in particular to our ladies, who are the most fair of face and wholesome in the whole world."

Another Saxon joined him at the table. He too was a hefty man. Muscles corded his back and his shoulders strained the seams of his rough shirt. The Normans looked at the new-comer. "And, make no mistake, you *will* pay for your food and drink tonight," the second Saxon said.

A thin and wrinkled Norman, a man of evil, weaselly looks, stared up at him with eyes peering, red and slitted. "You were right," he said to his friend, wrinkling his nose, "they do stink!"

The new-comer glared down. He showed his white teeth as he grabbed the Norman and hauled him from the bench. "You will apologise for your foul tongue to all good Saxons assembled here, and to the maid in the corner seat," he demanded. "Then I might let you go back to drinking your French wine piss!"

The Norman pulled out a hidden blade and struck at the Saxon. The knife pierced the Saxon's chest and heart, and he gasped, a terrible gurgling coming from his mouth, as he fell to his knees — the hilt of the knife protruding from his body. A trickle of blood ran from his mouth and dripped from his furred chin. His eyes glazed and, with a sigh, he fell to the floor, stone dead, his lifeblood draining into the dust! The inn stood still. No man breathed!

A huge hand clamped upon the Norman's neck. The Norman let out a cry. But his cry was stifled by a huge fist that caught him full on the chin, driving upward. His head went back and as it flopped forward again, teeth and blood littered onto the floor of the inn.

The other Normans rose as one and pushed back the bench, but they were too late. The first Saxon picked up the rough table and hurled it at them, knocking them back against the wall. More Saxons streamed across the floor of the inn and joined in the melee.

Fists flew and the Normans were quickly overpowered and lay, bleeding upon the floor. A Saxon man lifted a Norman head. The eyes were empty. "This one is dead!" he said. The crowd hushed. More heads were raised and bodies turned over. Of the group of Normans, fourteen were dead. The Saxons looked from one to another, not knowing what to do, but realising the gravity of the situation. "What do we do?" the first Saxon asked.

"They must be disposed of," the landlord said. "I don't want them in my alehouse."

"What of the two who are still alive? They will tell the tale once they come to their senses."

"Then they must not be alive to tell the tale," said another. And with that, he drew a dagger and finished the task, so that neither man could ever tell what happened in this world. The Norman bodies were quickly taken out through the back entrance, to a piece of rough land at the edge of the town, covered only with scrub willow and thorn thickets. Here they were left for the crows to pick at.

The Saxons slunk away and melted back into the

everyday scene of life in Dover. All hoped that the night's happenings had gone unnoticed by the people.

But, of course, the drama was not to end there. For it was only a matter of time before the bodies were discovered by the sickly stench of blood, their carcases strewn around, under mantles of crows, and the Count inevitably heard of the deaths of his men. In a blind fury, he gathered his troops and made his way to Dover. They approached the town in the early morning light, as the birds began to sing their songs in the trees and the sun rose over the eastern horizon.

The people of Dover were awaking and going about their morning business, still perhaps a little sleepily. People dragged themselves from their homes after a meagre breakfast, and began opening their shops to trade their goods with the world. Curls of smoke drifted from smoke-holes in roofs, and mingled with the mists drifting across the town.

Many a man and woman stopped and gazed at the first sight of a group of strange armed men cantering into their narrow streets. Traders hurriedly moved carts from their path and wondered at the sight. What was the to do? A group of Norman soldiers in their streets. Where were they going?

Suddenly, their leader held up his hand and the column of men and horses came to a halt in a small square. The Count looked around him at the gathering crowd. A look of derision was etched upon his features at the Saxon peasants now beholding him. *These people live like pigs*, he thought. *And they are about as worthless.*

"Here me!" he suddenly called. "I am Eustace, Count of Boulogne. Three nights past, a group of my men entered this town looking for entertainment. I am sure they drank in your alehouses, but at some hour, they were viciously assaulted and murdered by a criminal gang. What say you to that? If any man or woman here knows the murderers, they will reveal it to me now!"

The crowd looked from one to another. Many knew nothing of the happenings, though some had heard mutterings. Of those who did know, they also knew that a Saxon had been killed in the brawl, and the crowd stood mute.

"My Lord," ventured one man, "we know nothing of this terrible misdeed. It is indeed news to all of us. We give My Lord our deepest sorrow at this event."

"Your sorrow is not enough. I would have the men who did this!" came the reply. Eustace was not certain whether the people were truly in ignorance of the occurrence, or whether they feigned such to mock him. His anger was rising. He waited for a further moment.

"So you will not hand over the guilty men to justice!" he roared. "Then you offend me and all of the Norman people, who are your superiors!" He bawled an order to his men in Norman French and, oh, what an orgy of blood-letting ensued. The Norman soldiers spurred their horses into the crowd of startled onlookers, causing panic and mayhem as they slashed and lunged with their swords and spears. Most of the crowd were, of course, unarmed and unable to defend themselves. Nor could they escape easily in the close confines of the streets. Men and women were struck and beaten to the ground, gaping wounds in heads and necks spilling rivers of blood and brains onto the dust. Men, women and even children were trodden under the feet of horses in the madness. Truly, it was a hideous and miserable spectacle.

Screams of terror and roars of fighting men rent the air. Children's cries were pitiful, as they were forced to watch the carnage taking place in their home town. Quickly, news spread around the town of the atrocity occurring in their midst, and men began to arm themselves with whatever they could find. They ran toward the noise of the massacre and began to harry the Norman troops. It quickly became apparent to the Count that the town was arming and rising against him and his men, and, like the coward he was, he bellowed an order to retreat to his troops. Now they came together and turned to fight their way out of what was becoming a crowded street of armed Saxons. Some of the Normans never made it to the edge of the town and fell where they were struck by angry Saxons, their bodies mutilated in the most horrible ways. Gloved hands lay on the street, separated from their arms. Norman soldiers were pulled from their horses, their helmets torn off and throats slit from ear to ear by Saxon knives.

But, eventually, Eustace and his remaining men made the edge of the town and rode for their very lives across the country, leaving a baying mob behind them. Eustace now knew that he must make the hall of the king as quickly as his horses could carry him, and before the Saxons could raise the hue and cry against him. He rode for Gloucester, where he knew the king was in his usual autumn residence. Edward, he prayed, would be his protection against the wrath of the Saxons.

# CHAPTER SIX

The following day in our village, dawned grey again, and chill. A brittle cold wind was blowing down from the hills to the west. There was a great gathering of cloud over the hills that said that rain was on its way. We were in the fields again, planting crops and tending to the animals. My father, Tom and I were working one of Tom's strips, planting turnips, and had almost come to a pause for breath as my father turned the plough at the headland, to return along the next strip.

I looked up. I don't know why – perhaps a sixth sense, to peer down the valley. Between two walls of trees, along the riverbank, I could see a group of horsemen coming towards us. They did not make haste, but came at a slow trot, so there was no immediate alarm.

I called to my father and pointed. "Riders!" He pulled on the reins of the oxen and stopped the plough to turn and follow my gaze. His eyes narrowed to take in the scene. Tom stopped sowing his seed and watched with us, a look of anxiety spreading across his knotted brows.

"I think we must return to the village for more seed,

Tom," my father breathed. The old man nodded, though, in reality, we had plenty of seed for the time being, and so we set off across the field to our home. As luck would have it, we were not far from the stockade. Would the riders pull across and turn into the thegn's compound, or continue to our village? But as they came, they showed no sign of veering off to the thegn's hall.

We entered the village just before the party of riders. We stood there and watched as they poured into the compound. It was unusual to have such visitors to our humble abode. People spilled out of their homes and stood, staring at the obviously wealthy cavalcade. There were oohs and ahs from the children at the beautiful horses and tack assembled within our confines. The boys advanced as far as they dared to look at the array of weapons hanging from belts and saddles. Some of the younger girls hid behind their mothers' skirts at the sight of such fearsome warriors.

One warrior in particular looked even finer clad than the others. His clothes were of fine linen, and dyed in so many colours! He wore chain armour over his tunic, and had a great helmet with a nose-guard upon his head. At his belt hung a large sword, inlaid with sparkling red jewels in its hilt. A large shield, with a huge, polished boss, hung at his back, and a spear was in his hand. *This is Tostig,* I thought.

"Where is your smith?" the great man enquired.

"I am here, Sir," said Benjamin the smith, striding from his forge. "What can I do to serve you?" He nodded his head at the visitor.

The warrior stared at Benjamin. "Do you know who I am?" he asked; a menacing tone, I thought, to his voice.

"No, sir," replied Benjamin, innocently, though I knew that he did know to whom he spoke. "I have never seen you here before, Sir, but I can see from your very being that you must be a very important man." My father shifted his feet, nervously.

The warrior sat his horse a while and pondered Benjamin's words. Was he being insolent, or did he really not know who the visitor was? "I am the Earl Tostig," he haughtily announced. We all fell to our knees as if this had come as a great surprise to us. It would not do to show that we knew our illustrious guest was due. *Keep your eyes on the ground,* I told myself. But I could not resist glancing up to see what was happening.

Benjamin stood there, solid as a boulder, but bowed his head in deference. "My Lord, I did not know. I am but a simple man." Again, I felt the earl could not decipher whether Benjamin really was a 'simple man' or whether he was simply disrespectful.

The earl looked at him again for what felt like an eternity, stroked his chin with a gloved hand, and then seemed to decide that Benjamin probably was as 'simple' as he appeared. "One of our horses has cast a shoe," he said. "See to it!"

"It will be an honour, my Lord," Benjamin replied, bowing deeply. Again, uncertainty from the earl as to whether he was or wasn't being mocked. Benjamin looked at my father as he turned to return to his forge, a flicker of a smile upon his face. My father cast him a glance that said, 'Don't go too far', as we all stood again. I glanced across to the earl. *Don't stare!*

One of the soldiers led a horse across to the forge. It was clear to all of us that the animal was in some pain by its limp. And yet these men had still trotted it across the countryside to us. Benjamin took the horse and spoke softly to it. He gently raised the offending foot and looked at it. Taking a short steel from his range, he began to pick at the earth clogged in the hoof.

Suddenly, the horse let out a shriek and kicked out with its back foot. Benjamin, being an experienced man around horses, dodged the kick and no harm was done, but the horse was clearly distressed.

"What have you done to my horse?" the earl cried. "What sort of smith are you?"

"My Lord, this horse has been made to run for days without the shoe. Its foot has become soft and is rotting. That is what caused the pain when I cleaned the hoof."

"Do you dare to say that I mistreat my animals?" screamed the earl, becoming red in the face. "Seize him!" he cried. With that, soldiers slipped from their mounts, tumbled forward and grabbed Benjamin by the arms. They led him to the earl. He stood there, staring up, with lake-blue eyes, at the man in the saddle. The earl drew his great sword and we all gasped at what might be the outcome. My heart hammered in my breast! Even Benjamin, so defiant, began to pale. The earl took the sword and placed it beside Benjamin's head. With one quick slice, he took off the tall man's left ear. More gasps from the assembled throng. Benjamin's wife moaned a great moan, and fell to her knees. Two of the women grabbed her by the arms and stopped her falling to the earth. "That is for your insolence!" Tostig announced.

But Benjamin stood stock still, though it was obvious that pain was drilling into him. Blood ran down and stained the fabric of his shirt. His face was pale. His eyes narrowed as he spoke to the earl. "I will care for the horse now, with my Lord's permission."

The earl looked unsettled by this development. "Do it!" he snapped, and the soldiers released their grip on the huge smith. An old woman ran out from the crowd and handed Benjamin a piece of soft cloth to hold at his ear – the severed flesh still lying in the dust.

Benjamin returned to his work, blood still pouring from his wound. We could all feel the tension in his body as he fought to hide the pain, which must surely have been great. His breath came in great heaves. He gently cleaned the horse's hoof and was, eventually, able to fit a shoe. The beast still limped, but it was clear to all that it was much soothed now, and would soon recover.

"My Lord's horse is well," Benjamin said, between gritted teeth. We stood stock still, not daring to guess what might happen next. The earl simply nodded, looked at us with a sneer, wheeled the great horse he rode and led his men out of the village, toward the thegn's house. Benjamin strode across the village, picked up his ear from the dust and returned to the forge, where he nailed it to a post. "Let it remain there," he said, "lest anyone forget what happened here today." His wife, recovered now, from her shock, and able to stand unaided, ran to him and guided him back to their hut, to better tend his wound.

We all made our way back to our own homes to gather our senses. On the way, we passed the house of Anders, and saw him peering out from the doorway, from where he would have seen everything. My father paused. "What think you now?" he asked, and strode on.

# CHAPTER SEVEN

Upon leaving our village, Tostig and his men turned to Cerdic's hall. They rode in through the burg gate and dismounted. They say that Tostig then had a meeting and refreshment with Cerdic. I have heard from a servant boy that it went like this:

Tostig dismounted from his horse, which he passed to a boy to care for. From the hall door, Cerdic emerged, entered the compound and approached the earl. "My lord," he said, "this is indeed an honour for my humble house-hold. To have the Earl of Northumbria within my walls! You must come in and I will order refreshment for you and your men."

Tostig acknowledged the thegn courteously. "I would be pleased to break bread with you," he replied. Cerdic led his guest into the great hall, where he rid himself of cloak and gauntlets. They sat at the great table, Tostig looking around him; considering his new surroundings. I imagine it was a modest home to his eyes, though to ours it was very comfortable. Two of his housecarls sat near to him; presumably as bodyguards. His men filed in and occupied one of the side tables. Servants flitted hither and thither, bringing a fine platter of cold roast meat, cheese, relish, bread and fruit to the tables. An old servant poured wine into pewter goblets.

"What brings my Lord to our lands? To what do we owe this great honour?" Cerdic continued.

"I travel to York," Tostig replied. "I have been to Bamburg, assessing ... things, and I also visited Yeavering," he said, cautiously, obviously not at all keen to give details of his mission to Bamburg.

"Yeavering, my Lord? Why so?"

"Men say that Yeavering – the old Ad Gefrin - was the site of Edwin's fortress. And also that of Aelthelfrith, Oswald and Oswy. Bede tells us so in his *Historica Ecclesiastica gentis Angolorum* of AD731. I was keen to see the site," Tostig told him.

"And did you find the site interesting?"

"Indeed. There is no doubt that there was once a large fortress there. The signs show it."

Cerdic nodded his head. "And are you to visit our monastery? It is very beautiful."

"Indeed. I will stay the night at the monastery of St. Peter, along the valley, and travel the last miles tomorrow."

"Then we are all honoured!" proclaimed Cerdic, as enthusiastically as he could. "Brother Benedict, the Abbot will be delighted. Does he know that you plan to visit?" questioned Cerdic, though, of course, he already knew.

"He does," replied Tostig. "I sent men to inform him some days ago. I am sure that we will enjoy a pleasant evening, discussing events and how things fare in his diocese. And how goes it with you, Cerdic?" he asked. "Is all peaceful in the countryside? Are the people happy with their lot?"

Cerdic became more cautious now. What did Tostig

know and what did he suspect? But, despite all, he needed to make a show of reassurance to the earl.

"Things are very quiet, my Lord," he replied, cheerfully. "The churls labour in the fields, now that winter has lost its grip, and the people seem very happy. I have no trouble with them."

"Good!" came the barked reply, "though some of your churls are not as respectful to their betters as they might be."

"How so, my Lord," asked Cerdic, stiffening and becoming worried as to what might have happened or been said. Tostig related the story of Benjamin and his ear, seemingly with great relish. His housecarls sniggered as the tale unfolded. Cerdic, whilst horrified at the tale, knew that he must be seen to side with Tostig. "Then the smith received his just deserts," he said, as Tostig finished the tale. Tostig grunted, self-satisfied that he had made his mark on this part of his earldom. He ate his fill and drank his wine, still searching Cerdic for information about the district.

"And now we must continue to the monastery of St. Peter," he announced at length. "We shall leave you in peace to govern this small locale, and keep the peasants in check for us. It does not do for the common people to have ideas above their station."

"My Lord need have no concerns on that matter," Cerdic replied, trying to appear calm, though inwardly seething with anger at the treatment of his smith. "My Lord need never fear. I and my men will always serve his cause and care for his interests here in this small corner of his lands."

"Hmm," Tostig grunted again and left the hall to retrieve his horse and continue his journey. He gave Cerdic but a cursory wave of his gloved hand as he led his men out of the compound and along the banks of the river toward St. Peter's.

When Cerdic was sure that Tostig was long gone, and that he could not be seen, he quickly mounted a horse and rode the short distance to the village. His concern for Benjamin was evident to all. He spent some time in our humble home, huddled in conversation with the leading men from the village, before he left. As a young boy, I was not privy to that conversation, though I can imagine its content!

Tostig soon arrived at the monastery of St Peter. It was a large group of buildings by our standards, and was constructed largely of stone, dotted with lichens of differing colours. It had all of the domestic and workplace buildings necessary for a double house of some 150 monks and nuns. I always marvelled at it, whenever I visited.

The monastery complex comprised a number of buildings which included the chapel, dormitory, cloister, refectory, library, balneary for bathing, and an infirmary for ministering to the sick. There were also a number of buildings that facilitated the self-sufficiency of its inmates, and its service to the community. These included a hospice, and a range of agricultural and manufacturing buildings - a barn, a forge and a brewery.

Life within the monastery was governed by the rules of the community. It required that they remain single and celibate, and have little or no personal property. The degree to which the monastery might be socially separate from its surrounding secular community can vary but, in the case of St. Peter's, the monks and nuns had a good relationship with the people. They often provided us with such services as medical care and some teaching. The monastic order were much prized within our community.

Tostig and his men thundered up to the gates of the monastery. A monk swiftly opened the doors and admitted the earl and his entourage. They quickly brought their horses to a standstill and sat, waiting.

For a few moments, nothing happened. The air itself seemed to stand still, as if it too was waiting.

The great oak doors to the monastery's hall scraped open and the Abbot emerged into the sunlight. That in itself was an irritant to the earl. He would have expected to have been met by an assemblage of senior monks the moment he entered the confines of the monastery. The Abbot smiled at Tostig, as if naught was wrong. "Welcome, my Lord," he said, "one of my monks told me that you were approaching." A further slight to the earl. "I was tending to the spiritual wellbeing of a young monk who, I am afraid, might not be with us by the Sabbath."

Tostig seemed to digest this explanation. "I am sure that your dying monk must be of great concern to you. His spiritual health is, indeed, of utmost importance, before he meets his maker."

The Abbot nodded and gestured to Tostig to alight from his horse. He and his followers handed their mounts to a group of monks who had assembled for the purpose, and followed the Prior into the interior of the monastery. "You will need refreshment, my Lord," the Abbot remarked.

"No, we ate briefly with Cerdic the thegn. We will dine again this evening," replied the earl.

The Abbot looked surprised. "You have visited Cerdic?" he asked, uneasily, though trying to indicate that it was of little importance.

"Yes," replied Tostig. "One of my horses cast a shoe. Therefore, we stopped at the village to gain the services of the smith. Sadly for the smith, he needed a lesson in manners to his betters," Tostig continued. "But I am sure he will never forget the lesson he has learnt."

"How so, my Lord?" the Abbot probed deeper. Tostig related the tale again, and the Abbot listened solemnly. "It is to be hoped that his wound is cleaned carefully, and that infection does not set in. It would be a pity to lose such a proficient smith as Benjamin. I will send a brother to tend to him forthwith." He signalled to a brother standing in the corner.

"There will be no need, my lord Abbot," broke in Tostig. "I am certain the peasants in the village will tend to him well enough. There is no reason to trouble a brother hospitaller." The monk looked at the Abbot, but Benedict shook his head and gestured him away. Tostig missed the raised eyebrow from the abbot to the monk.

"I am sure you are right, my Lord," he smiled, though he was clearly unsettled by it.

"And now I must inspect your beautiful monastery," Tostig announced. The Abbot started. What could be the reason for an inspection? Did Tostig have intelligence of what was afoot? Was he on the look-out for signs of preparation? Or did he simply wish to look around a building he had never entered before? Who knew?

The Abbot rose from his seat and ushered the earl toward the cloisters. "I am honoured to take my Lord to tour our humble monastery," he said, and the party moved off to peer into every nook and cranny of the buildings, from library to sheep pens. As they progressed around the monastery, a hospitaller monk left the monastery via the back entrance and made his way, on horseback, to the village.

In the evening, once Tostig and his men were rested and refreshed, they joined the Abbot and senior brothers for the evening meal. The meal began with brown trout from the monastery's fish ponds. That consumed, a dish of roast quail was delivered to the Abbot's apartment.

"Quail," the earl commented. "You eat well, my brother Abbot."

"Nay, my Lord," Abbot Benedict responded, "In reality, we brothers dine meagrely, but when we knew that you would pay us a visit, our hearts burst with pride, and we resolved that your visit to us would be memorable to you, as befits a man of your status."

"Hmm," Tostig replied. "The sin of pride, Brother Benedict?"

"I fear so, my Lord, but we are all human and prone to some frailties, are we not?"

"Quite so."

The rest of the meal passed off well enough, with sweet cakes and wine to finish. But the atmosphere seemed, to the brothers, strained. They had no inkling as to whether their visitor also felt it. What was certain was that the resolve of Abbot Benedict and his senior brothers had strengthened in the same way that Cerdic's had. They were sure that the people of Brockford were also more hardened against their earl.

Tostig left early the following morning, and the sense of relief around the religious community was palpable. Abbot Benedict retired to his apartment for the rest of that day, to ponder on the happenings of the past days.

On the following Sunday, we all filed into the small but lovely church next to Cerdic's hall. We always attended mass on the Sabbath. My mother would not countenance anything else. The only family member missing was my grandmother, who rarely attended these days, due to the frailty of her years.

As we entered, we were surprised to see Abbot Benedict there, talking earnestly with Cerdic. Brother Mark was also in attendance, which was what we had expected. He approached as we entered and filed into the nave. He glanced around at us. "Aelric," he addressed my father. "Your family are gathered. But how goes your blessed mother?"

"She is frail, Brother Mark," my father replied, "and we are unsure how much she now understands."

The monk nodded understandingly. "I will visit her soon," he said.

"Thank you Brother," my father replied.

"Aelric, after the mass, the Abbot would speak to the men. Will you gather them?"

My father nodded.

Benjamin and his wife entered and I saw the Abbot glance up and speak to Cerdic. He left the thegn's side and made a beeline for Benjamin. The two spoke and the Abbot gave Benjamin a blessing. He then looked at the wound on the side of the huge smith's head. They spoke again and then the two took their respective seats.

The Abbot himself took mass, with the help of Brother Mark. I did not altogether understand his sermon, but my father seemed to read more into it than I did.

At the end of the service, my father led the men into a huddle whilst we made our way back to the village. Abbot Benedict and Brother Mark joined them, and we left them deep in conversation. My father did not return for some time. When he did, his face was grim.

# CHAPTER EIGHT

Days passed, and the news of Dover spread. Earl Godwin sat in his hall, considering what must be done concerning the situation in the town. He was surrounded by some of his most faithful supporters, including his sons. Godwin's sons were also powerful figures in England. Sweyn had now been allowed to return though Harold held his earldoms. Godwin's nephew, Beorn, was earl of Hertfordshire and Buckinghamshire. Godwin, it has to be said, had become the leader of the opposition to growing Norman influence.

"The men killed were of the retinue of the visiting Eustace II, Count of Boulogne. This is why the king is so infuriated by the event. We do not know the full circumstances, but I am told by those closer to the people of Dover that the Normans began a quarrel in an alehouse when they refused to pay, insulted a Saxon wench and killed a Saxon who had complained at their dishonour of Saxon men and women. The men of Dover reacted to protect their honour and that of their women.

"After the Norman corpses were found, Eustace took a troop to Dover and massacred innocent men and women like dogs, before the men of the town took arms and the Normans fled to the king at Gloucester. And there they remain, in the king's protection."

"We must consider how we move from here," observed Harold. "This cannot go unpunished!"

"The king demands," Godwin told his men, "that we punish _all_ of the people of Dover for the killings that happened there. He means in the same way as Leofric did to the people of Worcester, when he raised the town and left it a wasteland, and many of the people dead – even his own people. But I have heard nothing from the king concerning the atrocity carried out by Eustace's men.

"So, you now know the situation we find ourselves in."

"My Lord," spoke one retainer, "surely, we cannot defy the king! We must do his bidding."

"And if his bidding is seen by the people to favour those who are not even from this land, against his own people?" A murmur of agreement spread amongst the gathered throng. "We cannot do this thing that the king demands. What will our own people say, if they are treated as lesser men by their own king, and by their Earl of Wessex? How could we ever command them again? How could we ever call upon their support in the fyrd?"

"I agree," spoke up Harold. "We must find another way to bring this situation to a peaceful end that will satisfy all."

"What do you suggest we do?" asked Sweyn, fearing that he knew the answer that was to come. He shifted uneasily in his chair as Godwin gazed ahead of him, seemingly lost in thought.

Eventually, he shifted his gaze to his men. He scanned each face, wondering how they would react to what he would say. He knew that what he would suggest could be seen as treason, and could be the end for many of the men gathered before him. Would they support him or desert him? He would not know until he had put forward his thoughts and his plan for what must be done.

"The king is in Gloucester for the autumn, as is his custom. We must raise our supporters to meet the king, and ask again that he rescind this order, expel this Norman Count, and to make it clear to him that neither he nor we can ride, roughshod over the law and the people; his people – our people!"

Murmurs rose from the group. "But will the king not see a great number of armed men approaching him as treason?" a housecarl exclaimed. "What you suggest will bring the downfall of all of our houses!" Further murmuring.

"It will not be treason. It will be a delegation to speak to the king. I believe that it is the only way forward," argued another. "My Lord, the Earl, is right. We must join together and force the king to see that what he says is wrong."

"No! I will not do it!" yelled Coenwulf, a thegn of Godwin. "My men and villagers would never agree to rise up against the king!"

"If the king speaks to us and we reach a settlement, we will not be rising against him," pointed out Godwin. "You are either with us or against us! Which is it to be, Coenwulf?" He glared at the thegn. "How can it be right for the king to punish a whole town for the deeds of a few men, and yet let go unpunished a man who kills our own people in a rage of vengeance? Does the ancient law not say 'if two men quarrel over their cups and one endures it patiently, the other who was violent shall pay a fine of thirty shillings'? Then how can the people of Dover pay wergild for the families of these wronged men of Dover when, less than enduring violence, they were not even involved in the violence and did not commit any crime? Were they not the same or better as a man who *endures* the violence of another?"

The man looked about him. He lowered his head. Slowly, Coenwulf nodded his head. "What you say is true," he admitted. "I will follow you, though my heart is heavy."

"All of our hearts are heavy that it should come to this," agreed Godwin.

The assembled retainers looked from one to another, and one by one they nodded their assent to what Godwin had proposed. Each man left to gather together his own group of men who would support the march to meet the king.

A short while later, a large group of men were assembled at Winchester and, upon a cold and dreary morning, began the journey to Gloucester, where the king was in residence. Godwin had raised troops from Kent, Sussex and Wessex. Sweyn had mustered men from Oxford, Gloucester, Hereford, Somerset and Berkshire, and Harold raised the numbers by recruiting men from Essex, East Anglia, Huntingdon and Cambridgeshire.

The troops marched north, past Oxford and Bicester. From there, they cut north-west, past Cirencester, to Beverstone, which lay near to Gloucester. The journey was of eighty miles or so, but they could make twenty-five miles in a day, depending upon the conditions they found before them.

Oh, how they gave thanks on warm, dry days, when the sun beat down upon them and their clothing stayed dry. How they cursed when the rains came down upon them, soaking them to the skin in minutes and making the walking more difficult and uncomfortable.

Feet, normally hardened by long hours of toil in the fields, began to suffer from the constant plod, plod of the march.

They passed forests and smaller pockets of woodland – the home to deer, boar and any amount of other wild creatures. Buzzards screamed overhead and great red kites floated on the up-draughts of wind, searching the ground below them for the carrion on which they depended. Their huge wings flicked and turned, using every curl of air.

They passed villages and towns and fields full of people, busy at the work of putting food into mouths and preparing the land for the next year. Most times, the local people would stop in their chores and stare as the column passed by, not knowing the why or wherefore of the great train of men.

Sometimes, they would turn into burgs and compounds belonging to thegns. Some supported the march and lent men to it. Others simply supplied food and drink and a place to say for the night within the village; not daring to do less.

Slowly, they began to near their destination. What would their reception be? How would the king react? Would they be received graciously and fed and watered whilst the earls discussed the problems before them? Would their king react with fury and savagery, and many men not return to their homes? None knew.

Upon reaching the small village of Beverstone, Godwin decided that they would camp there, and approach Gloucester two days hence. It was, he knew, around 25 miles to where the king was residing.

This was a good place to camp. A village stood nearby, where they could purchase food from the locals, if they had it to spare. There was a water supply to quench men's and horses' thirst. There was good cover, to keep men and animals from the worst of the weather.

The troop of men soon made themselves as comfortable as they could, and camp fires were lit. There was no need for the caution of cold-camp – they were of no threat to any man, and felt no threat from another.

Two days later, Godwin's men were rested and clearing the camp to walk the last miles toward Gloucester. They all knew that the king would be aware of their presence in the area. Indeed, he would have known of it before they even set out. Every man was sure that the news would have spread and was probably widely known. Of course, they were correct. Upon first knowledge of the march, Edward had sent messages to his most trusted protectors, bidding them to make all haste to protect him. His loyal earls immediately sent messages to all parts of their territories, ordering fyrd armies to be assembled. The son of Eustace also rallied to the cry, and Edward could rest easily, knowing that a force would be in Gloucester to counter the 'threat' approaching.

The tranquillity of the camp was suddenly broken. As the men were gathering their meagre belongings, a rider dashed into camp. It was one of the 'wolves' that Godwin had posted at intervals to report on any movement from Gloucester. He dragged on the reins and brought his horse to a sliding halt. Hardly pausing for a heartbeat, he leapt from the steed and rushed to the now-alert Godwin and his sons.

"My Lord, a large body of men approaches from the north!"

"Do you know who leads them?" asked Godwin.

"I have seen the banner of the king, and also the banners of Mercia and Northumbria," the man reported.

"Leofric and Siward!" exclaimed Harold. "He has mustered troops against us!"

"Do we march forward to meet them?" asked Sweyn.

"No," replied his father. "We shall wait for them here. We mean them no harm, but we can defend this place if we are driven to do it."

Quickly, the earls and thegns mustered their men and placed them in the best positions to repel an attack, should it come.

After a short while, which seemed to the waiting men an eternity, horsemen approached their camp. Godwin's men were spread out across a stretch of common land, and along a woodland edge. The visitors rode up the incline of the common. At the head was a man Godwin and his sons recognised as one of the king's most trusted commanders. To each side of him rode Siward and Leofric. The new arrivals rode to within a hundred yards of each other, and then stopped.

Both sides stared at one another, Edward's courtiers presuming that they knew why the king's Earl of Wessex had marched to Gloucester, with so many supporters behind them.

Godwin strode forward to hail the leaders of Edward's men. "Siward, Leofric, Cenelm, I am here to speak with the king. I hope that he might see me today or tomorrow, but if not, perhaps you will take my good wishes and a message from me to King Edward, and bring to me his reply."

The Commander nodded his assent. "Tell me for what you would petition the king, and I will take either you or the message to him." Though, of course, he would certainly know the cause of the march.

"Tell the king that his Earl of Wessex means him no harm. The men I have with me are from Wessex, East Anglia and some from Mercia and other areas. They are not meant as a threat to him, but are zealous in my cause. I also believe that I have some support from men within the northern earldoms."

Leofric and Siward looked at one another. They knew it was probably true.

"Tell the king that I cannot find it within myself to carry out his instructions concerning the people of Dover – his own people - who are mostly innocent of any crime. I cannot punish innocent people, for the king or for the Lord in Heaven."

The courtier nodded again.

"I will not be a party to the destruction of Dover, as I was with Leofric when he punished his own people of Worcester, upon the King Harthacnut's command. (Worcester was the cathedral city of the Hwicce, Leofric's own people.) I dared not refuse then, though I did everything I could to lessen the harshness of the punishment, which was not in proportion to the crime committed. The death of two housecarls was serious, but did not call for the atonement of Harthacnut. Too many innocent men and women died in that terrible rage. I cannot carry out a similar punishment on Dover."

At that, Leofric bridled and a fury rose within him. Nevertheless, he held himself and simply glared at Godwin. He was furious at the mention of the sack of Worcester, but he too had been too afraid to go against the king, though what he did pained him greatly, and weighed heavily on his conscience.

Siward, seeing, as all men did, that Leofric was angry at Godwin's words, came forward to try to pour oil on the troubled waters.

"Godwin," he said, "you are Earl of Wessex. Your conference should be with King Edward, not with us. Come with us to Gloucester and speak with the king. You, your family and your men will be treated well, and as friends, as it should be between us. We have no quarrel. There is no need for arms in this dispute, but the reasoned argument of intelligent men. This, I am certain will be settled amicably between us."

Godwin turned his gaze on Leofric. "Leofric," he said, "I have always regarded you with honour. We were both younger men in the time of Harthacnut. We dared not stand up and refuse his order, as we surely would now. What is passed is passed. Neither of us is proud of what we did, but the fault was with Harthacnut, and not ourselves."

Leofric now rode forward and nodded his ascent. "Siward is right. You must come to Gloucester, with your sons and men, and we will hold conference. I swear unto you that, whatever has passed between us," (and here we must presume he meant the reference to his sack of Worcester and the slaughter of his own people), "I will be a fair mediator between you and the king."

And so it was agreed. The earls, king's men and the Saxon warriors made their slow progress the twenty-five miles to Gloucester and to the presence of King Edward the Confessor.

Once in Gloucester, his men and horses fed, watered and rested for a night, Godwin and his sons and senior followers entered the king's hall. Each man gave up his weapons, bowed low and bent their knee to their monarch. Edward nodded and welcomed them into his presence.

"Sire, I attend you this day," said the earl.

"Your business, I have no doubt, is the terrible deaths of our Norman friends at the hands of the people of Dover," the king replied.

Godwin then began to explain his position to the king, and outlined his opposition to the punishment of Dover, over the deaths of Norman soldiers and supporters of Eustace II.

"My Lord, it was a truly dreadful happening. Much of the violent crime we see is kindled by drunken quarrels. But the Normans had also killed a Saxon man. I understand that what happened next was a reaction to that original crime.

"I also understand that, two days later, the Count of Boulogne took armed men into Dover and massacred unarmed and innocent men, women and children in revenge. What punishment does My Lord have in mind for this crime? Let us meet with the Count and discuss the matter."

Edward looked confused and embarrassed by what his Earl of Wessex said. "The Count and his men have been safely transported to a safe castle. There will be no further revenge against a guest in our country. Eustace has my full protection."

Godwin's eyebrows flew upward. A murmur of dissent ran around the room from the assembled men of Godwin. The king's guard stiffened at the prospect that violence might break out at any moment. The air was heavy with menace as men looked around them, weighing up the strength of potential opposition forces. It now seemed that a civil war could ensue, and tear the land apart.

The Confessor argued that a foreign power had been hurt and humiliated in his kingdom. Did Godwin not know what friendship with the Norman rulers and nobility meant to Edward and England?

Of course Godwin understood, it was pointed out. He had no doubts at all about what the friendship of Normandy meant to the king. Was he not raised at the

Norman court? Did he not surround himself with Norman advisors and clerics? Though, of course, he was careful in the way in which he made his point!

"Sire, I cannot bring myself and my men to punish the good people of Dover in the way in which you demand. My men are, as we speak, continuing to enquire into the circumstances of the deaths of Eustace's men, **and** the Saxon dead, and when the Saxon murderers are brought to justice, they will feel the full force of the law upon them. But until that time, I must insist that the innocent are left alone to get on with their lives as best they can. I must also appeal to My Lord to banish the Norman murderers from our land, or risk the wrath of the English people, who will feel slighted by their king in this matter."

Edward coloured and anger rose within him. Who was this earl to '*insist*' that his orders should be dismissed? But he was also wise enough to know that battle with Godwin and his men would be folly, with the cream of England on both sides. Their loss would leave England open to its enemies, and might leave Edward himself open to further dissent within the kingdom.

Leofric intervened at this point, bringing his wisdom to the occasion. "My Lords, would a compromise be acceptable to all? Why do we not swap hostages as a sign of good-will and as security? Then we should meet at a new Witangemot in London. There we can discuss the situation again, when feelings have cooled."

Edward rose to his feet. All eyes followed him. What would he proclaim?

"Earl Godwin," he pronounced, "I have heard what you have said and listened to your argument. I must ponder your words further. So I say to you, return to your homes with honour. We will meet again at the London Gemot in just a few short weeks from now. Give to me the murderers

of the Norman men, and all will be well between us and
Eustace and his Normans. We will speak further of this at
that time." But Godwin was seething inside. How dare the
king still think to punish all of the people of Dover for the
crime of a few, and yet still take no action against the
Normans? It was not the way! How could the king NOT
punish the murderer of his own people? But what was to be
done?

The men of Godwin bowed low again and left the hall,
gathering their arms. Fed and watered again, they left
Gloucester for Wessex and East Anglia and all areas from
whence they came. Godwin and his sons were relieved that
violence had not been the outcome of the Gloucester
Gemot, but were still unhappy in their hearts at the
outcome. Would the murderers on either side ever be
caught or punished? Would Eustace be pardoned for his
actions? It was more than likely. Would Edward back down
in his demands for the punishment of Dover? It was
doubtful – he would be seen to lose face before the
Normans. What would he do? Only time would tell.

# CHAPTER NINE

Eventually, as is the way of the world, spring gradually turned to early summer. The birds of summer began to return to the land and winter birds began to leave us. Where they went and returned from, no one knew, but it was all part of nature's cycle. The sun shone down onto our village we called Brockford, and there was the drone of insects on the air. I always enjoyed this time of year. The living was so much easier for all. The bitter winds of winter were behind us and long summer days were here, at least for a while. The crops were growing well in the fields now. A mix of gentle rain and warm sunshine was always welcome to us.

But why was our village named Brockford, I hear you ask? I will tell you. Our village stood at a point in the river, some good miles upstream from Dunelm, where it could be forded easily, except in the worst weather. But why Brock-ford? Well, in our forest, we knew that many badgers lived their lives in the great holes they called home. We had no fear of the badger; he never did us harm, and we oft enjoyed watching his snuffling in the meadows as he foraged for food in the cool of evening. He would search out the piles of cow dung to turn over for the grubs it often contained.

Some people, I know, eat badger hams, but my mother would never have them. My father said that the great grey beasts did no harm to our livestock, though they could be a nuisance in the crops. But on balance, we left them alone. There was enough of the old religion left so that we respected the natural world around us, and believed that we must care for our world.

But back to my tale. Early summer was here, and we were out in the fields from dawn to dusk. In the meadows, the tall rich grass was growing well. The meadow was fenced around with hurdles now, and each man's share was fenced off with large stakes. The hay meadow needed to be protected, lest the cattle and sheep break in and spoil the grass. That would destroy the next winter's feed.

Two of the younger children were caught in the meadow, a short while before, chasing the butterflies that flitted amongst the wild flowers. They soon learnt the lesson that the meadow was to be left alone! Had the Reeve caught them, their father would have had to pay 6 pence!

We also had to fence the corn, as the animals would try to get in amongst that too. Guarding the hay and corn was the job of Wistan the hayward. He would watch early and late over the fields. If animals were amongst the crops, he would blow his horn and chase them from the fields. If a stray beast was found, he would take it to the pound, a square pen within the village. Then the owner would have to pay to get his beast back.

Wistan was always given the strips of land on the edges of the fields. That way, should animals break in, it would be his corn eaten first! It certainly encouraged the hayward to carry out his duties properly!

And so, it was as we all prepared for a day in the fields and woods that a tinker crossed our ford. We saw him come from afar, leading a broken down old horse, laden with panniers. He entered the village, calling his wares. The women came from their houses and we all turned from our tasks to see what the old man had brought. He had baskets of pots in one pannier, and trinkets in another. Two other panniers held salt – a substance my mother was always interested in, if she had any money left. But the most important thing he brought was news. The men always wanted to know what was happening in other places, and this time they were more interested than usual.

As children, we always wanted the tinkers to tell us stories they had heard on their travels.

The tinker did good trade with the villagers, selling a number of his clay pots, a few trinkets to some of the older girls, thinking about marriage and the local boys, and some blocks of salt to the wives.

The men sat with him and heard the latest news, and then it was our turn. "I suppose you would like to hear a tale." he said. We all nodded eagerly. "Then I will tell you the tale of 'The Hand of Bamburgh'," he said. He immediately had our attention:

"Well," said he. "Bamburgh Castle was built many years ago. It is said that it was the residence of old King Oswald. Now Oswald was the first Christian king to live there. Oswald was a good man, it seems, and his good deeds were well known, particularly to the holy men who lived there on the island of Lindisfarne. Now, St Aiden, who was the Bishop of Lindisfarne at this time, was so pleased with Oswald that he grasped him by the hand and said, "May this hand never consume nor wither." When Oswald was slain in battle, his hand was cut off and enclosed, they say, in a silver casket. It was placed in the church at Bamburgh, where it remained for generations. Men say that, when it was opened, the hand was no worse than the day it was severed from Oswald's body!"

"Do you know any more tales?" a child cried.

"Ah, yes," the tinker replied, his eyes twinkling, "but they will need to wait for another day." At that, he arose and gathered together his wares. One or two of the wives made last minute purchases and many stopped to chat with him, including my mother and the mother of Anders, who seemed to have a long and earnest conversation with the old man. At length, he left our village and continued his travels to who-knew-where. I often envied the tinkers their life on the road; it seemed so free compared with our lives of constant work on the land. But my mother said that a tinker's life was a hard one, wandering the villages and towns, selling their wares to keep body and soul together.

After the excitement of the tinker, we quickly resumed our daily tasks in the woods and fields. There was always hard work to be done.

As people made their way out into the fields, I long remember them singing the songs that made the day's toil seem easier:

Summer is i-cumen in,
Loudly sing cuckoo!
Groweth seed and bloweth mead,
And springeth the wood new.
Ewe bleateth after lamb,
Cow loweth after calf,
Bullock rouses and buck browses,
Merilly sing cuckoo!
Cuckoo, cuckoo, well sing thee, cuckoo,
Now cease thee never now.
Sing cuckoo now, sing cuckoo,

Sing cuckoo, sing cuckoo now!

I took my brothers and sisters to the forest to collect firewood, and to check upon the swine who fed there. My mother always wanted good firewood for the fires. Dry firewood was always best, but we also collected the damper stuff. My mother would store it up high off the ground, so that it dried well for the morrow.

We could see the swine rooting in the leaves and forest plants for food to eat. They seemed well enough and there was no sign of the wolves. They had moved to another part of their hunting grounds for now, as was their custom, so that one place should not be hunted out of game, but animals allowed to breed, to provide them with food in the future. Though we were afraid of them, and the men despised them for their preying on our flocks and herds, we nevertheless admired the way in which they too managed the land and kept nature in balance. Too many deer would eat themselves out of house and home! Sick animals also needed to be culled from the herds, lest their sickness spread. So, all in all, we grudgingly recognised the part they played in keeping our countryside healthy.

As nightfall approached and Mother Earth unrolled her cloak of darkness, we left the fields for home. The cattle and sheep were brought in for the night, and my sisters drove home the geese from the meadow beside the river. All was secured and we went to our homes to the mouth-watering smells of my mother's cooking and baking.

The following morning dawned and we arose to go about our tasks. We had not got far in our preparations when a great cry was given up. "Thieves! Thieves!" Everyone stopped what they were doing, looked toward the noise and then ran quickly to see what the trouble was.

The cry had come from Adam, who probably knew sheep better than any man amongst us. He had gone to release the sheep from their fold, only to find the gate open and some of the sheep gone! This was a disaster for the village. Could the sheep have broken out in the night and strayed? Unlikely. The sheep were also aware that wolves roamed the land, and that they were safer in the fold at night. (Sheep are not as stupid as many would believe!) No, this was the hand of man!

The men roamed around the fold, looking for signs of the night's happenings. It was not long before the recent tracks of sheep were found, leading from the fold. This was still no certain sign of their whereabouts, as the sheep tended to follow the same trails in and out of the fold every day. The tracks were fresh and the men followed them until they deviated from their usual path and ran along the bank of the river and up to the hill. This was indeed a sign! There were also the tracks of man! The men of the village grouped together and discussed what must be done. It was plain for all to see that the tracks must be followed until the sheep were found. Our village could not survive without its sheep to provide the wool for clothing, milk for cheese and meat for the table at special occasions. One man was sent to raise the hue and cry with Cerdic and apprise him of what was afoot.

Cerdic duly arrived, with three of his followers, on horseback. They would accompany the men in their search for the sheep and the apprehension of the thieves.

The men set off along the trail left by the thieves. I was not allowed to accompany them; my father said I was to stay at the village and carry out the tasks that he would no longer be able to do that day. I was disappointed, but even at that tender age I knew that the work must be done if we were to eat well throughout the year. So I shall tell it as I heard it.

Now Adam was an expert huntsman. He always came back with game from his trips into the forest, when other men brought naught. He followed the tracks like a dog with its nose to the ground. There had been an attempt to cover the tracks by sweeping them with branches, but that had simply left a wider trail in the grass. The trail led them over the hill and through a part of the forest, to emerge again looking down upon another village. Thegn, followers and men made their way down the hillside. The people of the village stopped in their chores and gazed at the visitors. Some ran back to the village and called to others, warning them of the imminent arrival.

A group of men came out to meet the visitors. A leading man held up a hand. "Greetings, Cerdic. What brings you and your men to our village?"

"I hope that it is a mistake," replied Cerdic, "but we come in search of a flock of sheep that have mysteriously disappeared from Brockford in the night."

"A flock of sheep, you say," said the man, appearing mystified as to why our sheep had disappeared or where they might be. "We have seen no strange sheep," he continued, "or we would have rounded them up and sent word to the villages."

"Then you will not object to my men searching the village, as the tracks would seem to lead here, despite the efforts of the thieves to cover them."

The men of the village looked at one another uncertainly. What should they do? They could not defy the thegn. After a moment of hesitation, the head man said, "Of course you may look for your sheep, but I am certain you will not find them here."

Cerdic made no reply, but gave the men orders which they promptly followed. All of the out-buildings – byres, folds and workshops – were searched. The men then turned their attention to the houses. Many houses gave shelter to both people and animals. Some had wooden separations between the people's area and that of the beasts. Others had a simple curtain of cloth. It was useful to have the animals in at some times, particularly during the depths of winter, where their bodies would provide much-needed heat.

Each house was searched – goods moved and partitions investigated. Nothing seemed to be amiss until one of the men cried out. "Sheep!" Other men ran to the house and flooded in. There, in a corner was a group of chests, arranged into a square against a corner wall. Upon them had been laid planks of rough wood, and goods were stored on top. At first it seemed a simple arrangement for dry storage, until the searcher had heard a bleat from beneath the planks.

The wood was rapidly removed to reveal ... the missing sheep. Cerdic spun around and addressed the head man. "Whose house is this?" he demanded to know.

"Sir, it belongs to Cuthred," he replied, hanging his head in shame.

"Brother of Anselm and uncle to Anders," my father breathed.

"Find him!" ordered Cerdic, and the men ran to their task. At first there was no sign of the miscreant, until one of the men saw a fair head amongst the grass.

"We have him!" he called, and the men ran to apprehend the fugitive. Cuthred sprinted toward the forest. He was undoubtedly fast upon his feet, and quickly approached the edge of the woodland. Should he disappear into the thickets, it could take some time to apprehend him. Two of the younger men gave great chase, but the gap between them seemed to widen. He had just entered the woodland when he started a large boar, rooting in the earth. The boar saw him late and leapt and turned to face him. Cuthred tried to leap to the side, but tripped on a tree root and tumbled to the earth in a heap. Strong hands grasped his arms.

He was quickly bundled in front of Cerdic. The villagers watched as their fellow was forced to his knees.

"What say you?" asked the thegn. "Are the sheep yours?" Cuthred looked at the floor and swallowed hard, as if wishing that the very ground would open up and swallow him, as in the old story. I believe these sheep to be stolen last night, from Brockford." Still no reply from the miserable churl.

"Did you not swear upon oath when you reached the age of 12, to abstain from all crime? This is the common oath of all good men, which buttresses all of our laws. You will know that, if found guilty of this offence, you and all your kin could be sorely punished!"

"I know not where they came from!" cried Cuthred.

"Then why hide in the corn?" retorted Cerdic. A muttering of agreement went up from the crowd, though many of his fellow villagers just stood, open-mouthed at the proceedings. Clearly, most were shocked and knew nothing of the hidden sheep. Cuthred hung his head again.

"Your case will be heard in the hundred court, though your guilt is obvious to all men," announced Cerdic. "Still, justice will be seen to be done. It is my obligation and that of the hundred to find any miscreant and bring him back to face justice and, if necessary, to punish the kin."

The hundred would organise the pursuit of all notable criminals who fled, and punishment could include exile. A criminal could be transported, with his kin group, to a different part of the country. Harsh methods these were, to be sure, but these were harsh times and criminals would not be tolerated. Indeed, it was not unheard of for men to be executed for stealing sheep and cattle!

Cuthred was led away by Cerdic's men, whilst his wife wailed and his fellow villagers looked shamed. What now would happen to Anders and his family?

At a later date, we all crowded into Cerdic's hall, where a number of the brothers were assembled, as well as 12 juratores, who had been sworn, and had been assembled to listen to and to swear to the truth of the happenings.

After hearing the evidence and listening to the submissions of both the complainants and the defendant, the juratores huddled in a corner and whispered to one another. They returned and Cerdic asked them to say what they had decided. Their leader arose and said, "My Lord, the sheep were found in Cuthred's house. He and his kin swear that they know not how the sheep got there. We believe him to be guilty, and probably others too, but from the testimony of the villagers and his kin, we would ask that it be put to ordeal."

Gasps from the assembled throng! Cerdic thought for a moment and then made his proclamation. "Cuthred, you can be tried by fire, hot water, cold water or consecrated bread. My decision is that it shall be by hot water." Further gasps from the audience. We all knew what this meant.

The punishment would be carried out in the church, by one of the brothers, before witnesses. A stone would be placed in a cauldron and the water heated until it boiled. Then the cauldron would be taken from the fire and allowed to cool a little, whilst prayers would be said.

Cuthred would then need to plunge his hand into the cauldron and take out the hot stone. He would be considered innocent if, after three days, his wounds were healed without festering. God would be his judge!

The following day, Cuthred was led to the church. We assembled at the door, whilst some of the men from our village and his entered, along with a number of the brothers.

A cauldron had been set up within, and the ordeal was ready. Cuthred was led in by Cerdic and his men. We waited – our breath seeming shallow, until a scream rent the air. The crowd gasped and then hushed. Women wept and men flinched, understanding the pain Cuthred had just undergone. Shortly after, a whimpering Cuthred, his hand swaddled in cloth, was led from the church and back to Cerdic's compound.

Three days later, everyone assembled yet again at the church. Cerdic and his men escorted Cuthred and his kin from his compound. A brother skilled in medicine was present, with his box of potions and ointments to treat whatever wounds God should see fit to impose on Cuthred.

Before everyone, the swaddling bands were unwrapped from the injured hand. The crowd gasped as they saw the terrible scalds of the flesh. Cuthred winced and whimpered as the last cloth was gently lifted from his tortured flesh by the brother.

Our medicine is based upon a deep knowledge of herbs and their properties. The Christian missionaries from Italy brought much medical knowledge from the Greek and Roman worlds. But for those injured in battle, or with injuries such as Cuthred had endured, many would have had a low chance of surviving. They were always prone to infections, which would cause the flesh to rot!

But every community had a person who specialized in knowing how to use plants for medicine. This knowledge would be handed down from generation to generation within the family. And we were more fortunate than most, as we had the brothers.

Cuthred looked down upon his red and blistered hand. Tears ran down his face, and a wail left his lips, as they did from his kinfolk. Cerdic examined the festering wound and then looked him in the eye. "Cuthred," he said, "The Lord has given us his decision, though it was never in doubt in my mind or in the mind of any decent man. You are found guilty of the crime of theft of sheep. Have you anything to say?"

"It was revenge," he muttered. "Revenge for the persecution of my kinsmen by the people of Brockford. They would expel my family in the winter. The old tinker told us so."

"They would expel your kinsman because he would betray his own villagers and his thegn to gain favour with powerful men!" replied Cerdic. The villagers knew to what he referred.

"Cuthred," he continued, "I will not banish you and your kin to exile." A visible look of relief spread over Cuthred's face, though uncertainty over what his punishment would be could still be seen in his eyes. "Nor will I cut off your hand, though I should!" Further relief, but puzzlement. "You and all your kin will remain in your villages, but lose the standing of free churls. You will, instead be classed as thralls. You will lose the right to all possessions, and will live a life of slavery and servitude to me and to your fellow villagers." Further gasps from the crowd and calls of "Justice is done!" from many of the assembled free men.

But the consequences of a man's drive for the favour of power! How horrific it was for his kin! A life of drudgery in full service to the thegn. No possessions – everything you have belonging to your master. The lowest of food and provisions, dependent upon the whim of another man, and not by your own efforts. And yet those efforts must still be made. No prospect of marriage for Anders and his brothers, except to another thrall. Their children born into slavery. The thoughts of that day haunted me for many a long day. How simple it was to bring disaster upon your family!

Oh, but it was not to end there. Did you think that things would be so easy for my people in those black days? No! Just two days later a messenger rode into the village. "Cuthred is gone!" he said.

The thegn and his men searched for many days, but no trace of him was to be found. Had he gone to Tostig? We could not know. And the tension rose around our villages! Oh, what days!

# CHAPTER TEN

Later, by some weeks, Godwin and his men made their way to the Witangemot in London. It would be held on the autumn equinox. Was that an omen? Perhaps. Edward built up a serious force of men and marched them south to London. He was clearly unwilling to risk a confrontation with his earl with inadequate forces to back his play.

Godwin took his troops and occupied Southwark. But all was not going well for the Earl of Wessex. Although the English felt great resentment at the happenings in Dover, and the king's position upon it, it seems they were less ready to oppose the king and fuel the ambitions of the earl and his sons. The fact that a Witangemot would be held was enough for many. They would slink back into the shadows and see what transpired from the talks. Perhaps self-preservation was the shrewd option, and Godric now saw a good portion of his support was falling away.

"How goes the assembly of support?" asked Godwin of his son, Harold, as he entered his father's erected tent.

"Coenwulf will not arrive. He will not bring his men. Hewald has sent a messenger also. He is not willing to

attend the Witangemot. There is no news from Aelthelwyne, nor Cynreow. We are lacking in strength by compar-
ison with Gloucester."

"Why do they desert me now, when we are strong
enough to stand before the king?" Godwin cried, despair in
his voice.

"It seems that, although the people of England desire to
see the foreigners punished for their heinous crime, not
enough are ready to stand behind us. They fear your ambi-
tion is more than to get justice for the English people, and
are not willing to be the weapons in a civil war between
ourselves and the king."

"Then our hand is weaker in this matter. We will have
to be cautious in our argument," Godwin decided, wearily.
"I fear that the Norman fawners and taletellers have fanned
the flames of the king's partiality against us."

But things were to get even worse for the Earl of
Wessex. The following day, a council meeting was arranged.
Godwin, his sons and their remaining followers made the
journey to the pre-determined meeting place. They had
been assured of safe conduct, and why would they consider
anything else? But as they arrived, each man in the Wessex
party looked carefully around him and became anxious at
the huge forces that the king had amassed. Siward and
Leofric were there, but there were so many others that
their hearts stopped at the show of power.

It was with a growing sense of unease that the party
dismounted and handed their horses to retainers. They
fingered their weapons and glanced from side to side before
surrendering their arms as custom decreed. Mounted on
great poles were the flags of the king's retinue, the double-
headed eagle of Leofric's Mercians stood out for Godwin.
Would Leofric remain the honest and fair intermediary he
had been in Gloucester, or would the affair in Worcester

and Godwin's reference to it sway his actions? Godwin knew that the matter still rankled within him. Perhaps it had not been wise to mention it at the Gemot in Gloucester. *How a few simple words can change the complexion of things!* he thought.

At length, the party approached the king and all bowed low to their sovereign. Edward nodded but said nothing. His eyes seemed to bore into the very soul of Godwin. The king was flanked by Siward of Northumbria and, of course Leofric. Godwin and his sons nodded graciously at the earls and received acknowledgment in return.

At that, Leofric stepped forward and addressed the gathered throng. "My Lord Godwin, you and your party are most welcome to this Gemot of London. It is dearly hoped by all that good can come from this meeting, and that all differences can be set aside on ... certain matters."

"Lord Godwin," he continued, "Do you have news of the regrettable happenings in Dover? Are we nearer to finding and punishing the perpetrators of the foul murders?"

Godwin arose from his kneeling position before the king and replied. "My lord Leofric, my men have made exhaustive searches and investigations in Dover, but have uncovered nothing of the murder of the Normans. We know that a fight took place in an alehouse after the Normans of Eustace had insulted the Saxons who were drinking there, and that they initially killed a Saxon in the fight. Of course, we know the outcome of that fight, but as to the combatants, we know naught. The innkeeper insists that he didn't know the Saxon fighters. It must be assumed that they were not residents of Dover, but merely passing through the port to an unknown destination, either in England or abroad. I fear that the chance of bringing them to justice is an increasingly impossible task."

"You mean that the people of Dover will not give them up!" barked the king. "They are covering the tracks of these murderers, and I will not have it!"

"Sire, I have no reason to believe that the good people of Dover are protecting these men." Godwin retorted. "Why would they, when they know that your retribution upon them could be terrible? The only fact we know for certain in this matter, is that Eustace and his men murdered innocent Saxons within the town of Dover when they could not tell him more."

At this, Edward leapt to his feet, a look of fury across his face. "Earl Godwin, you continue to insult a guest at my court, and yet you would protect vile murderers on your own side!"

"I protect no one, Sire. I simply ask for justice to be seen to be done on both sides. If I do apprehend the murderers of the Normans, they will be severely punished under the law. The fact that we cannot trace one set of killers is troublesome, but cannot be helped. However, we do know the identity of the other guilty party."

This was too much for Edward, and he arose again from his chair. Leofric saw how the situation was and stepped forward. "My lords, we need to consider this situation calmly. Harsh words will not help the cause of justice, and will only fan the flames of discord."

Edward stood stock still, and glared at Godwin and his retainers. An air of tension was tangible within the room. Men-at-arms of the king's household fingered the hilts of their long-swords and short 'seax' swords upon their belts. It seemed to all that the room had suddenly become unbearably hot. All eyes were upon the king and Godwin.

At length, Edward seemed to cool and spoke to the throng. "I will retire for a while and consider what has been said here today. Return after noon, and we will discuss it further, when we have all had time to reflect upon our words." He aimed that barb firmly at Godwin. The assembled men bowed low as Edward took his leave, surrounded by his own men-at-arms. Leofric and Siward swept after him, followed by some of the lesser Ealdormen and retainers.

Godwin and his men turned also, and left the chamber for their own encampment. A meal was brought forth, and many partook of the fare, but Godwin ignored the wooden platter before him and stared into space, brooding upon the morning's happenings. Why could the king not see the truth in what he said? Why had he lost so much favour so quickly? Why had some of his support dried up like a brief rain on a warm summer's day? What would the afternoon bring? Would Leofric reason with the king and the matter be resolved, or would he buttress Edward's stubborn position?

After a short repast, Godwin and his sons sat upon low stools, considering the outcome of this debate. "Do you think that the king will force our hand against the people of Dover?" asked Harold.

"He will not force my hand to do his dirty work," growled Godwin. "He must do his own, and then see what the people of England make of that."

"Surely, he would not go to the lengths of sending in his own troops?" questioned Gyrth.

"I doubt it," his father replied. "But I can see no easy way out of this situation."

As the party pondered, a messenger arrived. "The king returns to the hall," he said, bowed slightly and turned his horse to retrace his steps. Godwin, his sons and the followers he had left looked from one to another and rose to attend their sovereign.

The party of Wessex made their way to the great hall

and filed into their places. The king, Leofric and Siward all had a look of sombre sternness on their faces, and Godwin wondered what had been discussed over their platters. Had a decision already been made? Was there to be more discussion?

When all were seated, Leofric rose to his feet. "My lords, the king has pondered long upon the unfortunate situation we have before us today, and has made a decision upon what action will be taken this day." He stepped back and took his seat again.

The king looked long and hard at his assembled nobles, and seemed to dither uncertainly about what he was about to say. But he then fixed his stare upon Godwin and spoke in a tone that left no one in doubt about his feelings and intentions. "Earl Godwin, it is my decision that you, your sons and all family and close retainers will be exiled from this kingdom to await my pleasure." The crowd gasped! "My Earls of Mercia and Northumbria are in agreement upon this matter. You will have five days to leave England." And with that, he swept from the room with his retainers, leaving Godwin, his sons and supporters still seated in incredulity.

And so it was that Godwin and his sons took leave of the country of their birth. Godwin and Gyrth left these shores and joined Sweyn in exile in Flanders, whilst Harold travelled across the sea to Ireland, where he spent the winter with Dermot, king of Leinster.

But was that to be the end of the Godwins as a force in this country? Only time would tell.

# CHAPTER ELEVEN

Time passed and the summer progressed, as years are apt to do. Life around the village became busy with the tasks that were needed to be done. The grass in the hay meadows was high enough to hide a man now. Tall daisies lit it up and insects buzzed around it. Now was the time to mow the meadows. Everyone had a job to do now – even the smith. We all went to the meadows at dawn. Long scythes cut through the tall grasses with a swishing sound. The sweet-smelling grass fell in soft heaps. Oh, how I have always loved the smell of new-cut grass!

Scything looks easy, but it takes much practice. The one thing that no one wants is to cut their own feet! But eventually the grass was cut. After a few days we visited the fields again; this time armed with pitchforks. We children always loved this time. It was great fun to throw all the hay into the air and watch it land again. We used to throw the hay over each other and play-fight with it. But the purpose of the fun was serious. By turning it, it allows the sun's rays to reach it all and dry it out. If the weather was wet, my father worried so much that it would be spoilt. This would have been a true disaster! 'Make hay while the sun shines,' the older people would say, and they were right. Once dried out, we would stack it into hay ricks.

Of course, the villagers also had to make the hay for Cerdic the thegn. There was often a good deal of grumbling about this, but we did each get three quarts of wheat, a ram to use, a pat of butter and a piece of cheese. That was something always to be looked forward to!

I long remember the game that would be played at the end of the hay harvest. Each man from a family was allowed to take away with him as much of the thegn's hay as he could lift on his scythe. But, should the handle break, he must leave it where it falls. We would all crowd around to watch as our fathers tried to get a good bundle of hay. Old Tom, Lord bless him, could not carry much away. Mark, Luke and my father were able to carry away a goodly amount, but Adam always tried to be greedy, and oft times would he break the shaft of his scythe. How we would all laugh at that!

During the twilight of summer, the ricks looked ghostly in the meadows. They appeared as a group of strange spirits, standing there in the hay fields. I always imagined their long wild hair waving in the breeze, and their robes trailing over the stiff stalks of the remaining stubble.

This time of the year, when the summer sun beat down upon us, was a busy time for all, and more so this year, as we pondered what would happen when the men left to join the rebellion against Tostig.

But wherever you went in the village and its surrounds, you would find us all hard at work. There were roofs to mend against the winter storms. The mill needed repairs, and a number of the men gave their time to help in the task.

Benjamin the smith was hard at work, sharpening tools

on his stone and making new ones. There was much dairy work to be done too, with cows and ewes to milk and butter and cheese to make. My mother and aunt worked such long hours at this task. My grandmother, by this time, was unable to help, and spent her time sitting in the sun and watching what went on. I was unsure as to how much she understood things by now, but that she enjoyed the sunshine was enough for us.

One person who was always busy was old Margaret the beekeeper. We were all fond of old Margaret, and especially of her honey! The bees were very important to all in the village. It is all we had for sweetening. Old Margaret would make round hives from twigs. These she would set up in a warm place, where she could watch them, and from where the bees could visit the flowers.

My favourite time of year for the bees was always late summer, when old Margaret would drive the bees from one old hive, or skep as we called them, to a new one, so that she could get at the golden honey they had stored each year. She would often give us part of a comb to eat in our hands. We became very sticky, but oh, the taste!

Once the bees had filled their honeycombs, the honey harvest would begin. So much of the honey had to be given to Cerdic. The rest was for the villagers, though Margaret was always careful to leave enough in the hive for the bees in the winter. Dead bees in spring are of no use to any man or woman!

I recall waking one morning to a babble of voices outside. When I emerged, blinking into the sunlight, a small crowd had gathered outside Margaret's hut. I soon learned that she had risen early and discovered that one of her hives had gone! But how could a person take a full hive of bees without being badly stung for his trouble? It was not something I would ever want to attempt! We were perplexed by this riddle. Cerdic and his men searched the nearby villages, but nothing could be found of Margaret's hive. And a hive is not an easy thing to hide, even in a town! I recall Margaret's distress at losing a hive – it was a serious business for the entire village!

All the while, although we were all busy and consumed by the jobs which must be done if we were to survive the winter, the talk often returned to the question of Cuthred. He had escaped all patrols and searches, and had disappeared into thin air. But how was it possible? Had Cuthred gained access to Tostig and his men? Was he now in service to the earl? Did the earl know of the plans against him? News from visitors to Cerdic and the monastery seemed to suggest that Tostig knew nothing or suspected nothing – but surely he must? Only time would tell!

In July, came the great sheep-washing. Oh, how the sheep hated it. Oh, how we also hated it! But it had to be done. The sheep were driven into a great pen by the banks of the river, bleating all the while. Some of the men waded into the water and others would catch the sheep and push it into the river. How they kicked and struggled against the men. It took a strong man to handle them!

Once they were washed, the time came for the shearing. Each of the men would catch a sheep and turn it over. He would hold it, on its back, between his legs, and cut the thick fleece from its back with great iron shears – well sharpened by Benjamin. The most skilful men could take off a fleece in one piece. When the sheep struggled, they would sometimes be cut by the shears, and then tar would be dabbed onto the wound to stop the bleeding. But the men prided themselves on finishing the shearing without harming a single sheep.

Once finished, the sheep were turned out again to graze. They always looked shocked and a little forlorn, I always thought, though after a while, they seemed more comfortable without their thick coats in the summer heat.

Of course, Cerdic's sheep were also to wash and shear. More grumbling from some of the villagers! But still, he was a good thegn, and well-liked amongst the villagers, so we got on with it.

The end of July saw everyone busy in the fields again, reaping the corn, this time. Benjamin the smith had sharpened all the village sickles. They are much smaller than the scythes, and mean that a man has to bend to cut the corn. It was back-breaking work! But it was a humiliation if a man got behind with the cutting! As the corn is cut, it is bundled up and tied into sheaves.

One morning, just as we had begun the day's work, a rider rode swiftly over the ford and into to Cerdic's compound. We all looked and wondered what news he brought and so urgently. Tostig?

We did not have to wait for long. Shortly afterwards, Cerdic and a handful of his followers thundered up to the fields on horseback. We stopped in our chores and stared, a strange feeling of fear welled up in the pit of our stomachs. Cerdic reined in beside a group of men. I stood on the periphery of the group and listened to what would be said.

The thegn pulled tightly on the reins, dragging his horse back from its headlong gallop. "We have word from the monastery," he announced. "It seems a shepherd monk has sighted Cuthred at the edge of the forest, near to his village. We must apprehend him, if we are able."

"Go with God," my father replied, "and pray to the lord that he has said naught to Tostig's men."

"There have been soldiers moving around the country-side in recent weeks," replied Cerdic. "We must all be on our guard for an attack at any time. Should Tostig hear of what is afoot, he will spare no man, woman or child he thinks is a party to the plan."

My stomach churned and I will admit that I spent the rest of the day looking nervously around me and jumping at the least strange noise. We might be bringing in a good harvest, but would any of us live long enough to enjoy it? Would it lie burned in the barns and ricks. Would the fields be littered with our dead animals, as well as dead villagers? Who knew? My imagination ran riot.

By the end of the day, all of the thegn's corn was cut and stored in the great barn on Cerdic's land. Some of the corn was also given to the church, and stored in the tithe-barn. My mother explained to us that this was a gift to God to thank him for the harvest. We stacked our corn in our own rick behind the houses. Oh, but this was always an anxious time for the village. If the harvest was good, then we would have plenty of bread to eat for the rest of the year, but if the weather was wet and the harvest spoilt, then we would go hungry during the long months of winter. The best part of the harvest for we children was the Harvest Home festival at the end of the toil. Wistan, the Hayward was a happy man at such festivals.

But would there be a Harvest Home this year?

Just as we left the fields, with the sun dipping to the horizon and the day's work done to everyone's satisfaction, the group of riders reappeared on the hillside. This time, they rode slowly, allowing their tired mounts to breathe. They were in no hurry. We looked as we could, but there was no sign of Cuthred. Surely, they would bring him back to Cerdic's compound, if they found him. Or was he already dead and his body dumped for his kin to bury?

The riders approached and trotted across the ford. Cerdic drew rein again. "There is no sign of the outlaw," he said. "We have searched what we could of the forest, near to the sighting, but there is no trace of the man there."

"Could the old monk be mistaken?" my father asked.

"It might be," answered the thegn, "he is old and his eyes rheumy. But it is still a worrying thing, so close to the rebellion."

The men nodded and Cerdic and his men continued their progress to his compound, where food and drink would be waiting for both man and horse.

The next job would be my favourite! This was the time when the trees were laden with fruit! The branches hung low, this year, with the weight of the apples and pears. The plums were also ripening, and the first blackberries, sloes and nuts were beginning to show fruit. We would have a merry time, gathering in the crops of ripe, juicy fruit to eat around the fire! Wigmund the swineherd would spend his time in the woodland, knocking down the first acorns for his pigs to root for. How they always enjoyed the feast!

A short while later, with most of the harvest in and the yield looking to be good this year, Cerdic appeared one evening, in the village.

"My people," he said. "The time has come to hunt! You have all worked hard in the fields, and now we must take an opportunity to fill our larders with fresh meat, for our women to smoke and salt down for the winter. Who knows what this winter holds," he finished, cryptically. Though he could have been speaking of our fortune with the winter's weather, there was another side to it. Would the men return to their families to enjoy the fruits of their labours, or would many a woman find herself widowed and in desperate straits? We knew that the women and children would be cared for as best the village could, but life for any woman without a man to provide was always difficult.

The following morning, with a light dampness in the air, all was prepared. Cerdic and a handful of his men, and also a few of his women, appeared, he with a goshawk upon his wrist, its jesses jangling as he rode; its great hood covering its eyes and calming the bird.

Now, hawking consists of the training and flying of hawks for the purpose of catching other birds and game. From kings and their noblemen, to simple churls, all delight in following the sport on horseback and on foot, to watch the birds soaring high to gain the upward drafts of wind in order to swoop down upon some unsuspecting prey and take it to ground.

A huddle of dogs stood ready by the thegn's horse, tongues lolling and spittle drooling from their jaws. They knew what was to be and eagerly looked forward to the chase and the reward of offal later. Their handlers were afoot, and called them together to keep them from becoming too excited and straying. A number of the men, including my father and myself, were also ready to go to the forest, to see what we could catch for the stores. We carried bows and spears. My bow, made for a child, was much shorter than that of my father, but it was powerful enough to bring down small prey.

We progressed toward the forest edge. Cerdic looked around him at all times, looking for suitable prey for his hawk to pursue. A clump of bare earth moved and became a small hare. Set up from its form, it ran a few paces toward the field boundary. Cerdic uncovered the great hawk's head, let go of the jesses and threw the bird aloft. It circled whilst the hare snuggled into the pelt of rough grass, hoping not to be seen by the keen eyes above it. Perhaps it thought that flight would bring only more attention from the bird.

The hawk glided around the skies on open wings, its attention fixed upon the ground. It spotted the hare and closed in for the kill. The hare saw the bird and fled for the forest edge, but not quickly enough. The hawk swooped from the sky and grabbed the unfortunate beast in its huge claws. It flapped skyward again, the hare wriggling in its grasp, still alive. The bird flew to the gloved hand of Cerdic, who relieved it of its burden and passed it to a retainer, who quickly despatched it and shoved it into a great bag whilst Cerdic rewarded the bird with a morsel of flesh from his pouch.

We entered the forest quietly, not wanting to raise too many alarm calls from the creatures that lived there. Soft, green leaves swished like velvet as we passed. We had noted the direction of the wind before we entered, as we could not afford for the deer to get a scent of the hounds.

And it was the deer that lived within the forest and along its edges that most of us were keen to find. That was the quarry that would keep us fed over the winter, as well as any boar that might be encountered. I hoped that we would not find boar, as I had no great desire to confront one of the magnificent beasts; though I was happy enough to feast on their succulent meat.

We split up into small groups now, and spread ourselves through the woodland to see what we might raise. The odd bird arose from the ground before us, and some were caught and killed to fill the bags.

We entered a glade in the forest to behold the sight of a stag, browsing the young leaves of the trees. He had neither seen, heard nor smelt us coming, the wind being in our favour. My father signalled for us to shrink back and we crouched and mimicked the shapes of the trees and bushes. He slowly rose and drew his bow. He loosed an arrow at the great beast, and it roared as if in the rut as the sharp point entered its neck and exited from the other side. It reared up on its great hind legs and then slumped to the floor. As we approached, the stag, still living, thrashed its great antlers, but, in truth, it was over. We stood as its eyes became lifeless and its tongue lolled from its mouth, blood trickling from the corner onto the grass below.

The men quickly brought forward a stake that we had carried with us for the purpose. My father slit its throat to allow the blood to drain and we tied its hooves together around the stake. Two men lifted the stake onto their shoulders and carried the beast back to the woodland edge, where it was raised into the lower branches of a tree to allow it to hang. There, two young boys and an old man, armed with slings and short spears would guard the game until it could be carried home.

We made slow progress through the woodland, until I set up a brace of pheasants from a low bush. I raised my short spear and hurled it. I was lucky and it caught the cock bird across the head. The bird fell, stunned to the bushes below. I quickly scrambled into the thicket to retrieve 'my' bird, of which I was very proud, only to stumble upon something unexpected.

Within the bush was a beehive! It must surely be the

hive lost by Old Margaret to the thief in the night. I called to the men in my group, and they stood gazing in astonishment as they saw the open hive lying there, most of its honey gone.

We stared around us, wondering who could have left the hive here. Who were they? How had they fared against the bees? Where were they now? One of the men held a horn to his lips and blew a blast. This was not a time to think about alarming animals!

Through the undergrowth men appeared from all sides. They came to stare at the sight before them, through the bushes, Cerdic appeared and quickly ordered the men to spread throughout the wood, but in sight of one another when possible. We combed the undergrowth, but no one seemed to be within our reach. The deeper reaches of the forest are a hidden world, humming with the life of insects and birds.

Just as we thought the search would remain fruitless, a cry went up to my right. Our heads whirled to the sound. Across a clearing, a man had been spotted, low on his belly, snaking to the edge of a clearing. At the sound, he rose from behind a great tree trunk and ran. One of Cerdic's men raised his bow and an arrow thudded into the fleeing fugitive's right shoulder. Still he ran. The men followed, hard muscles running, sure feet on solid ground. The man's form was a flitting shadow through the trees as he bent his steps toward the deeper woodland. But the men were gaining on him, and now the dogs gave chase. He glanced backwards, uncertainty and fear etched across his face, and that was his great mistake. Another arrow followed into his back and yet another near to the base of his spine and his legs folded beneath him. We dashed to the scene to see Cuthred lying face down upon a cushion of moss. Two men raised him to his knees to face us. Blood soaked into the rough cloth of his shirt and came trickling from his mouth. A rattling in his chest showed that a lung was punctured.

Cerdic looked down upon the beaten man. His words were cold as ice and as hard as steel. His hard eyes showed no emotion. "Your time is near," he said, "tell me truly what has passed from your lips to others. If I find your words to be true, your family will be cared for. But if I find you lied ..."

"I have said nothing to any man," Cuthred managed to say, and I believed him. Surely, he would not lie now. He had nothing to gain; his time on this earth was done, but he would surely protect his kin.

Cerdic stood and was lost in thought. Could this man be trusted? Was the plot safe? He must believe that which the man told him. What choice did he have? If he lied, there was little that could be done now.

"I will believe you," he stated. He nodded to his men and the two began to drag the outlaw toward the woodland edge. It was futile, as Cuthred would be dead before they emerged from the trees.

We wandered home, deep in thought. The birds, deer and a great boar, killed by another group, were transported back to the village, to the delight of those left behind this morning. We would all share in the spoils. But the main topic of conversation in the village tonight would be Cuthred!

# CHAPTER TWELVE

Autumn was upon us soon enough, and the last grey tendrils of fog curled against a pale sky. The night airs were becoming chill now. But life went on and tasks still had to be done, regardless of the sword we all felt was hanging over us. I had noticed that my mother was becoming more agitated and less patient with us as the days wore on. I knew what was eating away at her soul. She tried to concentrate on the work to be done; her hustle and bustle was her way of putting it all to the back of her mind. But it was still there, lurking, waiting for a still moment to leap back to the forefront.

I knew too, that my father pondered more and more about what might lie ahead for us. Was he regretting now that he had said he would go? How could he not go? Was he regretting saying that I should go?

Was I regretting that he had said that I should go? I didn't know.

But, as I have said, life must go on. We could not afford to be idle. The corn still stood in the ricks and was not yet ready to be made into bread. The first task was to thresh it to beat the grain from the husk.

All around our village you could hear the thump, thump of the threshers at work. We would take the sheaf of corn and beat at the heads with jointed sticks called flails. This breaks the grain away from the stalk and helps release it from the outer husk.

All the while, the women would shovel up the grain and the empty shells, or chaff, and throw them high into the air, into the breeze. The simple effect of that is that the heavier grain − which we prized − fell to the floor, whilst the chaff was blown by the breeze into a separate pile. We called this winnowing. The children would look around at the ground to find any grain which had gone astray. When winter came, we would be grateful for every last seed!

The grain was poured into sacks, whilst the straw and chaff were kept for the cattle and sheep. Nothing was wasted. The good grain would need to be stored high and dry, away from autumn's dampness and also the mouths of the many mice that ran around the village, searching for scraps around the halls and out-buildings.

When my mother needed flour, my father and I would haul a sack of grain to the mill to be ground down, good and fine. The water turned the great wheel and that in turn moved the grinding stones. I seem to recall the great cog wheels of the mill were carved from hornbeam. The miller insisted on nothing less. They took the strain better and lasted longer, he said. In payment for grinding the corn, we had, of course, to give a proportion to the miller in return for his work in grinding it. We also had to provide some to Cerdic too, as was his right as thegn and owner of the mill.

Once home, my mother could make her bread. I have watched her many times, as she mixed the flour with clean water, that my father had filled from the river and decanted a number of times from one pot to another, in order to allow the tiny fragments of silt to settle out. She would then strain it through a clean cloth.

Once mixed, she formed it into flat loaves and we would take it to Cerdic's great oven, or she would bake small flatbreads herself over the fire. (To cook it in Cerdic's oven, my mother had to pay a loaf for the privilege.) Whichever way it was done, the smell was wonderful. Ah, I can smell it now!

Of course, our fathers were always thinking ahead, and ploughing had already begun for the setting of next year's corn. I loved to see all of the colours of the earth, as it turned again under the plough.

Oh, it was a time of joy, when the larders were filling again after looking very deplete of late. But even then, we all stopped from time to time and stared at the horizon. What we expected to see, I have no idea – perhaps troops from Tostig, come to take their revenge? Or perhaps it was just the time of year, when the shrivelling of the leaves starts and winter begins to get the upper hand. I knew that the time of our departure was near. I had seen Cerdic's men making preparations. I knew that wagons had arrived, carrying the arms that had been promised to us 'by a friend of Cerdic'. We all pretended not to know the mysterious benefactor, but all knew that the money to buy the 'goods' had come from the monastery.

But was it all work and doom and gloom? No. We were all determined to carry on as normal and to make the most of the time we had left ... had left? And so our Harvest Home arrived. On the Sunday, we all dressed in our 'better' clothes, though truth to tell, we had few clothes to wear – only what my mother could provide and the few pieces she bought from the tinkers when she had a few spare coins in her purse. The church bell called us all to the first service of the day; Matins. One of the senior brothers would attend to say Mass.

We were all very proud of our little church, as we'd all played a part in its building. At least, the adults had. We would proceed to the nave and either stand or kneel for the service. Only the old and infirm would have the comfort of a seat. On a step into the chancel, the monk would stand before us. The altar was to his rear. It was covered, I remember, in what I felt was a beautiful cloth of different colours. It was more beautiful than any cloth I'd ever seen in any home, though there were many similar ones in the monastery. Upon the altar were two shining candlesticks. I loved to watch as the tiny flames danced in the drafts like fairies in a woodland glade.

Around some of the walls were pictures, painted by the monks. They told of the stories of the Bible and the lives of the saints. I always looked at the picture of Daniel in the lions' den and marvelled at his courage, to stand there amidst wild beasts bigger than any I had ever seen. What, I wondered, would he have made of our wolves and great boars?

At the Mass, the monk would bless the Holy Water. Afterwards, one of Cerdic's men, the parish clerk, would take it and sprinkle a little on every house in blessing, so that we might live in peace and harmony during the following week. Things being as they were, this was something that we all fervently hoped!

I always wondered at our week. It was of seven days, as laid down in the Bible, and therefore a Christian week. And yet we named the days after Pagan gods and the heavens. Sunday was the day of the sun. Monday, the day of the moon. Tuesday was named for Tiw, the god of war. Wednesday for Woden, the god of magic and death, Thursday for Thor, the thunder god, Friday for Frige, the goddess of love. Saturday was named after Saturn, which, I believe is one of the heavenly bodies. Curious!

But I digress. Each family had brought a little something from their own stores to the church, for the Harvest Service, and these, along with offerings from the monastery fields, would be given, by the monks, to those in our community who were in most need. Cerdic, I noticed, had also made a generous contribution to this charity. He was indeed a good thegn. We could have had much worse!

Some people attended church again in the evening for Evensong, but for the rest of Sunday, and particularly for the Harvest Sunday, we mostly enjoyed ourselves.

All of we boys made ourselves a bow and arrows – they were useful in hunting small game for the pot – and we all practised hard, for it was a fine thing to be a good archer. We would make the bow from elm or yew, as they are both tough woods, but they will bend well and don't break easily under the terrible strains we put them under. The bowstring was made from hemp. For our arrows, we usually chose oak, ash or birch. Each arrow had a sharpened end, sometimes with an arrowhead, and goose feathers for the flights.

It takes a very strong man to bend an adult longbow and to string it ready for shooting. In one corner of a field, Cerdic had erected butts and, if the men were not using them, we boys would go there to practise.

We rough boys would also take part in wrestling, and indeed it was one of my favourite sports ... after archery, of course.

Sometimes, we would climb on each other's shoulders and the top two would wrestle. That was great fun, I always thought.

Some of the adults would take part in board games, such as 'Nine Men's Morris' or 'Fox and Geese'. But I was a young lad then, and needed to run off the seemingly bound-less energy of youth!

When I returned home in the late afternoon, to warm myself by the fire and enjoy some small morsel of my moth-er's cooking, my father was busily preparing leather helmets, clothing and weapons. He had two spears and shields and a small seax sword, which was to be mine, I learned. He was also sharpening some of our farming tools; honing the blades until they were sharp enough to sever flesh and their blades shone in the firelight.

My mother had cooked some small cakes and flavoured them with honey. My young brothers and sisters were already enjoying them. I picked up a couple and popped one into my mouth, savouring the sweet taste and the soft texture, melting in my mouth! I would not eat too much as I knew that in the evening, when the sun went down, we would all go to Cerdic's hall for the Harvest Supper. There would be duck and probably fish from the river. There would be more oat cakes and honey cakes. There would be pies and sausage, bread and paste and even pepper. There would be some of the early autumn fruits to delight our senses. We would drink pots of ale – perhaps too much in some cases! What a feast we would have! People would play pipes and other instruments, largely made by them from what they could find. And yet still they made a jolly sound.

There would be dancing, when the young lads and the girls would eye each other and shyly dance with those they favoured. Mind you, we were always careful to dance with other girls, lest people would get to know our youthful secrets! We were always conscious, also, not to leave out anyone from the gaiety, lest they should be hurt in their pride. My mother always stressed this to us. She was a kind and thoughtful woman.

I took a pot and poured myself a mug of ale and sat down beside my father. "It is to be soon then?" I asked.

He looked up from his work and permitted himself a smile. "They say we go the day after tomorrow," he said. "We meet with Cerdic tonight, at the Harvest Supper. We will make our final plans then; where we are to go and by what route."

I must admit that my heart leapt in my breast and then dropped as quickly to my stomach. So this was it then? We would soon be off. None knew if we should ever return.

I glanced at my mother, slowly grinding up a little of our corn in a hand quern she kept to grind smaller amounts of flour. She looked up as we spoke and I could see the fear in her eyes. She wiped an eye and pretended it was a mote of grit bothering her and then returned to her task.

My grandparents also looked over to us, following the conversation. At least my grandfather did. I was not sure that my grandmother really understood the gravity of the situation. She had once been a wise and contemplative woman, but age had taken its toll upon her body and her mind.

I'm not sure that my siblings really understood, or, indeed, how much they had been told. It was probably better that they knew as little of it as possible, save that we were to go away for a while with Cerdic. Perhaps the thought that we would be with our thegn would reassure them that we would take no harm and return to the bosom of our family.

Later in the evening, we made our way to Cerdic's hall. People were already gathering, chattering excitedly and laughing together. For how long, I thought? My mother and sisters dressed in their best peplos dresses, with their linen under-shift, covered by a woven outer dress, fastened at the shoulders with brooches, passed down from generation to generation. My father, grandfather and I had donned clean linen shirts and dyed over-shirts, with clean leggings.

As we entered, my mother ushered my younger siblings to the tables, where the food was laid. They would soon be enjoying themselves and would not notice my father and me sidling off to talk with Cerdic and the other men.

We gathered behind a curtain and stood whilst Cerdic waited for all to assemble. Once he was satisfied that we were all there, he spoke to us.

"We leave the day after tomorrow. You have the day tomorrow to finish any tasks you might have begun, and to leave things in the hands of your families. We must trust them that they will work hard to keep our holdings in the manner in which we would approve. There is little other choice."

We looked at each other. So much was to be loaded onto other shoulders.

"I will leave some of my older men here to guard the village from outlaws and bandits who might be roaming the country. Your families will come to no harm." We moved uneasily. I was sure he meant what he said, but no man could guarantee that this would be the case. There were many lawless, desperate men roaming the countryside, trying to survive, whilst outside the law for whatever reason.

"We march south. We should make York in a few short days. As far as anyone is aware, Tostig's men know nothing of this rebellion. Men will join us as we march and others will meet with us at York."

A murmur ran around the crowd of men. It seemed that the whole of the area was up in arms against our Lord Tostig. We would be well supported in our mission to rid ourselves of this canker. It was as we had been told. Benjamin the smith fingered the side of his head where his ear had once been. I was sure that an idea had planted itself in Benjamin's head, that it would be he who dealt death to Tostig, in revenge for his injury.

"I know that you will have your weapons prepared. You are all fine men. We *will* prevail in this matter. Tostig will go and life for us will be better. It has been decided to call upon Morcar, a noble of Mercia to be our lord." He paused. "Until the day, then." he said. We all nodded.

Just as we were turning to leave, Cerdic held me by the shoulder. "You are a brave young man, John," he said, staring down at me. "You will do well with us, and will return safely to your family. I swear it."

A young man! He was addressing me! I had never thought of myself as a 'brave young man', but my heart burst with pride at the thegn's words. I was truly a man!

# CHAPTER THIRTEEN

On a fine autumn day, as the sun squeezed above the horizon, we were finally ready for the march to York. Oh, how my mother wept. My aunt too. And in my grandfather's eyes, there was more moisture than usual. He clasped us to him and held us tightly. My grandmother sat upon her bed and stared at us. "Have you ploughed?" she asked my father. "All is well, Mother," he soothed her, "The work is done." I am not sure she fully understood what we were about to do, nor what the outcome might be. My siblings too picked up the mood and began to sob, and clung to us. My father and I tried to smile away their worries, but to no avail.

At length, we had collected together our possessions for the coming events; not much really – a shield and spear each, an axe, the seax, a couple of sharpened sickles and knives. I took my bow and a leather quiver of arrows. We also took a bag of dry food and a leather skin of ale. The rest of our food and drink would have to be supplied by Cerdic or well-wishers, or caught and collected along the way on the journey.

Other men of the village began to congregate in the

centre. They too were hauling their freight strapped to their backs. Families all around us were in each other's arms, clinging and whispering good wishes into ears. Tears ran down many cheeks and some of the women had set up a keening wail.

I think I can imagine how they felt by the way I felt. Suddenly, I did not want to leave the village and my mother behind. I did not want to say goodbye to my grandparents and brothers and sisters. I was a man, but inside I think I was still just a boy. But I knew that it had to be so. I had to march with my father and the men to right the wrongs done by Tostig, and to free ourselves of his tyranny. He had badly treated the people of Northumbria for too long, brutalising and taxing until many could barely survive, whilst he lived in luxury in York with his Danish house-carls. It was said that he ate meat daily, and drank wine!

As the dawn sky brightened, Cerdic rode into the village, his men in tow, and sat his horse in the middle of us. "My villagers and friends," he began, "this is a sad time for all of us as we leave our families; they worrying that we might not survive, and us worrying about how they will fare in our absence. It should never have come to this, but we can no longer continue to live like whipped dogs, our money and goods taken from us by Tostig and his men. But of one thing you can be certain. We will make good account of ourselves in York, and I pledge that I will do everything in my power to bring safely home all of the men of these villages."

With that, he wheeled his horse and left through the village gate, followed by his household men and finally by us, his churls, armed as best we could to face Tostig's housecarls. We looked back as we marched away, trying for just one last look at our families. A wailing rose again and many of the women followed us out of the village until they realised that they could go no further in our tracks. And there they waited until we were out of sight, around a bend in the river. South we marched to York!

The day's march began well. Everyone seemed in better spirits once we had left the village behind and marched for an hour or two. Men began to sing and to whistle tunes. Some began to tell humorous stories and riddles, and to laugh out loud. I suppose that is what men do when they know that they face the uncertainty of battle. It must be a man's way of dealing with the unknown ahead. The dread of battle and of not returning to the village we had known all our lives, and our families left there to fend for themselves.

The leaves had now left most of the trees, except those that never fully shed in the winter, but cast all year round. Many of the people of the villages we passed were busily going about the autumn tasks, which, they prayed, would ensure their survival through the winter. Men were ploughing, keeping their eyes fixed straight ahead to make good straight furrows. Boys drove the oxen, shouting and flicking their long whips to drive the beast faster. Oh, it is cold, hard work, ploughing in the chill of autumn!

In the midst of all of this work, a church bell pealed out. Now everyone stopped and dropped to one knee to pray. The people know that when the Sanctus bell rings, their rector is holding the daily service in praise of God.

By midday, the men in the fields we passed had unhitched the oxen and fed them some hay. Their lords would provide a meal for those working his land. It might be a 'wet' meal, with ale, or a 'dry' one, without. Everyone loves a wet meal, with bread, cheese, a little meat and ale. After the meal, it is always back to work again, until the Ave bell rings from the church, and all stop to say a short prayer again. That is always the welcome signal to go back to their homes again, see to the oxen and settle to their own suppers.

Other people we passed were cutting wood and carting it back to their villages. We use wood for so many things in our lives. And we need to stock up the firewood for the winter season ahead. What we would do without it, I have no idea! I have always thought that we must take great care of our forests, and farm only what we need, lest they disappear from our landscape. What a disasterous day that would be!

From one great wood, a group of boys was bringing the swine in for the winter. They were fat from gorging on the acorns. Soon, it would be the great pig-killing day, when the excess swine would be slaughtered for the winter, and either pickled in great tubs or salted down, or hung in the rafters to smoke over the fire. I always hated this time, as animals we had seen grow from babes would be brought to the end of their lives. But I could almost taste the roast meat to which the people would treat themselves! Oh, the running fat of the pig's rind!

There would be cattle and sheep to slaughter too, and fish to catch and pickle. Nuts would need to be collected, before the squirrels took them all. I had always enjoyed watching the squirrels in the wood, running up and down the bark of trees, chasing on the forest floor and burying their nuts where they thought others would not find them. Oft times, I am sure, they forgot themselves and these nuts grew to be forest trees, to provide further food to the feast.

The women of the villages sat outside their homes in the autumn sunshine, making the thick winter clothes that would be needed soon.

Wherever we passed a village – though we did try to avoid them in order to maintain the element of secrecy and surprise for Tostig's men - the people would stop and stare at the column of men marching south. Many would already know our purpose, though others would not and would wonder.

As we travelled, more men joined our column, as villagers came from their own compounds and burghs. There were some strange sights, as with a giant of a man, dressed in leather, whom, we were told, was a village blacksmith. Our smith, Benjamin, quickly sought his company, and the two soon fell to talking about their craft. I saw him glance and point to Benjamin's missing ear, and watched as Benjamin was told him the tale of its loss. The giant nodded solemnly.

By the end of the first day, we had travelled around 25 miles, so they said. We settled ourselves in the lee of a wood, sheltered from the north winds. But still, the night air was chill. We lit fires and huddled into our cloaks whilst warming some pottage we had hauled with us. On the way, we had collected some fruit and nuts from the wayside, with which to supplement our poor meal.

As we sat there, men began to mingle with others from different villages. I have to say that the feeling around the camp was one of optimism mixed with grim determination to do what had to be done. A man approached us and settled himself before our fire. He was a slight man, with a grey beard and a scar that ran from one eye to the corner of his mouth. I thought, at first, that it made him look sinister, though he proved to be good company.

Men around the fire told tales they knew of the past and the history of our people, which I always enjoyed. In a lull in the conversation, the stranger spoke up. "I know of a tale that I heard when I travelled in the south. It concerns a king of ancient times. Would you hear it?"

"We will," my father replied, and I pricked up my ears for a new story that I had not heard before.

"It is said," he began, "that a great king lived in the land of the East Angles. Now this king was called Raedwald. He lived many centuries past, and was a powerful king. He was the son of Tytilla of East Anglia, and a member of the house of Wuffingas. It is said that, at first, he bowed the knee to Aelthelbert of Kent. But later, his own power grew.

Legend has it that he was the leader of a great army that fought our kingdom of Northumbria at the Battle of the River Idle. There he defeated Aelthelfrith, our lord, and installed Edwin, who bowed his own knee, as the new king of Northumbria. I did hear that, in that battle, Aelthelfrith and Raedwald's own son, Raegenhere, were both killed. They say that the battle was fierce and long and that the River Idle was foul with the blood of Englishmen".

There was a muttering at the thought of our kingdom of Northumbria being defeated by this king, but my father bade the tale-teller to continue. I could not wait to hear the rest of the tales about him.

A new hero to hear about!

"I heard that he became the most powerful ruler that the land had ever seen, and many tales were told about his courage and wisdom."

"Well now, this man, according to the Venerable Bede, became the Bretwalda, the over-king of the whole land."

I had heard of Bede from the monks. He was a great man of letters, who had written much about the history of our people and the Christian church. Though that is about all I knew at that time.

"It is said by Bede, that Raedwald was the first king to become a Christian, though he also kept a pagan temple. I suppose he wanted to make sure that he displeased no deity!

"But the thing I heard that most amazed me was after

Raedwald's death," the man continued. "It is but a story, and I do not know how much of it is true."

Now our appetite for the tale grew even stronger!

"They do say that when Raedwald died, he was buried in a great mound, near to a wood bridge over the River Debn. And certainly, there are mounds to be seen to this day. But they say that Raedwald's grave was unparalleled in its richness. They say that the great king was laid to rest in a ship, many feet long, which had seen action on the high seas."

Eyes opened wide at the thought of the riches buried with this man, though, of course, none would ever dare to seek it out, for fear of angering God, in whose care this king had been placed.

"In the centre of this great ship was a hoard of jewellery, silver bowls and drinking cups, and weapons of all kinds, encrusted with jewels."

Now eyes widened even more, and jaws dropped open as the tail unfolded.

"One tale I heard tells of a huge sceptre, in the form of a whetstone, though one that was never used. It seems that it was the symbol of office of the Bretwalda. They say that the jewellery and weapons could only have been made by the best goldsmith in the world!"

Further gasps from the assembled throng, which had slowly grown as the tale unfolded. *Please stop him from saying, 'they say',* I thought.

"But the most amazing thing that they say is buried with the king is a great helmet. It is said that it is decorated with animals and warriors. The helmet, they say, has a face mask, with eye-holes and a nose plate. It has, they told me, a great boar's head as a symbol of the man's strength, and also a great dragon's head. Of course, no man knows whether this is all true, and I suppose no man will ever know the truth."

I knew that night that I would dream of the great helmet and the man who wore it. Would I ever be as brave as he? I doubted it! But could the story really be true? I hoped so.

The following day, we crossed the River Tees, where it was shallow enough to wade across, and made our way as far south as Aelfereton, (Northallerton). Here we stopped to eat and drink. It was, my father said, named after a farm that once stood there, belonging to a man called Aelfere. He often told me such things and taught me a little of the history of the land he had learned from the monks. I was always fascinated to hear about such things. Indeed, I was never happier than when learning from the monks of the monastery. How could anyone not?

Once across the Tees, the thegns consulted and decided to send out 'wolves' to scout the area. They all felt that it could now become dangerous for us, as we would be more likely, at any time, to run into patrols of Tostig's men. That would have been a serious situation, as there could be no doubt that a force would then be sent against us.

The people we met along the road were, in general, kind to us. Though we did try to skirt around settlements, we could not avoid them all. We were often given food and drink, and, at our halt that day, we enjoyed a meal of local fish and bread. Cerdic also moved around our party, with his men, distributing half an apple each and a pot of ale.

As we moved on, a group of men approached us from the east. They were, they told us, from a place called Thraesk, (Thirsk). It was, I thought, a strange name, but I have much later learnt that it is a Viking name, meaning 'lake' or 'fen'. It was settled around a small beck that ran into the much larger River Swale – another Norse name. Of course, we must remember that this has always been a Scandinavian area, and, indeed, York itself was the Danish capital of Northern England. Many men looked upon that era with fondness.

Some of the men had come from the small hamlets of Ainderby and Quernhow, around five miles west of Thraesk. Ainderby too is a Viking name, meaning the village belonging to Eindrithi, whilst Quernhow means 'mill-hill'. I suppose that this is taken from the quern stones we use to grind our corn, and a 'howe' is, of course, a hill. The hill at Quernhow is but a small mound, on the old Roman road that men call 'Dere Street'.

It was at the crossing of a bright, bubbling stream, near to a large stretch of woodland that the worst almost happened. Just as the sun passed its highest point in the sky and began to fall again to the west, and we considered that a halt might be called to rest our bones, a rider suddenly thundered toward us. It was one of the 'wolves'. He dragged his mount to a standstill and leapt from the saddle. "Hide the force!" he yelled, "a patrol approaches from the south!"

At once, pandemonium broke out within the ranks. What was to do? At once orders were barked by the leading thegns. "Get ye to the trees! Hide yourselves! Get down and blend into the landscape! Show no bright colours! Let no man neither breathe nor whimper!"

My father grabbed my arm. "Run for the trees!" he called. I was not to ask twice. I ran like a fox into the nearest thicket. Would the woodland be enough to hide us from the eagle eyes of the patrol? There were few leaves left on the trees now. We dove behind a low bank, behind a holly tree and took our breaths in short gasps. We crawled up to the bank's ridge and peered out into the surrounding farmland. After what seemed like hours, but was but a few minutes, a patrol of around twenty men-at-arms appeared, mounted on large horses. They were well armed, though not for a serious battle. Indeed, we could, perhaps, have taken them, but that might only have alerted other forces, if the men did not return.

The patrol rode toward the track upon which we had been walking, and the leader held up his hand. He and the other men looked closely at the ground. *They have found our trail*, I thought. The men broke ranks and wandered their horses around the area, scanning every bent blade of grass and each footmark in the dust.

They lifted their heads and stared around them. Would they see where we had run for the wood? Each man turned his horse slowly, and peered into the middle distance. The leader spoke, though we could not catch his words on the wind. He pointed in a number of directions, and it was clear that a discussion was taking place.

At that point, somewhere in the trees above me, a woodpecker began to rap out its territorial hammering on a tree. My breath stopped in my breast as a soldier turned in the saddle and stared across, directly at us. He had to see us. But then one of the other men called to him and his attention was drawn in another direction. There was a bellowing of cattle and shouts of herders.

At that moment, from around a bend in the track came a small herd of around thirty cattle and their cowherds. They were driving the cattle south, in the direction in which we had been travelling. The soldiers watched them approach and then stop a short distance away, as the leading cattle detected the smell of horses and men on the breeze.

One of the cowherds approached the men-at-arms and spoke. Again, we had no idea of the course of the conversation. The soldier pointed to the ground and swept his arm in the direction we had come. The man shook his head and shrugged his broad shoulders.

Was the soldier leader asking if he'd seen a large moving party? Had the cowherds seen us? Would they tell the patrol what they had seen? Again, the cowherd shook his head and looked puzzled. He pointed to the cattle and at the track behind him and ahead. The soldiers looked around them again and then, seemingly satisfied by the idea that the track had probably been made by herds of animals, they wheeled their horses and continued on their way. A collective sigh of relief was almost audible.

It was decided, by our leaders, that to move directly south toward York would not be the best course of action. We would need to divert our tracks. And so, from there, we moved west, toward the small town of Rypum. It was a goodly way out of our preferred direction, but I think all agreed that avoiding the troops was the best option.

As we skirted around Rypum (Ripon), one of the bands of men who had recently joined us and now travelled with us told us of the origins of the small town.

"It has a folk-name," he said. I must have looked puzzled by this, as he continued. "It means that it has a tribal name. It is named after the people who first settled here. They do say that the name used to be Hrypis. It was the meeting place for a tribe known as the Hrype."

I liked this settlement that I could see in the distance. It seemed to me to be a gentle place to live, with a landscape softer than the one I knew at home.

When we settled for the night, I asked our new friend, Oswald, to tell me more about Rypum.

"Well," he said, "I will tell you what I know. I was told by a monk that a beautiful monastery once stood there, between the trees you see in the distance. They say that it was Alfrith who built it, and monks came from the land of the Scots to settle it. But, it seems, when we Northumbrians converted from the Celtic to the Roman church, the monks refused to change and were sent away. Now, when St Wilfrid was Bishop of York, he was given the monastery and became its abbot."

"Who was Wilfrid?" I asked him. He looked startled that I did not know this, but smiled at me, patiently. It is always important to be patient with children – they are not born with knowledge.

Well, Wilfrid was a powerful man, and spoke out at the Synod of Whitby, supporting the change from Celtic church to Rome.

In that same year, Wilfrid was given the Bishopric of Lindisfarne, the Holy Island off our coast. But old Wilfrid found that the monks there were set in their Celtic ways too, and so he moved the whole of the Bishopric to York!"

"After that, he built the monastery here, at Rypum. They say that men came from France and Italy to help build it. Imagine that!"

"But nought stands there now of the old church. They say that it was destroyed by the Vikings in a raid, many, many years ago. All that remains, of that *old* church, so I hear, is the old crypt."

"Just a small church stands there now." But then he brightened. "Who knows, perhaps someone will come along and rebuild a great church there someday."

I awoke the following day shivering in the cold of an autumn dawn. Already, some of our fighters were up and about, collecting their goods and trying to eat a breakfast of bread, cheese and a little ale. I lay awhile and listened to the wind breathe amongst the trees. My father shook me, gazing down at me, his face stubbled by new growth.

"We must awake and away, my son," he announced. He

ruffled my hair and smiled. "The life of a soldier is a hard one."

I pulled myself back to the present and stumbled up, grasping a hunk of bread and hard cheese in my fist. Would I ever be warm again? A soldiers' camp, I soon learned, is cold, filthy, noisy and full of confusion. I sat there for a moment, chewing on my breakfast and swallowing it with a gulp of ale. I stared at the nearby woodland. I always found peace in the solace of trees and old woodland, where we can reflect upon our lives. A vixen emerged from a thicket edge, took a glance at us and trotted by, towards a dense bush.

Soon we were on our way again. We could not afford to waste time in our journey. We needed to be at York soon, before news of our columns spread to ears we would rather not hear it.

We walked roughly east now, for around sixteen miles, until we reached Birdforth, (Easingwold). Here we sat a while at the Birdforth Beck, where we ate some lunch. It is said that the settlement is linked to St Chad, though I cannot be sure. It is here that tribes would meet with their weapons and touch the chief's spear to show allegiance to the king. And here were we, marching to make war upon the king's man!

After our meal, we then turned south again, to continue our journey to York. We should make the area before nightfall, and set up camp. I looked forward to that, as some of the men had caught a brace of hares and a young deer, which we could share between us, so long as our campfires did not attract undue attention!

As we began to reach the area around York, our leaders diverted our tracks again, toward another stretch of thick woodland. We entered along a small trail; possibly a badger track, judging by the badger dung pits and a few snuffle holes, where the badgers had dug for worms; which meant that it took our column some time to enter the cover of the trees.

The 'wolves' returned and reported no further sightings of patrols in the immediate area. A message which was gratefully received!

Once within the thickets, it was decided that we could, indeed, light campfires and cook some warm food. That lifted my spirits, as the days seemed to get colder as the journey wore on.

"No one should discover our fires, as long as we are careful," announced Cerdic, as he moved amongst us, inquiring about each man's health and delivering a few morsels of food to cheer and sustain us.

And so we quickly lit a number of fires, whilst a few of the men butchered the wild animals they had caught upon the way. Oh, how my mouth watered as the meat was spitted and hung over the fire! My father produced a little bread and cheese and some smoked fish that he had been carrying with him. He had also refilled our leather bag of ale at a village we passed, so we could at least have an option other than the water from the stream.

As the meat cooked, we sat there, many of us, I'm sure pondering what might have been the outcome should the patrol have discovered us. Would we have killed the men? Could we have killed them? I had no idea what it would be like to kill a man. Oh, I had helped my father many times killing pigs and sheep, and had also killed birds and small animals in the woodland, with my bow. But how would it feel if I had to slay a man?

Once the deer meat was cooked well enough - just enough to brown the outside, whilst leaving a little of the inner pink – my father took the piece and carved it into slices. He laid out two slices to each man in our small group onto the wooden platters we carried. Oh, the taste! Fresh venison was indeed a treat! I savoured every mouthful and chewed every piece until it was little more than a mush in order to eke out every morsel of flavour.

Once finished, I lay back against a tree trunk to nibble on a few nuts I had saved. All at once, a cry came up from another part of the camp. I could hear the thud of running feet on the earth.

We all rose and looked in the direction of the shout. Suddenly, through the trees a man ran. He was ragged and his feet wrapped in cloths. His face showed the growth of many days and he was certainly in need of a wash in the stream!

He darted between the trees and bushes like a wild animal. He saw us and our fire and swerved away, only to be checked by the enormous body of the smith who had befriended Benjamin. He rose from the ground at exactly the right moment, so that our fugitive ran straight into his huge chest. It was as if he had collided with a tree! He dropped to the earth and lay there, stunned.

Quickly, the smith bent down and hauled him to his feet by the rags on his back. Still the man looked around him with glazed eyes, almost unaware of where he was. He shook his head and his senses began to return. He stared up at the gigantic smith and cowered from him. Soon more men appeared and held on to him.

Cerdic and some of the other thegns arrived and the man was shoved to his knees whilst they questioned him. From where had he come? To where was he going? What was he doing in the wood? It seemed that he was a mendicant vagrant, who simply wandered from town to village, begging for his food and shelter. He had, he said, smelled our food cooking and had seen the campfires as he looked for a place to bed down for the night. All he wished, he pleaded, was to be freed to move on and find somewhere to shelter.

The thegns considered his story. Could they believe him? Was he really who and what he said, or would he make straight for York to arouse the garrison and, perhaps find favour with Tostig's men? It was decided that he would spend the night with us, under close guard, and would travel with us to York when we moved on.

In the meantime, all fires would be extinguished in case they were spotted by others in the area. Somewhat disappointed by this development, we huddled up closely, wrapped in our cloaks to await the next dawn.

# CHAPTER FOURTEEN

On the following steel-cold morning, the sun rose unwillingly, it seemed, from behind a smudge of cloud. We arose and went about our business, washing briefly in the clay-cold waters of a nearby stream and eating a tasty breakfast of bread, cheese and a little left-over cold venison. We all wanted to have enough energy to see us through what could be a difficult day.

'Wolves' had been out all night; some in York, posing as travellers passing through, on pilgrimage. Now the riders began to come in, reporting to the thegns before caring for the horses and taking breakfast themselves. They would remain in camp today, resting, and watching the vagrant, whilst we moved carefully and cautiously into York and its surrounds.

One of the 'wolves' who rode in dismounted and went immediately to the thegns. "Tostig is absent," he reported. "He hunts with the king." All ears pricked up at this information. What did it mean for our cause? Would we still go in, or have to wait until Tostig returned? Certainly, we could not rid the world of the earl as things stood. *Have we wasted our time, and put ourselves and our families in mortal danger?*

Much discussion followed, with some diverse views forcefully argued until it was decided by a majority of thegns that we should continue in our campaign and see where the fates led us.

It was under these circumstances that we began our march to York. It was agreed that we should not attack the city as a 'mob', but should enter within the walls a few at a time until we were all assembled at strategic points. From there, we would advance on Tostig's residence and his housecarls until we held it and them, should any survive, and bend them to our will. The administrative buildings would also have to be taken and secured if we were to succeed in our plan.

And so, my father and I, accompanied by Benjamin the smith, Peter the miller, Gilbert Chaffinch the fowler, Tom Mouse and Luke the churl made our way to York. I was amazed at the walls, rebuilt by the Danes, and by the great gateways through which people passed in and out of the city.

Eventually, we approached and passed through a gateway into Copprgate. Copprgate, or as people seemed to call it Coppergate. It was a row of small tenement houses, fronting the street. They appeared to be, in the main, constructed of vertical posts in the ground, around which strong and flexible withies had been woven to make walls. They stood around 15 feet wide and 20 feet long, I estimated. Their construction seemed quite strong, but, I thought, being so closely packed, must be very vulnerable should fire break out. Indeed, I am sure that many were destroyed by fire and rebuilt from time to time. I guessed also that their walls would need to be repaired regularly, as they would almost certainly rot and decay into the dust.

There were small apertures in the walls to let in light, and some would probably be lime-washed inside to help make the inside brighter.

There were also some dwellings of a higher status. Here seemed to be manufacturing industries. There was a jeweller displaying his wares at a table in an open fronted shop, whilst keeping an eagle eye on travellers such as we were meant to be. There were also a number of shops manufacturing wooden cups on a pole lathe, from which the street got its name. The name did not derive from the metal, but from two Danish words – 'coppr' meaning a cup and 'gata' which meant street. So Copprgate is 'cup-makers' street'. I also noticed smithing and iron-making and leather-working shops along the way. It was certainly different to our small settlement! My eyes were everywhere.

We came upon a tavern, and my father and the other men decided that we should take some refreshment. We entered the building and looked around us. The floor was slightly lower than street level and had mats of brushwood upon the earthen floor to provide some insulation from the cold, hard earth. In the centre of the floor was a stone hearth, where a low log fire burned, helping to heat the building, but providing a smoky atmosphere. Along the sides, part of the floor was planked and benches ran along there.

We sat at a bench and a large man with an enormous belly sidled up to us. He looked us up and down before asking what re required. "We'll take a jug of ale and a morsel of food you might have," my father told him. He nodded and shuffled away to a back room. At length, he returned with a clay jug of ale and pots for each of us. He repeated the journey and returned with a wooden platter of bread and some dried up mutton. We ate the meal gladly. The bread was actually quite good, though the meat had seen better days and took a good deal of chewing before it could be swallowed.

The ale was watery, but provided us with something with which to wet our mouths. And it was probably safer than drinking the local water. I had noticed a well shaft beside the river. It was constructed from a hollow tree trunk – probably black poplar by the look of it. It was revetted with basic wattle and daub. No doubt it provided water for the community, but was, I thought probably unclean and we were better off with ale! Around the well and along the streets in general, were levels of cess and rubbish such as I had never seen. The smell was unlike anything I had ever encountered, even in the winter quarters of our animals! Certainly, the villagers would have had something to say, should anyone have fouled our village in this manner. I later learned that the local population was largely infested with whip-worm and maw-worm, and was little surprised as conditions seemed perfect for these parasites to flourish.

The innkeeper shuffled over again and leaned his great frame against a wall. I wondered if the willow withies would stand the strain, but they seemed to comply.

"And what brings you to York?" he asked. The men stiffened but tried to seem untroubled by the question.

"We are come to see if there might be opportunity for trade in our goods and skills," my father replied.

"And what skills would you have to offer?" the innkeeper questioned.

"This man is a smith, and we are all free churls who have wool to trade. It seems a busy city. You must see people from everywhere," my father added, casually.

"Oh, strangers are a part of everyday life in a large settlement like York," the man agreed. "We have a thriving city. Why, traders come here from all over the world –

Denmark, Flanders, Saxony, Jutland, Normandy, the low-countries, the far north and Ireland. They come to trade their goods and services, as you do."

It was hard to believe that so many people from so many parts of the world were in the same city as me. Oh, I had seen travellers moving through our land, coming and going from the monastery and travelling from town to town to sell their wares, but to think that so many were all together here, was amazing to a young boy from the countryside.

"Will you be looking for shelter for the night?" the innkeeper asked.

"We will soon be moving on," my father told him, which was a surprise to me, as the agreement was to spend the night in York, to allow all of the columns to arrive, and then to strike in the following morning. We finished our food and ale and left the tavern. "We could not take shelter there," my father told us, "I had no liking for the innkeeper. He asks questions. I could not be sure we would be safe." And so we made our way further into the centre of York to find a bed for the night.

I was still amazed by the filth of the streets of this large settlement. *How could people live like this?* There were piles of rotting vegetation, swirling around in the breeze with dusty soil and domestic rubbish. In places, even animal remains seemed to have been simply dumped at the back of the very houses the people lived in. It appears that all this was not helped by the regular flooding of the two rivers that ran through York. Or perhaps it made it better! Who could say?

At the end of one row of tenement buildings, were a number of pits. Some were filling up with rubbish, some were cesspits, full of human waste and pieces of fabric, with which the people cleaned themselves, and some were even wells, from which people drew their water to drink.

As people constantly dug and filled these pits, it resulted in waste simply lying on the surface, and these attracted the attention of scavengers, such as dogs and red kites who picked amongst it. I could not get used to the smells I was encountering for the first time. Oh, how I longed for the fresh air of our village.

We walked the streets of York for some time, scouting the lie of the land and finding important landmark buildings. We found Tostig's abode and his offices, from where his men administered the region. We watched as men-at-arms strode around, going about their business. We counted them as we went along. Soon we had our bearings around the city, and knew the way to and around the important buildings.

We passed many more traders, calling their wares. Potters made their pots on slow kick-wheels and fired them in kilns, supported on clay arches. Their pots were glazed in orange, green, brown and yellow.

One man was busily making combs, strap-ends, toggles, boxes, pins, gaming pieces and pottery stamps from animal bones and antlers. We watched for a while, whilst the man used an animal jawbone to practise his intricate incised decoration.

Benjamin looked on in fascination as a metalworker worked on smelted iron to forge a spearhead from a single piece of metal. He gradually flattened the metal and then folded it to form an open tube, where the shaft would be inserted. We admired some of the pattern-welded swords hanging on an inner wall. These had been forged by repeatedly folding and hammering a bar of good iron to craft a tough structure of layered metal. The strips of steel were then twisted and hammered together to produce a pattern of entwined lines along the length of the weapon.

Butchers and fishmongers bawled out their wares to the passing women. The butcher, with a mailed fist, cut meat into chops with a great cleaver. A wine merchant advertised Rhenish wine. Other merchants sold luxury goods, about which we could only dream; oils, perfumes, jewels and precious metals, spices like pepper and cumin, ivory, and other goods. The merchants would ship out Anglo-Saxon goods and return with these fantastic cargoes. I am sure they made healthy profits and, the law had it that should a merchant travel across the seas three times, at his own expense, then he would be made a thegn. A wonderful thing, but not without its risks!

Finally, we turned our steps to another alehouse, to seek a bed. We entered by a low doorway into another room with its earthen floor below that of the street. The smell here, too, was not pleasant; mud, dirt and domestic rubbish seemed to have been trampled into the floor, which was carelessly strewn with rushes, some of which seemed to have been there for some time.

We looked at each other, but my father nodded. "There will be few people who will want to spend the night here, I suppose," he said, "so we should, at least, be left alone."

Another innkeeper came toward us. This one was much smaller than the first. "What can I do for you?" he asked, and wiped his nose on his filthy sleeve.

"We would have somewhere to spend the night," my father replied. "We will be moving on at dawn."

The innkeeper looked us up and down. "You can rent a room and pay, or you can sleep here without payment, if you take food and drink," he sniffled.

"We will be happy to sleep here, by the fire," my father

replied. We will eat and drink here when the sun goes down."

The man nodded.

That night, I have to say, was not a comfortable, nor a pleasant one. We slept fitfully on the benches around the alehouse.

On the following morning, a light drizzle fell, damping down the dust of the streets. We ate a meagre meal of dry bread, stale cheese, a platter of eels and ale, provided by the innkeeper and moved out of our hovel of an inn.

We had all of our weapons with us, hidden within the clothes and the bags we carried with us. We knew where we must assemble with others of our group. Soon, a number of us were loitering in the shade of a small group of trees in an open market square. The usual traders were there, but we had no interest, now, in their goods. We knew where we would need to go.

Suddenly, it seemed the square near to the earl's residence filled with men from every direction. I noted that traders began to look up from their business and stare at the gathering crowd. Cerdic rode into our midst and raised a hand. Men drew their weapons and pointed them menacingly at the locals. Screams and shouts rang out as the people of York realised that something very serious was happening. Many ran from us into buildings and alleyways.

Cerdic sat his horse in the middle of the square and spoke to the panicking locals. "Stay yourselves still, and nothing evil will happen to you! We have no quarrel with you, but with the earl. We would rid Northumbria of his presence and have someone else to rule over us."

At that, the crowd began to look at each other uncertainly. Then some of the men nodded at one another and they began to cheer us. At that moment, it appeared, the panic was over and the people seemed happy to have us there amongst them. They too had no great fondness for Tostig, and would not be sorry to see his demise. A large man, well dressed and obviously a prosperous merchant, strode toward Cerdic. Some of his men raised their swords in defence of their master. The merchant raised his hands to his shoulders to show that he carried no weapons and the ripple of tension diffused.

"Sir," he said, "Do what you will. No one in this town will stand in your way, other than Tostig's housecarls and men-at-arms." And with that, he retreated backwards into the crowd. Another roar went up from the crowd.

Now Cerdic led our force to the gates of the residence. The guards on duty were already alert to something happening in the vicinity, but they did not seem to know what it might be. Perhaps it was nothing but a silly quarrel between some of the people? Perhaps a thief apprehended?

Cerdic knocked hard at the gate with the pommel of his great sword and there was the scuffling of feet behind it and on the wall above. The soldiers began to open the doors until one of their number upon the wall cried out a warning. Then they tried to force it closed again, but to no avail. They were too late. A great iron bar had been inserted into the gap and the gates were now forced open by the sheer weight of numbers behind it.

The men-at-arms fell back. Some ran from us. Others stood their ground and drew swords. From the building in front of us, Tostig's Danish housecarls decanted and ran across the bailey toward us, swords in hands and shields on arms. The polished bosses on their shields shone like wolves' eyes. Our shieldwall was now raised and the two sides clashed together with a roar and a clatter or weapons.

I was well behind the shieldwall, but still seemed to feel the great thud. Our men pushed, shields overlapping and swords and spears pointing down to try to inflict maximum injury to the legs and feet of our opponent, and also over the shields to strike downward at heads.

Now more men were piling into the courtyard and the pressure behind me grew. I was unsure of what to do. My father had warned me to stay back, but I was being gradually forced forward to the line. There was no room to unleash an arrow from a bow, so I drew my seax and waited to see to where I would be pushed.

A large arm came over my shoulder and hurled me to one side as the man behind me tried to make his way to the front. I stumbled then and fell to the floor, fearing all the while that I would end my days here, crushed to death beneath the pounding feet of the warring factions. I managed to scramble to my knees and could see a gap between the legs of the two men in front of me; one of them my father. I wormed my way forward – surely it was better to die fighting than to be squashed like a fly in the dust!

As I crawled through, I found myself beneath the shields of my father and his partner to the right. I could see the feet of the opposing soldiers, as they slammed their swords into my father's shield. I was suddenly gripped by the thought that I must help, and so, crept forward until I lay between the defences. Now I took my seax and rammed it hard into the foot of a soldier. His feet were shod only in leather, as violent action had not been anticipated, and my sharpened weapon passed through as easily as a knife through cheese. The man screamed and looked at his foot disbelievingly, the blood now pouring from it into the earth. His shield dropped down to his chest. It was his last mistake. As he took his eye off my father and the others, my father's spear took him in his mouth. I heard him gurgle as blood rose from his throat to his mouth and spattered down upon me. I had seen my father kill a man! I was shocked, and, very evidently, so was my father, because he seemed to stop for a moment and stare at the man, who stared back with sightless eyes and slumped to the floor before him.

This was the opening our fighters had needed! Now we pushed again and again, and their shieldwall defences collapsed. They staggered backward, falling over each other in their haste to escape. With a great cheer, we, of course, piled forward. Now swords and spears flashed in the sun and men screamed on both sides as they died or received horrible injuries. I looked on as one of the men from our village collapsed in a heap with a great gaping wound in his head. Blood ran from it and grey brain matter oozed from the slit in his skull. What would we tell his wife and children?

Now the men-at-arms and housecarls fought their way backward to the great building. They held the doorways and battled us from there. But soon, as bodies piled up, they began to retreat again and we found ourselves inside. Again the battle raged and blood smeared the floor in great pools, making it greasy. I could smell it – I can smell it still.

It soon became obvious to us that the housecarls could not resist us, however manfully they fought on, in desperation. My father was in the thick of the fighting, and I feared for his safety. What would my mother say if I went home without him? How would we all manage if he were not there for us?

Unable to see over the melee of fighters, I clawed my way to the side of the great hall. There, I clambered onto a table, to better see for myself what was happening. I quickly kicked off the table the meal that had been set and steadied myself. It was probably a stupid thing to do, as I made myself more vulnerable to attack, towering over the men as I now did. I watched anxiously as the fighting raged. I watched my father thrust with a captured sword and batter with his shield. It was a strange sight for a young boy. The gentle father I had always known, now in battle, fighting for his very life!

At that moment, my world seemed to go into a slow dream-state. I could see that a Danish housecarl was approaching my father from the side, and that my father had no knowledge of his position. I could see the housecarl's intention – to thrust his sword into my father's back. At that point, almost in a trance, I gripped my bow and drew an arrow from my quiver. I nocked it into the bowstring and drew with all my might. Mine was only a boy's bow, but it could still deliver an arrow with force over a short distance. I drew the bow up to my eye and aimed for the housecarl's neck, where he was not covered. I let loose the arrow and saw it find its mark in the man's throat. He stopped, almost puzzled as to what was happening, and then he fell, clutching his bleeding throat.

I knew that he was dying. I had killed him! I had killed a man!

My father glanced briefly at the man, and then turned to see where the arrow had come from. He saw me standing there on the table, my bow in my hand and a white, shocked face. He looked at me and I looked at him. And then he gave a grim smile and turned his attention back to the battle.

When I could control the shivering within my body, I dragged myself back to the reality in which I found myself. Now I dug down again into my quiver and withdrew more arrows. I nocked more into my bowstring and began to fire. I don't know how many men I killed or injured on that day.

I didn't want to know. I knew that I had done it and that was almost too much for me. I tried to put it to the back of my mind.

Soon, it seemed, the battle was over and the bodies of all of the housecarls and men-at-arms lay huddled on the floor. Blood seeped from wounds and sank into the earth between the planking of the wooden floor. Bodies of some of our men also lay there and many cried in pain at injuries they had received. But not one of Tostig's men could cry in pain. None were alive to do it. Englishman and Dane alike from Tostig's retinue had gone to meet their maker on that day!

A strange silence now fell upon the place. And then Cerdic called to us. "Search the fortress. Take every weapon and any gold, silver and money you can find. Bring it to me, that I might set guards upon it."

And so it was that we began looting Tostig's fortress. I had never seen such riches, and have never seen the like since. Bags and pots of gold and coins were stacked up. The most beautiful jewellery I had ever seen!

Weapons of all description were heaped upon the floor.

We stared in amazement. But Cerdic soon had the situation under control, and his own men began carrying them out and loading them into carts at the gates.

Now we left the scene of the carnage and filed out onto the streets. We knew that what had happened here had been replicated in other areas of York. There would be many more dead and injured to care for today.

When we emerged into the narrow cobbled street, the locals seemed in shock. Slowly, they appeared from buildings to stare at us. I felt very conscious of myself.

Cerdic stood his horse and addressed them. "People of York, know you this day that Tostig's housecarls and soldiers-at-arms are no more. Our men have spared none.

Tostig is not here today, or he too might have been laying there, his own throat cut! Riders have already gone out to the king. We will now petition the king to banish Tostig from the region, and to give us an earl who will protect the people, whilst maintaining order. We must now march south to meet the king and his advisors and ask for Morcar, younger brother of Edwin, Earl of Mercia, to become our overlord. We will leave men from the local area here to protect you and maintain order."

A great cheer went up and a cry of 'Morcar' from every voice filled the air. We shook our weapons and laughed and cried in equal amounts, as the tension began to leave us and the understanding of what we had done began to dawn upon us.

I stood there, with tears coursing down my cheeks, when my father reached me and wrapped his great arms around me. "John," he whispered, "you saved my life today. Without you, I would now be cold on the ground. This day, you became a warrior!"

# CHAPTER FIFTEEN

The following morn saw us formed up again into columns – this time not disguising the fact that we were a force of men on a sacred mission to release our people from the tyranny of Tostig and his followers. I noticed the small innkeeper staring at us. *Are these the very men who spent the night in my inn?*

Now we marched out of York, through the great Viking gates in the walls and onto the road south. It would, they told us, take at least six days of hard marching to make Northampton, where we would be joined by Earl Edwin and his forces. Here, also, we were to meet up with the king's representative, who would speak to us and hear of our petition. I had no doubt that people already knew, or shortly would, the situation, and I wondered about the reaction at the deposition of the earl.

It was a long and arduous journey, as we had all suspected. We spent many nights huddled together, soaking and cold, listening to the tongues in the trees as a recent break in the weather closed again like a trap. We were, at least, better provisioned from our brief stay in

York. And we could now light our fires and cook meals without the fear of discovery. Now we feared no man, and it was certain that nothing less than a powerful force could overcome us easily. Of course, we all knew that many of the king's nobles could easily put together just such a force.

We passed many villages and towns, most of which I had never heard of in my short life, but also towns whose names I did know, such as Nottingham; though it was only the names I knew, and little else. In just seven days – one more than we had planned – we settled in a meadow on the very outskirts of Northampton. We set up our camp there and settled to wait for whatever might come.

It was in noon of the following day, as the sun rose high and shadows shrank, that a scout rode into our camp with the message that a large body of men were approaching our camp from the north-west. We grabbed weapons and leather armour and stood to watch the approach. As the force neared our field, it halted behind a well-dressed man on a great white horse. The forces behind him were bristling with weapons.

All at once, one of our thegns called out, "I see the banner of Mercia. It is Edwin and Morcar!" We let lose a communal sigh of relief and I felt tension from my body seep away. This was the man whom we were due to meet. He was the brother of the man we wanted as our earl. More importantly, he was not the feared force from the king!

The force moved forward again, slowly, toward our position. Our thegns mounted and met them at a short distance. We were not privy to the conversation, but it was obvious that the discourse was cordial. Then the thegns turned their horses and led Edwin and his men to our camp. Here, they soon set up their own camp. Indeed, I was amazed at how quickly a band of professional soldiers could make camp and make themselves comfortable. We had much to learn from their efficiency!

We passed the evening huddled in cloaks against the wind, though at least the rain had now ceased to soak us. We cooked and ate a meal from some of the reserves we still had from York, and some we had collected along the way. Edwin's men too were well provisioned, and a man-at-arms gave me the leg of a bird to eat, which I greatly enjoyed.

As the dawn broke, we all rose from our humble beds upon the meadow and began to prepare for our promised meeting. I came to the conclusion, again, that soldiers' camps are filthy places, and I thought that the owners of the meadow would be dismayed when they saw the damage done and the rubbish strewn about the site.

Once organised, we began the march into Northampton. Now one of our thegns unfurled the red and gold banner of Northumbria over our heads. It was joined by the flag of Mercia. At last we really felt like a proper army – a fyrd, rather than a gaggle of churls, somewhat out of our depth in challenging the established order of the kingdom.

As we entered the town of Northampton, my eyes were everywhere. I had seen some amazing sights over the last few days, but I never tired of looking at the many different places and things we passed. Who would I see today? Some said that it would be the famous Earl Harold!

Shortly, we approached the centre of the town and there we halted and waited. Edwin and the thegns gathered together at the front and we arranged ourselves behind them. We did not know for sure what would face us, and so each man had his weapons – many of them looted from Tostig's men – easily to hand.

After what seemed to me a long, long time, a whisper ran around the crowd that Harold himself and his entourage, along with a small troop of men approached us. At its head was a man who could only be the Earl himself. He was backed by a few retainers, but no great force of men. Harold had come to us without arms, trusting that we wished him no harm. It was a brave thing to do, under the circumstances, but a master stroke of diplomacy.

The two sides met and greetings were exchanged. We all stood, rigid, waiting to see what transpired. More talk. Then all of the leading men dismounted their horses and moved to a large hall to our left, not far from where I stood, along with my father and the other men from the village. Once the leaders had entered, we all surged forward to the entrance. My father held up a great arm and pushed back a couple of smaller men. He manoeuvred me toward the entrance and I knew no more until we were both inside and looking through a gap into the room. Was I really in the room with Earl Harold and his men? This was the king's right-hand-man! Was I really witnessing this scene, or was it simply the foolish dream of a young boy?

The nobles sat themselves around a great table. Food and ale were soon brought and more pleasantries were exchanged.

And now, it was down to business. Harold sat back in his chair and spoke. "My good men of Northumbria, you have come today to petition the king on a matter of great importance."

One of the thegns, Aelthelwyne, spoke first. "My lord Earl, we have been to York and have taken the area. There has been much bloodshed, and Earl Tostig's housecarls and men are mostly dead or have fled. It was with a heavy heart that we took this action, but we could no longer bear to live under the yoke of your brother, the earl."

"I hear too, that you have looted the residence and armouries of York?"

"We have, my Lord, I will not lie to you. We took the monies we found there to recompense the people of Northumbria, who have suffered long under the weight of taxes of Tostig, with which he paid great amounts to Danish housecarls and mercenaries."

"What say others of your number?" Harold asked.

Now Cerdic himself spoke up. "My Lord, what Aethelwyne says is the truth. We can no longer live under the unjust and cruel rule of your brother." At this, he turned and gestured behind him and Benjamin the smith was jostled forward by one of Cerdic's men. "Earl Harold, this is my smith, Benjamin. You will note the loss of an ear." Harold nodded and peered at the side of Benjamin's head. "This ear was cut off by Tostig for no other reason than that the smith explained to him that one of his horses was lame and its foot rotting from being forced to run for days without a shoe or care."

Harold nodded and sat back to think about what he had just heard. It could not be pleasant for him to hear such things about his own kin. Now other thegns came forward and told Harold stories of the lives they led in Northumbria. Harold listened patiently, it must be said, to all of the evidence before him.

Eventually, he turned to Edwin, who had sat listening to the discourse, but had said nothing. "My Lord Edwin," he began, "have you a word to say in this matter?"

"Nay, Lord. I am a noble of Mercia, and my only involvement in this is that the men of Northumbria would take my brother, Morcar, as their earl. I am here only as a third party in this debate."

At this, Harold raised his eyebrows and looked surprised, though I doubted that it was as much a surprise as it seemed. His men would have felt out how the land lay before this meeting, and I was sure he would be well informed.

"And Morcar," he asked, "are you willing to be Earl of Northumbria, as these people seem to want? They are a wild lot," he joked, and a rumble of laugher ran around us.

"If the people of Northumbria would have me as their earl, then I am humbled and would be glad to serve them, no matter how wild they might be," Morcar replied. Further laughter spread.

Harold sat a while and pondered. His men looked from one to another and to him. He turned and muttered to his closest advisors and they returned their advice.

At length, and after much pondering, it seemed, Harold spoke again. "My Lords, good people of Northumbria, I have listened patiently, I hope you agree, to what has been brought to me this day. I must now return to Oxford and meet with the king, I will take to him the message you have given me. I will tell him of all I have heard and seen, and then, the king being a wise and just man, I am certain that agreement on the way forward can be reached. I can say no more."

Men now nodded enthusiastically and smiled at one another. It seemed that Harold had given us fair hearing and might even support our claim to the king, even against his own brother.

"Return to your homes in the north. Collect together all of the provisions you will need to feed your families over this winter. The Royal Council will meet soon, and you will hear the king's decision."

With that, we were all shoved back out of the door again and into the narrow streets of Northampton. Our leaders emerged first and moved us further back, so that Harold and his entourage could leave in safety.

As the Earl left, Cerdic turned to us. "I feel that my

lord, Earl Harold has already made up his mind what the king will think!" He smiled a knowing smile. And now we must prepare for a long journey home.

That night, we slept in an inn in Northampton, somewhat better than those in York. The following morning we set out on our long journey home. And what a journey! It was, we thought, around 200 miles to walk before we felt the floors of our own homes beneath our feet! I will not bore you with the tales of long marches in cold weather, nor camps with food roughly cooked over an open fire, or nights spent wet and cold in a cloak.

It took us two whole weeks to walk back to our home in Northumbria. We had injured to help along, and goods to carry. I remember it as yesterday when we rounded the bend in the river and sighted our village. My brother was collecting wood at the woodland edge when he saw us. He dropped his bundle of sticks and ran for the village, calling, shouting, screaming, to alert my mother. Now people spilled out of the village and ran toward us. I could see my mother running. We also began to run and we met and threw arms around each other, tears streaming down our faces. My grandfather also appeared and came to greet us.

Other villagers poured out and ran, only stopping when they realised that their loved ones were not with us. Some of us shook our heads sadly. Shrieking, they dropped to their knees and buried their faces. How they must feel! We were in ecstasy, whilst they were in utter misery!

We walked with our families back to the village. All the while, though my mother was obviously delighted to see us fit and well, I felt that there was an underlying current of unease. We entered our home and threw down our baggage. Our family flooded around us like a swirling river. I hugged my siblings and they held me tightly. They scrambled into my father's arms and hung around his neck. My aunt greeted us warmly, tears in her eyes too.

My father looked around. "Where is my mother?" he asked. I threw glances around the room then. She was nowhere to be seen. We looked at my mother and she hung her head.

"Ealde modor (grandmother)?" I cried.

My grandfather came to us and took a hand of each of us. "She is with God," he said. "She passed on two weeks ago" – the day we had turned for home. "We have buried her near to the church. She is at rest now."

And now it was my turn to burst into tears. My father simply sat down where he was, shaking his head in disbelief. "She has gone and I was not there with her."

"It was God's will, and we must accept it, no matter how hard," my grandfather told him. "She did not suffer. We simply found her dead in the morning. She had slipped away peacefully in her sleep." That at least was some comfort.

"I will go to her," my father announced, and he rose to his feet and left the house. We all followed in his wake. At the side of the church was a new grave. We knelt at the verge and stared at the freshly turned earth. My father spoke. "Mother, we are home – John and I. We are well and our mission is complete, I think. I am sorry I was not there at your end, but I put you into the hands of God." Each of us said a silent prayer, and then we rose and returned home, with a mixture of sadness and gladness in our hearts.

It was said, later, that some of the men marching north again had not all done so honourably, though I saw none of this and can neither confirm nor deny it. It is said that some of the northern men did much harm about Northampton. Some slew men, and burned houses and corn; or took all the cattle that they could find; which, I heard, amounted to many thousands. It is further said that even some slaves were taken, so that some Shires were the worse for many winters. I would be sad if I learned that this was true. These people had done us no harm. It simply engraved on the hearts and minds of others that we in the north were truly wild. How sad!

Some few weeks later, a rider approached and rode into Cerdic's compound. Soon, the rider and Cerdic appeared in the village. He pulled his horse to a standstill and beamed at us all, as we gathered there before him.

"My people," he said, "this messenger brings news. It seems that Earl Godwin has persuaded King Edward to accede to our demands. Tostig, at first, refused to accept his deposition, but Edward has outlawed him from the land. We have Morcar as our earl."

The cheer we set up could probably be heard in Oxford! There was such laughing and slapping of backs. Many danced in wild abandon.

Sometime later I was to hear what had happened at the meeting of Tostig, Harold and the king.

Tostig had barged into the room where the earl and the king sat deep in conversation. "Will you allow this dishonour to our family?" he screamed at Harold. Earl and king turned to look at him. "Have I not served my king well? 'Twas not long since we hunted together, and now this! What do you mean to do about it?" he raged at the king. That was never a good idea. Edward might not be the strongest king the country had known, but nor was he to be insulted and browbeaten.

Now Edward glowered at him. "Tostig, you forget to whom you speak! I have heard Earl Harold and I have listened to what the people of Northumbria told him. And now my instincts tell me that I would do well to strip you of the earldom."

Tostig coloured purple! "Ah, so, it is my brother who plots against me!" he blustered, almost choking on the words. "It is my own brother who foments this uprising against me! I see it all now!"

"You speak nonsense!" Harold told him. "I listened to the people of the north. I listened to thegn and churl alike, and heard the same stories of oppression from every mouth. You have alienated the people of Northumbria yourself. It is no person's doing but your own!"

Tostig stood now and glared at his brother. "And you would see Morcar in my place! What sort of brother are you?"

"In the times in which we live, we must unite England. I have told you this before. We know not what lies ahead of us, and a disunited kingdom is one which can fall easily."

The reality was that Harold was indeed worried about the kingdom falling. Edward was old and becoming more frail, and William of Normandy was looming as a threat to the crown upon the horizon. Harold had to have the support of the north if he was to face this threat.

Now Edward spoke again. "It is my decree that you, Tostig, shall take your household and will leave this land until I say further."

And so it was that Tostig and his family took a ship and sailed to refuge at the court of Count Baldwin V, his brother-in-law. Here, it is said that he even tried to make a pact with William. In the spring of 1066, Tostig and a fleet, provided by Baldwin, set sail and landed on the Isle of Wight, where money and provisions were collected. He then raided the coast as far as Sandwich. However, his brother, Harold, called out both his land and sea forces against him. He moved north with his ships and tried to forge an alliance with his brother, Gyrth, who spurned him. He now set his sights on the land of the East Angles and further north, but Edwin and Morcar were more than a match for him. Finally, deserted by his men, he fled to Scotland, to the court of King Malcolm III, where he plotted his revenge!

# PART TWO

## CHAPTER SIXTEEN

As the end of 1065 approached, old King Edward the Confessor fell ill and became as a living dead man, and was unable to awaken himself. He had not, by then, they said, finalised his own preference as to who should follow him to the throne. He had no son to follow him.

It was on the 5th January of 1066 that Edward passed on to the hands of his maker, but had, briefly I hear, woken from his living death and become able to point toward his Earl of Wessex and commend his widow's safety and protection to Harold. Of course, no man knew for certain what the intent of this might be. This sign was accepted to mean, by many, that Edward had indeed chosen Harold as his successor to the throne, though others said that it was more of a curse!

So now three noblemen raised claims to the crown of England. Harold himself, King Harald of Norway and, of course, William of Normandy. William claimed that Edward had promised him the succession, and, when ship-wrecked years before, Harold Godwinson had sworn to help him, William, to ascend to the English throne.

But there was, it seems, confusion upon all of this, as the English succession was not definitely inherited from father to son, nor decided by the dying monarch, but by the Witangemot. This was the great assembly of the land's leading men which would come together upon the king's death to select a new king.

Of course, there had once been another player in the game! It seems that, many years before, Edward Aetheling, son of Edmund Ironside and Ealgyth had been exiled to the continent. It is said that Canute was behind it, and sent Edward and his brother, when only a few short months old to the 'care' of Olof Skotkonung, his half-brother, where they were to be murdered! But instead, it seems, the boys were saved and sent a long way from these shores, to a place called Kiev, where the Queen was Olof's daughter.

Many years later, when Edward the Confessor received the news that Edward Aetheling was alive, and not murdered foully in his cradle, The Confessor immediately sent for him and, some said, made him his heir. It was, the king thought, the only chance of succession within his own royal household.

And so it was that Edward Aetheling came home to England in the August of 1057.

Oh, but it was not to be long, for, when he arrived on these shores, it seems he was not allowed to speak to the king. The Confessor was a pious king, but was weak in his dealings with his Earl of Wessex. And worse was to come, for, it seems, Edward Aetheling was dead within two days of touching England's shore! The cause of his death? No man knows for certain, but he had a powerful claim to the throne and many powerful enemies here who would find life easier if he were not a player in the game! Many say that he was murdered! But by whom? We can only wonder, perhaps? So this laid the succession open and a simmering dispute between Harold and William.

When the Witenagemot met the day following the king's death, they selected Harold as the man they thought should succeed Edward to the throne of England, and said that he should be crowned without delay. This was, not least, because all of the nobles of the land happened to be already in Westminster for the annual feast of the Epiphany.

On a following morn, Harold and his supporters approached Westminster Abbey. Harold was mounted on a large white horse, bedecked with the most beautiful tack. The men dismounted and grooms took the horses. Harold looked around at his men. "Well," he said, "let us have this issue settled."

The attendant nobles and thegns all nodded their agreement and made their way through a crowd which opened and closed behind them like a wave upon the sea, to the great front doors. As they approached, the huge doors swung open. Harold and his men entered the great church to be met by members of the senior clergy. Within the abbey sat most of the nobles of England, waiting to see their new monarch crowned as God's representative in the land.

Harold was taken to a small chamber and prepared for the ceremony. His outer cloak was removed and the anointing gown slipped over his head. It is but a simple garment, which is worn during the anointing. It is plain white and shows no decoration. Over this was an ermine cape with a train of crimson velvet cloth.

And so, Harold entered the Abbey proper, bedecked in the gown and the robe.

Harold and his attendants, Archbishop Stigand and clergy processed forward to where the great seat was placed. All eyes turned to view him. Harold took his place upon the chair and gazed around him as certain officials made their way to the north, south, east and west of the Abbey.

And then Archbishop Stigand began the ceremony. "My Lords," he said, "I here present unto ye, Harold, your undoubted King. Wherefore all you who are come this day to do your homage and service, are you willing to do the same?"

"Aye!" the cry was given out.

"Does any man challenge his claim?" There was silence in the abbey. Despite what they might have thought, no man would risk a challenge to their powerful Earl of Wessex, if he desired to live to see another dawn!

Stigand then approached Harold and administered the oath. "Harold, Earl of Wessex, do you promise and swear to govern the people of this Kingdom of England according to the laws of this land?"

"I solemnly swear so to do," came the reply.

"Will you, to the best of your power, cause Law and Justice, in Mercy, to be executed in all your judgments?"

"I will."

"Will you maintain and preserve inviolable the settlement of the Church?"

"I swear to do. All of these things I have said, I promise and swear to do."

At that point, a cleric approached the great chair and held out to Harold a copy of the Bible. "Here is Wisdom. This is the royal Law. These are the lively Oracles of God." Harold held out a hand and accepted the Bible.

At that, the religious ceremony continued. Now clerics approached Harold and removed the crimson robe. He now wore only the anointing gown. A canopy was brought forward and held over Harold's head by four nobles for this, most sacred part of the ceremony – the anointing. Now Stigand poured sacred oil from a container onto a great spoon, and anointed the head, hands and heart of his new king. Then, there followed a blessing.

Following that, clerics brought forward the crown and presented it to Stigand, who placed it firmly upon Harold's head. He was then dressed again in his ermine and crimson robe. Into his hands were placed a golden orb and a sceptre. His great sword was returned to him and buckled on. Now Harold stood and looked out over the assembled throng.

As one, they all stood and each man called out "I do become your liege man of life and limb, and of earthly worship; and faith and truth will I bear unto you, to live and die, against all manner of folks. So help me God."

The clergy assembled then gave their own oath of allegiance, followed by the various members of Harold's own family – now the royal family!

Upon withdrawing from the abbey and the assembled throng, Harold embraced his brothers and senior supporters. "It is good. My father's vision is accomplished this day. This family has become the greatest family in the kingdom. I have no doubt that he looks down upon us from God's Heaven with satisfaction at the events of this day."

"And what of the Norwegian and William the Bastard?" one retainer dared to ask.

Harold turned upon the man. "What of them? I am the anointed and crowned King of England. Let them dare to challenge me!"

The retainer blanched at the rebuke from his new sovereign and bowed his head low. "My Lord, I am sure that none would dare to challenge you, but if they were foolish enough, they would suffer ignominious defeat at your hands, supported by every hand here today."

Harold nodded and proceeded on his way to the post-coronation banquet.

It was upon a cold and frosty morning in the early January of the year 1066, that a messenger rode up to the great fortress of William of Normandy. The guards at the gate shivered in their great winter cloaks and ice covered the fish ponds and glittered in the weak winter sun.

Upon arrival, the gates were opened and the man cantered into the bailey of the fortress. A groom ran out of the steaming stables upon hearing the hoof-beats pound on earth as hard as iron, to collect the horse and rub it down and feed it, before leading it to a warm stall with fresh straw upon the earth.

The man wasted no time in approaching the door of the fortress. Two guards threw spears out in outstretched arms to block his way. "Out of my way, fools!" he snapped. "I am here upon the Duke's business!"

At this, the door opened and one of William's clerks, who had seen the arrival, ordered the guards to stand down, and led the messenger into the building. They progressed until they came to double doors which were open. Into the presence of William, his brothers Odo and Robert and his cabal of advisors the messenger strode. He bent his knee to the Duke and then stood and identified himself.

"My Lord, my name is Wilibald. I am come to you with news." With that, he presented a scroll of parchment to a servant, who passed it into William's hands. The Duke untied the cord and unrolled the scroll, studying carefully the message therein. His face clouded.

William stood. "The Confessor is dead!" he announced. "And the English have crowned Harold as their king!" The assembled advisors and counsellors gasped at the implication.

Though I have never seen William in the flesh, except at great distance, I have heard reports of him. It seems that he was a tall, robust and burly man, with a harsh voice. It is said that he could pull bows that other men could not even bend. He was, apparently, an unequalled horseman and warrior.

It is said also that he laboured under two tutors as a young man, though his achievements in education are unclear. His main pastime, it seems, was hunting.

I believe that he could be a cruel and greedy man, though his devotion to his wife, Matilda, appears to have been strong and gentle. That then is one thing to be said in his favour.

"What must we do, Lord?" one man timorously asked, when William sat down.

"We must go to England and take what is ours," was the reply. The men in council looked at one another, unsure as to what to think. William intended to invade England, defeat Harold and snatch the crown for himself and Normandy. This was a huge undertaking. Harold was a great general of his troops, and would be more powerful now that he was king.

"Tell us what you plan to do," Odo requested of his brother.

"I would have 700 warships built and readied. We shall build them at Dives-sur-Mer. I will fill them with warriors and men at arms and all provisions that we shall need, and we will sail to England. Gather together all of my most senior supporters. We will plan this and execute it together."

Some days later, William's great hall was packed with nobles, all speaking of the news that had shocked Normandy and caused consternation to all. It was common knowledge that William had pledged to seize the English throne from the anointed king of that land, and many had reservations about the whole business. There was chatter and whispered mutterings from all assembled; most speaking cautiously – it would not do to be on the wrong side of the outcome! But many were, in their own hearts, uneasy at the thought of what was to come.

William and his senior officials entered the room from the rear, to the surprise of many of the throng, who quickly stopped in their conversations! All looked upon their Duke, who made his way to a great table, which had been spread with grand food. Around the hall were further tables for the general assembly and all now sat in anticipation of what was to come. Food was delivered by servants and all men waited for their leader. Now William picked up a bowl and spooned out the venison broth he had been served. The rest of the men followed suit.

After a meal of soup, roast goose, quail, suckling pig, cheese and sweet cakes, washed down with Frankish wine, William, at last, wiped his face and sat looking out over his men. At length he addressed them.

"My lords, you all know of the happenings in England. The old king is dead and Harold usurps the throne, which should, by right, be mine. I am decided on the course of action I must take. I will have a great navy of ships build upon the coast. I will equip them with everything we will need for a successful campaign to regain my title. What say you of that?"

There was much muttering and William scanned his audience for signs of support or dissent.

A noble arose from one of the tables close to the king. "My Lord," he said, "Harold was chosen, it is said, by the Great Witan of England to be their king. If that is the will of his people, how can we justify reversing that will by force of arms?"

Again, mutterings of support rippled around the gathering, the nobles more brave and confident now that one of their number had spoken up.

William again cast his gaze around them. The muttering stopped where his gaze fell. "I was promised the throne by no less than Edward the Confessor himself. He said that I should follow him as his rightful heir."

More mumbling. Another man rose to his feet. The mumbling stopped. "My Duke, we cannot be sure that we could defeat a man such as Harold Godwinson. He is indeed a powerful man and has great backing amongst his people. We would be fighting not in Normandy, but on foreign soil, with all its attendant dangers." Further mumbling of support.

William now rose to his full height upon his feet. His face a mask of anger. "This is the talk of women. Have I no warriors in Normandy who will follow me?" Silence fell upon the hall.

Then the figure of a bishop stood. "Duke William," he said, "we are all your devoted followers, but think upon this. Harold is already crowned, and therefore, in the sight of God, he has become the Lord's representative in England. It has been done by religious custom and is binding in religious law." The bishop quickly sat, the colour draining from his cheeks. A shiver ran down his spine.

William rose again. "Harold Godwinson, Earl of Wessex, was shipwrecked upon our shores, at Ponthieu. There, he was captured by Count Guy and taken to Beaurain. We went to where he was held and had him released into our care. Did he not then accompany us into battle against Conan of Brittany? Did he not distinguish himself by rescuing two of our soldiers from the quicksand at Mont St Michel, for which we were all eternally grateful? Yes. From there, Harold fought with us, pursuing Conan to Dinan, where we made him surrender the fortress at the point of a spear!" Chuckles and agreement came from the nobles and fighting men who remembered it.

"Here, did I not present Harold with weapons and arms? Did I not knight him into our order? And here it was that Harold swore an oath upon sacred relics to me that he would support my claim to the English throne. Has he not perjured himself of this oath?"

A great roar went up from the crowd. "It is true!"

"I heard him!"

"He did make the oath!"

"My lords," William cried, "Harold *is* a strong man. His courage cannot be in question. But what are these gifts to him if he has no honour? Surely, honour is all."

The hall erupted with cheers. "We will follow Duke William," they cried.

The bishop stood again. "My Lord, Harold did make a sacred oath and has broken that bond. Go to England with the blessing of the church." Nobles now flocked to William's cause and plans were made to sail to England and right what they saw as a terrible wrong.

# CHAPTER SEVENTEEN

It was not to be long before Harold's spies in Normandy returned with news of William's plans. But the new incumbent on the English throne was confident that William could not throw an army at him that could not be defeated on English soil.

Nevertheless, he wisely gathered together troops from his southern areas on the Isle of Wight and along some of the 'Saxon Shore'. There they waited for the Norman fleet that was being gradually assembled.

But William was nothing if not a skilled planner! He was making sure that every last provision and every last weapon was collected and noted. He knew that only the most detailed planning and preparation would be enough to defeat the Saxons of England.

He visited the sites regularly, and strode around with his advisers and administrators, counting and recounting, checking and rechecking until satisfied that all was to his satisfaction.

"How goes it, Simeon?"

"My Lord, all goes well. Provisions are coming in and are being stored ready for loading. All is within the time."

"Excellent!" and he strode on.

He watched his troops practise their fighting skills. Archers at the butts, men-at-arms fighting at close quarters, shield walls being drilled, cavalry exercising their great horses, galloping at targets, hurling spears and wielding swords. And he insisted that every horse was rubbed down and well fed before the cavalrymen could eat and rest themselves.

But an early invasion was not to be. The weather, and in particular, the winds were not as favourable as they might have been. William paced the harbour, watching the skies, feeling the winds in his face and speaking with his captains.

"What think you? Will we sail soon?" he asked of a gnarled and sun-bronzed seaman who was staring out over the crashing waves.

"My Lord, none can say. This weather is wrong for us. We need a change in the winds otherwise we will put our fleet in danger, and could suffer great losses."

And so it was, day after day, until William and many others began to think that it was God's will that they should not take to the sea and invade the island across it. Of course, William would not have said this in public, nor dare anyone suggest it in company, but a feeling of unease was growing in the ranks and amongst the nobles.

The fleet was still in port almost seven months after the day it should have sailed, with William champing at the bit and furious that he could not progress.

On September 8th, with his supplies running low and his men becoming bored, Harold Godwinson was persuaded to stand his troops down and disband them to their homes. It seemed now that the threatened invasion would not happen, at least for the time being. Harold's men tramped away and returned to the villages and burghs they had come from, to prepare for the winter with their families, whilst Harold and his closest supporters left and made their way wearily back to London.

But trouble was brewing in the north! On that very same day the Norwegian, Harald Hardrada, (hard ruler), lay off the mouth of the River Tyne. "Haul down the sail!" he bawled to his captain of boat. Men ran to unhitch the arm from the cleats on the mast and furl the sail so that the wind would carry them no further. Now work began to unplug the oar holes and the great oars were lifted from the bowels of the ship and slid into place.

Harald's fleet of ships lay low in the water, so full were they of men, weapons and everything an army would need to mount a challenge to the established order of England. Now the men strained at the oars and they bent as they felt the force of the water. The men at the steering oars heaved on the poles to gradually turn the boats shoreward and towards the mouth of the Tyne.

Within the hour, Hardrada had stepped from boat to oar and from oar to land, raising his sword into the air and, to great cheers, claimed the English throne for himself. And here he was met and joined by another who would support his claim and fight for his cause … Tostig!

As the ships were being drawn up onto the beaches and mudflats by straining men, the two men approached each other. Tostig held up his hand in greeting. "My Lord Harald," he cried. "It is a fine sight to see your long-ships and men arriving on these English shores."

"Tostig, you are well?"

"I am. Now come with me and we shall take refreshment."

As they left, Tostig gazed around at the Norsemen hauling the ships and unloading their cargoes. They surely were a fierce lot of warriors. Tostig shuddered involuntarily at the thought of facing these men in battle. Soon, his own brother would see this for himself and quake in his boots! The same brother who had, unwisely, unseated him from the earldom of Northumbria. He knew that Harold Godwinson would not be able to ignore this incursion into England. Oh, how he would have his revenge! How good it would feel to see Harold kneeling before him as he awaited his inevitable fate. (He knew that Harold would never beg for his life!) He could feel it now, that elation that victory would bring. What would he say to his brother? He rehearsed words in a speech that he would, one day, deliver, he was certain. He would have to get it right, as his brother could only die once!

But, of course, word was spreading fast concerning the arrival of Hardrada and Tostig to the earldom of Northumbria. Morcar was the first to hear it, of course, whilst in his stronghold of Bamburgh, upon the Northumbrian coast. Indeed, his own men had spotted the sails of the Norwegian craft as they glided south. The monks of Lindisfarne were amongst those who were pleased to see them pass, but worried about their presence in the land and what it meant for their religious houses.

(But it was not such an unexpected happening. Harald's intentions were well enough known, and indeed over the summer months, Edwin and his followers had transported many of their forces from Mercia on the west coast of England, by boat anticipating the peril that lay ahead.)

Messengers were now sent, hotfoot, to relay the news to the nobles of Northumbria, and to Edwin, that their worst fears were coming true. Immediately, Northumbrian troops began to be gathered and mustered to counter the Norse threat. In truth, much of the preparation had already been in hand.

Morcar sat in his hall, surrounded by his nobles from close at hand. He pondered, a look of worry etched across his brows. *Am I well enough prepared? Could I face down and defeat an army of Norsemen, led by Harald Hardrada and supported by the treacherous Tostig? Why, oh why had Tostig been banished and not slain when the opportunity arose, for his mistreatment of the people of Northumbria? He was a mischief that the land could well do without! But then, would a brother slay a brother in those circumstances? Probably not.* But Morcar was under no illusions that Harold would slay his brother now, should the opportunity arise.

"My nobles," he began. "Intelligence from scouts in the field says that Hardrada and Tostig have now mustered a combined force and will soon head for York, where they intend to make a stand. We must now make our move. I have given orders that as many troops as we can raise should quickly be stirred and readied."

Morcar turned as the door to the chamber was opened and a messenger, flushed of face, entered the room. "My Lord, I have news of Edwin."

Morcar's eyes widened. "Tell me the news, and may God make it good news."

"My Lord, Edwin and troops are already mobilised and heading for York. The Mercian boats are moored upon the river Wharfe, just 10 miles downstream of its meeting with the Ouse."

"It is good. I know that my brother has gathered the greatest force he can muster from his own men and we have called upon the local fyrd. This area has long been a Nordic land – indeed as little as thirty years ago – but I am confident that we can rely upon the loyalty of our local men. Did they not rise up to cast Tostig from this land only a short time ago? And that devil's spawn is now in league with Hardrada."

"My Lord, Edwin bids that you should muster immediately and meet him at Fulford, to fend off this attack upon Northumbria's capital."

"Thank God!" exclaimed Morcar. "My brother is ready and stands with me, as I knew he would. Now we can move against the Norsemen and the disreputable wretch who calls himself a son of Godwin!"

After further discussion, Morcar dismissed his nobles to go about their duties, with new orders for the battle ahead.

Morcar travelled south on that same day and, as September progressed, troops assembled and made their way from north, south, west and east, avoiding contact with the Norsemen on the way. On the 20th day of that same month, Morcar and Edwin, his brother, met and arranged their combined troops upon the land between the Northumbrian capital and the invading Viking hoards. They knew – nay, all knew - that their task was to halt the progress and snuff out the mission of Hardrada and Tostig in taking York as their military base in the battle for England. And what a battle it would be!

Morcar's troops were now assembled and bedded in at Fulford, well before the Viking force could reach the area. But, in truth, it was not a large army.

In the Norse camp, Hardrada and Tostig were huddled in conversation regarding the best way to outflank and defeat the forces of Northumbria and Mercia. They too had their spies, and knew what was afoot.

A huge Norseman, with a great red beard entered his leader's tent. His long red hair flowed down over his shoulders to the shoulder blades and his arms were bedecked with the arm-rings which showed that he had excelled in battle against his leader's enemies.

"My Lord, the scouts have arrived with intelligence. It seems that Morcar and Edwin have blocked our progress to York."

"Have they, by Odin! Well, let them try to resist us. We shall skin them alive and boil their innards for the dogs!"

"How many troops do they command?" questioned Tostig.

"My Lord, we estimate their forces at between 3000 and 5000 men. There are around 300 housecarls."

"Only that?" said Harald, his brows raised. "How many thegns will Morcar have?"

"Around five thousand," answered Tostig, "from my recollection."

"So none too many on the battlefield then? Their confidence cannot be high."

"And us? What is our fighting total?" questioned Tostig. "How many will we put into the field?"

Hardrada pondered. "We have around three hundred ships, and some smaller craft. Around forty men to a ship. Between nine and twelve thousand, though not all are warriors. I must leave a goodly party with the ships, here at Riccall, upon the Ouse. We can put around six thousand into the field against Morcar."

"Could we field more? I have some."

"You have *some*, Tostig. Most of the men are mine, and I cannot chance putting all into the field at once. We will defeat Morcar and Edwin, have no fear! They are Anglo-Saxons. We are Norse!"

Tostig threw him a glance but decided not to challenge the Norseman on the insult.

And now it was Morcar's turn to plot and plan. He knew that his force was but limited. "We need to bring Hardrada and his lapdog to us at a choke-point," he explained to his commanders. "Here at Fulford the land is marshy and soft. The space between the marshes and the river is no more than six hundred yards. In front of us will be the stream that drains the marsh into the river. It is the most advantageous point I can find in which to deploy our forces."

Edwin looked out over the land. "You are right, brother. It is an excellent vantage point from our stand. The Norsemen will have need to trail northward," he pondered, "though some could be deployed to follow the riverbank from Riccall. We must be alert to that. Send men out to watch that route. But our position here blocks the southern approach well. The land has provided us with a solid position!"

A housecarl spoke up. "The Norse will find the land that they must stand upon is bog, whereas we will stand upon firm ground."

"Aye," said Morcar, now giving orders to his commanders. "The stream twists and turns, so we must spread our troops along its banks for around three hundred paces. Place there, around a thousand men, in three or four ranks. Place the warriors to the front and the fyrdmen in the rear. Let the rest of the army flank us on the firm ground."

Morcar knew well enough that his flanks would need to be protected, lest the Norsemen send troops around to his rear, where he would be caught like a fish in a trap! But the river and the marsh, he knew would also play their part in watching his sides.

And so it was that Hardrada's troops began their advance to scout the position. Norsemen and the Saxons now looked out over the area. Morcar had chosen well. This was an excellent place to halt their progress. The river ran to their one side and marshy ground lay to the other. It would not be easy to find a ford for the stream, for it lay in a trench some three paces wide and more than half a man's height deep. More boggy land lay before the Saxon positions.

But Hardrada also eyed the land and considered his position. "There is a weakness to Morcar's plans," he said, at length. "There is some high ground, over there. From there, we can view the battlefield. The way the land lies there," he pointed into the distance, "hinders the Saxon flanks in communicating with one another. Should one flank collapse, the other would know nothing of it until we attacked them from the rear. And only then when we were almost upon them."

"And they would have little chance to retreat before we drove them into the marshes behind them," pointed out Tostig.

The two men looked at one another and grinned.

Harald signalled back to one of his commanders. They in turn signalled to three groups of Norse warriors who began to move forward. "To this side," he explained to Tostig, "I have sent my troops who are the least experienced warriors. The ground there is very wet, and will be difficult to manoeuvre, but it will make it more difficult for them to retreat if their nerve fails them!" He gave Tostig a knowing look. The two men laughed.

The troops moved slowly forward over the next hours. The most fearsome warriors were grouped along the river-bank, on the firmer and drier land. They were dressed in leather, chain mail and iron helmets. Most of the Anglo-

Saxon Fyrd had much less of the highly protective wear, and for most of them, leather had to suffice.

As the two armies built up their numbers and faced each other, the usual barrage of insults and threats began. Even when the two sides could not understand the language, the intent was obvious. "It is important to un-nerve the opposition, with the hope that they will either turn and flee or will enter the battle with their confidence at rock bottom," Hardrada said.

Before the whole strength of the Viking warriors could assemble, Morcar wisely decided to pre-empt the enemy. "Let the left flank strike," he called to his officers. Now they assembled, shield to shield and the hand-to-hand fighting began. Swords, spears and axes thudded into shields on both sides. Both sides pushed back with the large bosses on their shield-fronts. Arrows struck into shields and many were shattered into splinters by the force of arms.

As the land was wet and slippery, many men lost their footing and plunged backward into the swampy land. Now each side struck where they could. Once the contact was close, the spears were used less, in favour of the long, double-bladed battle-axes Blades rose and fell and cracked helmets and skulls alike and the waters ran red with the blood of both sides. Bloodied bodies floated in the marsh, and were pushed aside as the fighters fought to gain any advantage. A film of greasy red began to spread across the surface of the water.

The Saxon forces pressed well to begin with, and the Norsemen were forced back up the track from whence they came. But as the land became wetter, the troops found themselves wading through deep water and clumps of reeds. Now they found they could not press further. Many were exhausted, after much fighting and pushing and shoving and the constant drain on energy of wading through the water.

Now the two ranks of the most elite fighters were locked in the combat of the shield-wall. Throats were pierced by the long spears. Heads were cracked open by the swords and axes. Men fell when arrows poured over the shield wall and found their targets. Corpses fell to the ground and began to build up until the two sides began to lose contact.

Harald retreated from the hand-to-hand combat and returned to the hill. Standing upon his vantage point, he saw that his troops were beginning to fall back, and he knew that he had to react. He turned to an aide; a giant of a man with his blond hair streaming in the wind behind him. "Move more men to the centre and push forward. Our forces are greater by the river, and we must push forward there." The man nodded and disappeared to deliver the order.

With that, Harald left the vantage point again and waded back into the fray, sweeping his great sword from side to side and cracking skulls and slicing necks where he could. One Anglo-Saxon leapt forward to face him, a look of steely determination in his eyes. The Viking king grinned and bared his teeth. "It is a good day to die, Saxon," he hissed. The two men circled in the mud. The Saxon feinted to the right and then leapt back and stabbed to the left. Harald caught the blow with his shield and countered with a great sweep onto the Saxon's shield.

Now the Saxon skipped to one side again and aimed a shot at the Viking's sword arm. The blow landed and Harald winced. He would have a bruise there by the dawn. Another prod with the Saxon's sword nicked the Viking's arm and drew a little blood that seeped out between the rings of chain armour. Harald looked down, surprised. But the blow did not deter the Norseman. With a quick shift of his feet, he brought another great blow to the Saxon's shield, which split it from top to bottom. The wood hung only by the shreds of leather that covered the face. The Anglo-Saxon warrior stared at the shield and shook it to try to dislodge the shards that were now no more than an encumbrance to him. It was that momentary loss of concentration that sealed his fate and ensured that this was, indeed, the day he died.

Harald pressed forward and pushed the broken shield aside. He buried his sword into the other man's stomach and pulled upward, so that the Saxon was filleted. His guts burst forth and fell to the earth before him. He stared down with a look of astonishment upon his face, before he fell to the earth with a groan, his eyes wide but unseeing.

Now the Anglo-Saxons were forced to give ground to their foes. Here, upon the riverbank, Edwin himself and his fyrdmen fought hard to hold the ground, but crumbled under the force of Norsemen who now surged forward toward their positions. Within a short time, the group were separated from the rest of their forces and began to retreat to the safety of York. How many made it is unclear. Some certainly were lucky enough to escape the massacre that was materialising in front of them.

The setback at the riverbank was not a critical hindrance to begin with. Indeed, Morcar's troops were beginning to overcome the Vikings at another point. But now some of the Norse warriors were on firmer ground on the side originally occupied by the Anglo-Saxons and they were gradually forced to retreat along the line of the ditch and toward Morcar's position.

Slowly, the Viking force fought their way across a stream and up a hill. It was never easy to fight uphill, but the Vikings came in such numbers that they were an unstoppable force, and the Anglo-Saxons were less than an immovable object!

It was less than an hour of hard fighting before the Anglo-Saxons were wedged out of their positions along the side of the stream. Now things were rapidly turning for the worst! Of course, not all of the Anglo-Saxons and their leaders were fully aware of the worsening situation behind them, as it was, as Harald had predicted, happening behind a low hill.

Now the riverbank Vikings were lying behind half of the Saxon ranks, along a track. More Vikings were pouring in, only to find that the battle scene was so crowded by their own men, locked in mortal combat with the Saxons, that they were forced to make their way around from another side. Across the marshland they waded, weapons held in the air above them to avoid them becoming too slippery to handle. After a short while, Hardrada led his men up and away from the river, just as the fresh late arrivals were beginning to take up positions from the other direction.

Now Morcar and Edwin found themselves in even more trouble. They were fighting on three sides — never an easy thing to do. They were also cut off from others of their cohorts of troops and could only retreat down the track toward York.

What they did not know, could not know, was that their escape route was largely cut off and they were heading to their deaths.

Soon they found that the ground fell away steeply. More Vikings were sited on higher ground behind them and others forcing them backward toward a great gash in the land. Their God, it seemed, had deserted them, and Odin was to triumph on that dreadful day! There was naught that they could do. Either they fell to their end, were cut down or crushed underfoot. It is said that the streams ran red with Saxon blood that day, and the tales were told in Viking halls for generations after.

The fight was fought. York lay open to the invaders, and the surrender was quickly agreed. I did hear, though, that the Vikings were certainly not without loss that day, and the Anglo-Saxon warriors were by no means humiliated. It is, perhaps, the only comfort that English people can take from the whole sorry story.

Harald and Tostig made their way swiftly to the city to organise their troops and to re-provision. Hardrada had already warned his commanders that their troops should not loot, kill or desecrate the city, and, to their credit, no harm came to York or its inhabitants that day, save for a few hostages who were taken. The people of York, in their turn, recognised Harald as their king and agreed to join forces with him in the forthcoming struggle with Harold Godwinson that all men knew must happen.

"We must now return to Riccall and our ships. Some of my men will remain here to keep the peace – though I doubt that will be a problem. We will take 100 hostages and move south to win this kingdom," he told Tostig. "Muster your troops again. We two shall meet again at the hall nearby Stamford Bridge that my scouts have reconnoitred."

"I will look forward to the meeting with the greatest pleasure!" Tostig chuckled. "And then we will see what my brother does."

# CHAPTER EIGHTEEN

Now Tostig and Harald Hardrada thought that they had the country by the throat! They had defeated Morcar and Edwin, and York was theirs. Had the people of York themselves not declared their support and allegiance to Harald? Of course they had. You must remember that Northumbria had been a Danish area for many a long year and there was no love lost for West Saxons! It was, however, strange that the people should accept back the West Saxon, Tostig, having been glad to see the back of him just a short while previously. However, it is strange what people will accept when they see vastly superior forces breathing down their necks!

But peril was much closer at hand for Harald and Tostig than they thought! Had they imagined that Harold, England's new king, was unaware of what was planned and what was happening in his kingdom? How foolish!

Harold was still preoccupied with the threatened Norman invasion, but had, of course, anticipated the invasion of the Norse king, and knew that his own brother was hand-in-hand with Harald Hardrada. When he had received word that Hardrada was off his shores with a fleet, he had mobilised his troops for a forced march northward. Harold had led his men to Northumbria from London in just four short days. An amazing feat!

But forces did not just come from the south. I recall my father and I attending a meeting with Cerdic, where the situation was discussed. We met at Cerdic's hall one evening, after we had finished our chores for the day and had eaten. We filed into the hall and seated ourselves at the long tables.

"My friends," Cerdic began. "I have some grave news. Tostig is again in Northumbria."

Gasps and cries of "No!" rose up from the hall.

"It is true. He comes under the protection of Harald Hardrada, the king of the Norse, in order to take Northumbria and then for the Norwegian to take the throne of England from Harold Godwinson. Hardrada and Tostig have defeated Morcar and Edwin at Fulford." Further gasps and shaking of heads.

"What is to be done, Cerdic?" my father asked. "We cannot allow Tostig to rule over us again. His retribution would be great upon every man who deposed him."

"You are right, Aelric. We must act. I have heard that Harold Godwinson marches north as we speak with a great force of men. They expect to be near York in four days. It is much to ask but will you fight again to free our land?"

"Aye!" came the roar, though I could see in every man's face a look of fear and sadness. They had fought well and rid themselves of Tostig, and now he had returned. Was all of the bloodshed for naught? What would happen to us if Hardrada became king and Tostig, his dog, reclaimed the land of Northumbria? It would go badly for everyone! It was hard to even imagine the bleak future that lay ahead of us if Tostig Godwinson returned!

The following day was one of frantic preparation. We still had the weapons we were given to fight Tostig, and also many that we had taken from his troops and his armoury. They were prepared and sharpened. Arrows were collected together and new ones quickly made. Food was collected for the new march to York.

My mother was inconsolable at the thought that we should put ourselves back into mortal danger. She had seen us go before and rejoiced when we returned. Now she must do it all over again. Would we return this time? Who knew? The odds were not good. Again, she threw herself into the tasks that had to be done. Autumn was here again, and it was a busy time for all of us.

My grandfather, too, looked down in the depths of despair. At first he had supported us and had been proud to see us go, and had rejoiced with the rest of the village to see our return. Now we were going again. What would happen if we did not return? How could he look after the family if we were dead? He was no longer a young, fit man.

The people I most felt for were the families of the men who did not return the last time. For them, it all came flooding back. The memories. The pain. The bitterness. They looked at us almost accusingly as we made our rushed preparations. The tears fell again and were wiped aside by woollen sleeves.

And then the time to leave came - again. We rose before dawn - again. We packed up our food - again. We dressed in our leathers - again. We picked up our weapons - again. We left ... *again!*

As we walked south, this time we knew what to expect. Well, almost. Last time we took on Tostig's Danish house-carls. This time we took on a whole Norse army, along with Flemish mercenaries recruited by Tostig as well! The old feelings came flooding back. Did we really want to be there? What would we see? What would we do? Would we return, or was this the time when we met our maker?

We walked south on a punishing schedule – much faster than we had before – and we marched long into the night. We reached the area of York within just four days. How we did it, I will never know. Once arrived in the area, we met up with other parties again. One of their thegns informed us that we needed to walk close to a place called the Stamford Bridge. It lay just nine miles to the east of York, and so it added little extra to our journey.

As we approached to the south of the Stamford Bridge area, we needed to be careful not to show ourselves to the Vikings, who did not seem to know that either we or Harold's men were in the region. That was very odd. Where were their spies? The night we arrived, we met up with some of Harold's forces and endured a cold camp. We could not afford to show our positions by lighting fires.

There was a story told by men of something that happened before the battle. They do say that a man rode bravely into the camp of Tostig and Hardrada and offered to talk.

"Tostig," he said, "even at this late hour, I can promise you your earldom back, should you rise up against the Norseman."

It seems that Tostig had asked a question in reply. "And what would Harold Godwinson give to Harald Hardrada to encourage him to make terms?"

The rider replied, "Hardrada will be given nothing more than seven feet of ground, as he is taller than other men." But no terms could be achieved, and the rider left the camp empty handed, with the Norsemen watching in amazement.

Hardrada turned to Tostig, who still stood there, gazing in the direction in which the rider had left. "That was a brave man who rode, unprotected, into our camp to try to negotiate terms for Harold. Do you know the man?"

"I do," replied Tostig, coming back from the trance he seemed to have slipped into. "That man was Harold Godwinson; my brother."

Harald Hardrada swivelled his gaze upon Tostig. He shook his head in amazement. "I have never seen such bravery in all of my years," he mused.

Now whether this tale is true, I cannot say, but it is the story that men tell of that day.

There is no settlement at Stamford Bridge. It seems the name describes a point on the River Derwent, with a stone ford and a bridge. I could see how this name had come about as, within the riverbed there lies a great outcropping of stone, over which the river falls in a small waterfall. When the level of the river is low, it is possible for a man on foot or on horse to cross the river.

Around a mile to the south, lay a small settlement used by the Romans, when they settled our land. Here, on the banks of the river, stood a bridge that carried a track for animals and wagons. I know not whether it still exists.

It was around these two features that Harold and his thegns planned their attack on the Norse army.

"We will force a two-pronged attack upon them," Harold told his followers. "We shall make use both of the ford and the bridge."

"The scouts report that the Vikings are divided. Some few of their troops are upon the western bank, with the bulk on the east. They have left most of their armour and weapons in the bowels of their ships; the weather being fine and warm," interjected a housecarl.

"Then that is the way we will attack," confirmed the king.

And so we marched. We arrived first on the western bank, as Harold had ordered. When the Vikings realised that we were attacking, chaos reigned in their camp, as men ran hither and thither, frantically collecting what armour and weapons they had with them. But, for them, it was too late.

We approached around a hill and quickly charged down onto the Norse troops. We had no need of a shield wall yet, as the Vikings were in disarray. Instead, we rushed them and began to hack and lunge at them with our weapons. I followed my father, armed with a spear, my seax and bow.

My father raised a great axe above his head and struck down a Viking who was struggling into a mail shirt. The axe caught him on the shoulder, and almost cut his arm from his body. It hung there, attached only by shattered bone and sinew. My father stopped and stared at the man briefly, realising what he had done yet again, when he had thought his battle days were over. But, as the man fell to the earth, a scream upon his lips, my father hit him again and his head exploded in a fountain of blood and grey brains.

I was now occupied with a young Viking who had managed to reach a sword and was frenziedly fighting with one of Harold's men. It seemed to me that the Viking had the better of it. I ran in behind the man and thrust my seax into his ribs from behind. He swung his head to see where the blow had come from and his jaw dropped to see a young boy standing there, with his blood dripping from a short sword. He took his eyes off Harold's man for a split second, and that was enough for the Saxon to swing his sword and slash the Viking across the back of his neck, below the line of his helmet. I was amazed that he did not seem to die immediately, but swung his own sword back. But it was to no avail, for I stepped up again and sank my seax into his belly. Now he sank to the earth and we two knew that he would take no further part in this battle, or any other.

I had done it again. I had killed a man, all be it with help. Now my blood was up and I looked around for further prey.

I drew my bow and nocked an arrow into it. I focused my aim on a Viking just a few paces away, who was recovering his breath after killing a Saxon with his great sword. He leaned back to stretch his back muscles and, as he did, I sent an arrow into his spine. He stood stock still for a brief moment of time and then fell upon his face in the dirt. Dead to this world.

By now most of the Norsemen on the western bank were slain, and those who survived were running for the bridge to join their comrades on the other side. We hurried after them, as more of our troops arrived in the second prong of the attack.

As we approached the bridge, I witnessed a happening that I would never have believed had I not seen it with my own eyes. The bridge was a choke-point over which it would take our troops some time to cross, and the more time the Vikings could buy, the better for them. A huge Norseman, his hair streaming out over his shoulders and long whiskers hanging down to his chest, stood upon the bridge, a sword in one hand and a double-bladed Danish axe in the other. He blocked the bridge and defied any man to challenge him. A strapping Saxon warrior stepped forward onto the bridge and engaged him in combat, whilst our troops cheered him on. It was futile. The Saxon was dead in a heartbeat and splashed into the river below! Now men looked at each other. One of us would need to take him, if we were to cross the bridge and finish the job we had started. Failure was not an option.

Another man bravely stepped forward, his shield held in front of him and a spear in his hand. The two parried blows for a while, until the Saxon dropped his guard for a lunge of the spear. It missed its mark. The Norseman didn't, and another Saxon fell into the water.

The warrior gave out a huge roar at this, and his fellows on the other bank cheered their approval.

Now more men stepped forward, but each time, it was the same story. The Saxon dead were building up in the river below, until almost forty bodies floated there.

But now my father nudged me and nodded his head. I looked upstream to see a barrel floating downstream. Was this a Viking trick? What was about to happen?

As the barrel floated under the bridge, ignored by the Viking above it and those on the bank, it suddenly stopped midstream. A Saxon soldier, satisfied that the huge Dane could not see him, climbed silently from the barrel and sent it on its way. In his hand was a long, sharp spear.

The Saxon looked up and saw exactly where the Dane was standing, legs apart, ready to repel all attacks. Stealthily, he pushed the spearhead through the laths of the bridge and rammed hard. Catching the warrior in his backside and plunging the spearhead into the man's bowels. The Norseman stood there, a look of amazement and horror etched upon his face, before looking down to where his bowels were now emptying onto the bridge and into the water. A gush of red blood followed, soaking the Saxon beneath the bridge, as he stood there still, forcing the spear further up into the Viking's intestines.

At length, the Viking died as he stood and fell forward. Now our soldiers had their chance to cheer and we poured across the bridge as quickly as the space would allow.

But the Vikings had taken the opportunity to regroup. They formed a shield wall to face us. But we poured forward and formed up in a line before the Norsemen. We locked our shields – and I am proud to say that I became a full member of the shield wall on that day – and we charged.

Oh, how the battle raged! Despite the fact that the Danish army and Tostig's troops were at a huge disadvantage, not having all of their armour and weapons with them, they fought like wolves. I held a grudging respect for them on that day.

And I blooded myself again, a number of times, as Vikings fell under my seax, spear and from the deadly barbs of my bow. Now I was truly an Anglo-Saxon warrior!

Men fell now, littering the ground with blood-soaked bodies. Heads lay separated from their bodies. Limbs lay at strange angles to their bodies upon the ground. The cries and moans of the injured were terrible to hear. I shall never forget it. Indeed, I still wake at nights, as an old man and remember that scene from you youth.

Slowly, slowly, under huge pressure, the Viking army began to break down and disintegrate. Our men forced their way forward now and, with a great heave, broke through the Norse shield wall.

I recall seeing the man I later learned was Harald Hardrada himself, fighting with great courage and ferocity near to my own position. He was, undoubtedly, a great warrior. But now he was outflanked by our forces. Having gutted a Saxon soldier and chopped his head from his body, he turned to see if reinforcements were arriving behind him and, as he turned back to the fray, an arrow caught him where his throat and chest met, cutting off the very air he breathed. Blood fountained from his lips and I could actually hear the gurgling sound as he fell to the floor, suffocating and drowning in his own juices.

And what of Tostig? I saw him die too. Not far to my right, a group of our men were locked in combat with a knot of Tostig's troops. Their commander was in the thick of it. One of the men in our party was Benjamin, the smith, who seemed to have been drawn to Tostig like a wasp to a honeypot. He barged his way through the lines and stared Tostig in the eye. He smiled and lifted the leather helmet upon his head to reveal his missing ear. I am unsure as to whether Tostig knew the significance or even remembered Benjamin, but he turned to face the huge man.

The two were soon tied in battle, first one way and then the other, for some considerable time. Each man panted to drag the precious air into his burning lungs. But after a while, Benjamin struck a heavy blow to Tostig's shield, laying him flat as he tripped over a body behind him. Now the smith saw his change and pounced. He kicked aside Tostig's shield and plunged his sword, taken from one of Tostig's own men, into the West Saxon's chest. Tostig looked up at him, a look of shock upon his face. Benjamin bent down and took off Tostig's helmet. With the keen edge of his sword, he cut off the man's left ear. I could not swear to the fact that Tostig recognised him at that moment, but I somehow hoped he did. Benjamin tucked the ear into his pocket and, when we returned home, he nailed it to the post beside his own.

In the later stages, the reinforcements Harald had been watching for arrived from the ships at Riccall. They were led by Eystein Orri, who was the betrothed of Hardrada's own daughter. But it was too late. These men, unlike their allies, were fully equipped for battle, but such had been the hurried march in the hot sunshine, that many men fell and died of exhaustion even as they arrived.

Their arrival did, for a while, cause us problems, but, in truth, the battle was now over. Orri himself was slain by one of the Saxons and the Vikings fled for their lives.

Many of our troops pursued them, killing them where they found them, and many, it is said, were drowned in the rivers before they could reach safety.

I have heard it said that so many men died on that day that the soil of the field wherein the slaughter took place was whitened by bleached bones for seventy years after the battle.

For us, the journey to home lay ahead. But for Harold Godwinson, it was not yet over. It now seemed that William of Normandy was invading our shores from the south, and Harold's men would need to march south again to face another foe!

# CHAPTER NINETEEN

That evening we huddled around campfires, largely made up of broken Viking and Saxon shields and the fractured shafts of spears and arrows.

King Harold had accepted a truce from the few Norwegians who were left standing. Harald Hardrada's own son, Olaf, was amongst those captured after the battle, and many wanted him killed or kept as a hostage to ensure that the Norse did not return to our shores. But Harold Godwinson would have none of it. "They will return to their homes," he told us, "now that they have given a solemn oath that they will not attack England again."

What, I wondered, was the value of a Viking's oath?

But, in truth, I could not see how they could harry us again after the losses they had suffered. Over three hundred ships had hauled up on our shores, but only twenty-four ships were needed to take the survivors back to their homeland. I gather that they slunk away with their tails between their legs to Orkney for the winter. (The Earl of Orkney had been in their number.) In the spring, when the weather improved and the crashing seas calmed a little, Olaf went back to his native Norway. He and his brother, Magnus, shared their father's kingdom between them. Their brotherly love seems to have extended beyond that of Harold and Tostig!

As we were eating a meagre meal, cooked over a campfire, Cerdic approached us. He sat down upon his heels and warmed his hands at the flames. "So, you will return to Brockford in a day or two," he said. We looked at him across the fire.

"But you will be returning with us," my father said.

"No," Cerdic replied, gazing into the fire. "Harold is certain that the Normans will attack our southern shores within days. I have said that I will ride south to South Wessex with him." There was a long pause. "But I could not ask you to do the same. You have land and families to attend to, and you have seen enough of conflict and death. You must return to your homes. I will take some of my armed men with me."

My father and I looked at each other. The other men had heard the conversation too, and glanced around, from one to another. I looked into my father's eyes. I could see indecision there. Of course, he had the responsibility of a family. He had my mother and my aunt. He had my grandfather and, of course, he had the overwhelming responsibility of my brothers and sisters.

"Father," I said, "I will go with Cerdic. I am a warrior now. I know that I can fight well, though I am not yet full grown."

My father stared at me, and I could see his brain in motion. Nay, it was in turmoil. What was he to do? At length, he said, "No, John, *you* will not go. *We* will go."

"But what of the family?" I asked him.

"They will survive. And I know that the people of the village and Cerdic's men will not see them starve until we return. But will the kingdom survive? And what would your mother say if I let you go off to fight alone?" He grinned from ear to ear.

I could well imagine it!

And so it was that we were to march south and fight again for Harold, our king, against the menace of Normandy.

I later heard of the return of some of our number to the village. They were the older men and those whose family had no other strong adult to carry out the heavy work of providing for the winter. As with the last time, the village turned out to greet them home and, when my mother realised that we were not with them, she fell into a dead faint. She had to be carried back to our home and cared for by my aunt until she regained her senses.

Once she was again in the land of the living, one of the men explained to her that we were not dead and what we were doing. It seems that she was still inconsolable and that she wailed for many days afterwards. After all, we had come through two battles already – what were the odds of us coming home alive from another?

Three days after Stamford Bridge, on September 28th, Harold was proved right. The Normans, under 'William the Bastard' landed on our southern coast. Now we had to rush our war-weary army south to meet this new invasion. Would there ever be peace in our lives, I wondered?

William, whilst we were fighting for our lives at Stamford Bridge, had sailed his great fleet to St Valery-sur-Somme, and here he waited until the conditions were favourable. At last, the winds turned to blow in the right direction, and William immediately unfurled his sails for England, just two days after Stamford Bridge.

In his great fleet were seven hundred ships, it is said, of Viking design, led by his flagship, the Mora. This great ship, I was told, had a huge carved figurehead on its prow.

William and his troops made landfall at Pevensey, just outside the small fishing village of Hastings. As they arrived, it seems that upon landing, William fell, face down in the breaking waves, which his forces saw as a bad omen and gasps were heard all around. But he picked himself up, his hands full of sand, and declared himself King of England, by calling out, "See, my lords, by the splendour of God, I have taken possession of England with both my hands. It is now mine and what is mine is yours." and that, it seems, gave his men much better heart, and a huge cheer went up.

Once ashore, William gave an order, which, in itself, worried his followers. "We will empty our boats and then we will break up and burn many of the ships that have carried us across the sea." His men looked at each other. That would mean that there would be little chance of retreat to Normandy, should they fail to conquer England. They would stand or die!

The first of William's forces to come ashore were his archers; bows strung tight and quivers full of arrows. They were to be the protection force from any attack from the English troops. But, of course, there was no resistance to their invasion.

Quickly, the ships were unloaded by the sailors and squires, carrying huge piles of weapons, shields and saddles.

The great warhorses were disembarked and settled again on hard ground.

Almost immediately, William set his men to work building a great earth embankment across the harbour mouth and his carpenters built a castle of wood upon the top of a hill, so that William's troops could watch for any sign of Harold and his men, and could defend themselves from attack.

At length, the knights landed. They too were fully armed against attack, and protected by mail hauberks. Each man gathered his weapons, helmet and shield, mounted his warhorse and formed up into groups to ride off into the English countryside.

And it was then that the killing and pillaging began.

As one group of Normans rode into the English land-scape, they came across a village. They stood their horses in a coppice of trees upon the hill above. Down below, the people went about their business, taking in the crops and storing food for the winter ahead, oblivious to the menace watching them from on high. The Normans took care not to stare directly at one person for any length of time as it is said that a stare can be felt.

The Norman commander smiled to himself. "Leave not one man, woman or child alive." he said. "Take all stores that might be useful to us. After that, burn everything to the ground. We must make our mark on these people. Let them see what will happen, should they resist Norman rule in this land!"

At a brief wave of his hand, the Norman soldiers galloped their horses down the hill toward the village. Villagers looked up to see what the commotion was, and fled in terror at the sight of the force bearing down upon them. Who were these warriors from Hell? But it was to no avail. The Normans rampaged through the fields and houses, slashing with their swords, stabbing with their spears until blood spattered the earth all around. An old man ran from the field he was working in, but a Norman bore down upon him. He flashed his sword and the man's head flew into the air and rolled in the dirt. His body fell to the ground and spurted blood to feed the soil.

A woman stood in the village, her arms spread, appealing to the Normans to cease their bloody carnage. A small child screamed as it held to her skirts, hiding behind its mother. A soldier dismounted his horse and strode toward her. She appealed to him again. "Sir, spare us! I know not why you kill us, nor what we have done to deserve it!" He looked her in the eye and thrust his sword into her breast. Her eyes opened in shock and she looked down at the red stain spreading across her chest. Then she sank to the ground and sighed as the breath of life left her. The child screamed again and the Norman turned and sliced her head in two with one blow of the great sword.

They carried on the slaughter mercilessly, killing every poor churl they came across, along with their wives and children. They threw blazing brands into thatch and burned their farms and houses. They killed the squealing livestock in the fields and stole all of the provisions they could find to take back to William and his great force.

Once the carnage was over, the Normans looked about them with satisfaction of a job well done. They laughed and joked. Their only disappointment was that they had found no gold or silver.

As they left, they stabbed every corpse again, to ensure that no one lived, and then they laughed again as they rode off to find their next victims. And this terrible scene was repeated across South Wessex. The grim reaper had indeed visited our lands.

We arose one morning, with clouds scudding across a blue sky. We ate a quick breakfast and then gathered together our gear. Harold had marched his troops the 180 miles north, in just a few short days, and now we were to do something similar, down the old Roman road of Ermine Street. We passed by villages, small towns, farmland, hills, valleys and, eventually, land as flat as a table. At Waltham Abbey, he stopped the column and went to pray, and we hoped that God was listening! We marched between thirty and forty miles per day, we reckoned, and eventually arrived in London. I had never seen such a place!

It was October 6th, I think, when we arrived. We remained in the city for six days, whilst Harold and his men recruited more forces from the middle lands and in the south. That gave us time to rest and to wander the streets of the great city and marvel at its sights, sounds and smells. The houses were much as we'd seen in York, but there were many more of them, and the streets felt more cramped. Sadly, it was no cleaner than York either! But the hustle and bustle of a city that was full of craftsmen, making and selling their wares, and travellers and merchants buying and selling these same wares, and also the myriad exotic goods from many lands! My mind was a whirl with it all!

Harold, for any faults he had, was very well liked in the south of England and troops soon began to rally to his cause. Most people had been impressed by the way he had dealt with the threat from the north, and found him a wise, just and merciful king. But now Harold learned what was happening to his people in the countryside near to Hastings, and it made him angry – perhaps too angry, and he became more eager to quickly stand against the Norman invaders.

Harold gave the command for his fleet to assemble again off the coast of South Wessex, though the Normans had landed and fortified their surroundings by now. I suppose he hoped it deterred any further ships from entering our waters.

Once a substantial army was gathered in London, we began the march south. It was a beautiful part of the country, I thought. After never really straying far from my own valley, I had now seen quite a considerable part of the land, and each part was different. This part of the country was gentle and crops seemed to grow well there. I could well imagine that life there was somewhat easier here than it was for us in the north.

Harold had hoped to take the Normans by surprise, in the same way that he had caught out the Norsemen. But the Normans were a different prospect to the Vikings, and they were brave enough warriors, and certainly not easy to defeat!

As we marched, we noticed mounted men on the ridges and in the woodland edges, just far enough away to be safe from our attack. My father nudged me. "We are being watched," he said, pointing to a distant rise in the land. "And they are not Saxon churls. Not on horses like those. They are Norman warriors." I stared at the mounted warriors. For some reason, to a young boy, they looked huge, and were obviously well armed. I suddenly felt very intimidated. I had experienced that feeling before when we saw the Norsemen, but somehow this was different. Somehow these men were more terrifying. An omen, perhaps?

We later learned that one of the men in the hills was one of William's leading thegns – Vitalis – and it was he who had ridden back at speed to tell William of our approach.

It had now become obvious that our element of surprise had gone and we would have to think through our tactics again. I was close to Harold and his commanders when the discussion took place. "What are we to do now, Lord?" one thegn asked.

Harold sat his horse and thought for a while. "The Normans know that we are coming. They would have expected it, but now they know where we are and how strong we are. We will march to a point of advantage and await our enemy there, where we can join them in battle." And so we marched again to a place called Senlac, a few miles from the Norman lines. And here we were to stand!

As we made our way to the battleground, we noticed the smoke rising into the sky from the villages and farmsteads that were still being burned and pillaged by William's men. By night, we could see the glow of burning timber and thatch lighting up the cloud base. It made every man feel sad and uneasy. We had all left villages like these, and could sympathise with the ordinary people whose lives and livelihoods were ending under the terror of Norman swords and fire.

Harold and his commanders had deployed the force well, we thought. We were covering the road from the port of Hastings to London. Behind us was a great forest of Anderida. The local men referred to it as the 'weald', which, I think, is the same as our Anglian word in the north of 'wold' meaning 'forest'.

It was a strange area, and I'd watched it apprehensively as we passed. It seemed sparsely populated and forbidding, and most folk seemed to live around its edges. (I was quite sure, however, that there would probably be any number of desperate men who were not keen to be caught by the forces of law living there, in the moody forest depths!) There were many long drove-ways through the forest, where people would move their animals from one place to another, perhaps for summer grazing. I understand that much of its depths were also used for hunting by the earls of South Wessex and their nobles. It would, I thought, make an excellent if somewhat frightening refuge and I bore it in mind!

Before our lines, the ground fell away sharply in a long slope, which tilted up again at the bottom. And here we set up camp.

As we sat there on the evening after we had arrived, cooking a meal over the fire, a group of riders approached and rode into camp. We leapt to our feet, fearing an attack. But they were Harold's spies, sent out to see how the Norman preparations for battle and conquest were progressing. These men had learned enough Norman French, and so could penetrate the enemy lines without attracting too much attention. They dismounted their horses and rushed to Harold. We later heard the story they had told him.

"My Lord," their leader had said, "we come with strange news. We have seen the Normans and there would seem to be more priests in their number than there are soldiers!"

Harold smiled at this and replied to his men, "Those whom you have seen in such numbers are not priests, but stout soldiers, as they will soon make us feel." It seems that the spies were mistaken. The custom in England is for only priests to have short cropped hair and clean shaven faces, but in Normandy, Harold knew from his time amongst them, that the soldiers too kept their hair short and their faces clean of hair.

I pondered our situation. Our army was mostly made up of infantry troops. Some of the higher lords and housecarls had horses, but even they tended to dismount and fight on foot when battle commenced. The housecarls were the main body of our forces. These were the warriors and men-at-arms who were sworn to the king and protected both himself and the realm. They were a magnificent sight, as they stood there, in their cone-shaped helmets and chain-mail hauberks, carrying their great shields. Most carried the huge Danish battle-axes and every man was equipped with a good sword.

As for the rest of us – the fyrd – we were but the reserve soldiers that the king and his nobles could call upon to defend the kingdom. We had our leather clothing and a few had mail armour, but our weapons were poor by compari-son. Nevertheless, we were an important element to the English force! And we were proud of it!

Now I look back upon it, the Norman army assembled against us were different in many ways. They were merce-naries from Normandy, Brittany, Flanders and other areas of France. Some, they said, even came from Italy.

Much of the Norman army was made up of cavalry troops. It has to be said that they were among the best soldiers that any of us had ever seen. They carried heavy armour, along with a lance and great sword. Sadly, we were soon to learn just how effective they were! Once an enemy line was breached, they would take full advantage of any gap to break up our formation.

The Normans also had many missile troops. We had never seen so many before. The bows they used were much shorter than the ones we favoured, and could be drawn much shorter. They also had a most strange bow, mounted on a cross-stock that shot projectiles called bolts. They pulled in the horizontal plane, rather than vertical, like ours. Our housecarls told us they were called crossbows.

Our great defence against them, of course, would be the shield-wall. Our men would lock ranks and stand firm together. There never was a better defence against archery than the shield-wall, and so it proved in the battle.

And now the time was come. We were sorted into groups and ordered into positions by the thegns and Harold's commanders. Our weapons were sharp. Our shields were strong. Our nerves were taut. Stomachs churned. Men ran to the woods and evacuated their bowels, before returning to their positions. Others turned and lost their meagre breakfast into the grass. Was this it? Would this be the day we died? Would we see another dawn? What of our families? All of these thoughts swirled in our minds.

The Norman troops were assembled at the bottom of Senlac Hill. We could see the weak sun glint on mail and plate armour. We could hear the clump of their feet as they assembled. They had so many horses! I had never seen so many of the beasts gathered together in one place! The overbearing smell was of sweat, soiled clothing and the acrid stink of vomit.

The shield-wall came together along the ridge-line. Shields were locked, one over another. I was in the second row and I will admit that I prayed to God that the men in front of me would not fall, so that I was forced into the front row. Was that cowardice – I don't know. I crossed myself, hoping that God above would spare me.

It seems that William had decided upon a tactic of weakening us with a barrage of arrows. As soon as we were formed and they were formed, their bowmen stepped forward and suddenly the air was full of the buzz of arrows. They flew at us like a flock of starlings heading for their roost in the dusk.

Almost immediately came the thud, thud of arrow

heads burying themselves in the leather and lime wood of
the shields. The clang as they hit the shield bosses. The
front row held their shields in front of them and we, in the
rows further backward held them above our heads. Volley
after volley winged their way toward us, each archer hoping
that they carried death with them. I held my shield and
prayed that no arrow should penetrate it. I flinched as
arrows thumped into my protection and peeped through at
me on the underside. But we resisted the assault and were
heartened to realise that few of our men had fallen.

William now decided that his archers had done enough
to at least soften us up, so that his infantry could strike at
us. And so the Normans charged up the hill toward us and I
felt my stomach churn again at what I knew was coming.
No man who has not stood in the shield wall can have any
appreciation of the sheer horror of it all. And no man can
call himself a warrior if he has not stood there, in that wall
of death.

As the Normans stormed toward us, with battle cries
rending the air, we threw down everything we had to hand:
javelins, arrows, even stones from the fields. Still they came
forward and we doubled our efforts. And it seemed we had
been successful as the bombardment inflicted terrible
damage to our opponents. Men fell to the earth, our stones
having smashed into faces, reducing them to a bloody pulp,
and spears and arrows burying themselves into heads,
throats and chests. One man, I saw, was screaming abuse at
us when an arrow loosed from behind me entered his
mouth and exited through the back of his throat. His head
went back and his eyes widened in disbelief and shock.
Blood spurted from his mouth and covered the man
beside him.

Now the Norman lines began to break up, and a great
cheer went up from our lines. But the Normans pulled

themselves back to their task and continued their charge. God knows, they were brave warriors, driven by their commanders and wound taut by bloodlust.

The Norman troops eventually reached our line and it was hand-to-hand combat. My God, it was terrible! I have never felt such a clash as the two sides came together! The men in front of us swung swords, maces and axes, and thrust their spears. The weapons came back dripping red with the blood of Norman warriors and the grey of brain tissue. Men fell and their comrades had to clamber over their dead and dying compatriots to reach us.

But not all went our way. For Saxon men were falling too and we were called to fill the gaps and hold the wall. I heaved with the others to hold our position and keep the shield-wall in place. Sweat ran down my face and trickled in rivulets down my body. I realised that some of the dampness was not sweat and that I had peed myself. Still we heaved. Still the two sides chopped and stabbed. Still men fell with screams upon their lips. They knew that they would never see Normandy or their English villages again!

I was dismayed when the two men in front of me fell to the ground, their lifeblood spilling upon the grass. I felt myself heaved forward into the front row and immediately held my shield and swung the sword I had taken at York at the screaming Norman facing me. I caught him on the side of the head with the flat of the blade and his head jerked under the force. He looked at me, surprised that a lad would even have the temerity to face him. In that split second, I swung the sword again and it slashed across his face, opening the slit of his mouth from ear to ear. He opened his torn mouth to scream and the flaps of his cheeks opened wide to reveal the bone that lay beneath it. I stared in horror at the face, but recovered to thrust again with my sword at the stunned warrior, driving the tip into his throat. He gave a shriek and fell, gurgling, to the floor.

Now my own bloodlust was up. I was a boy-warrior and I was now excited and enjoying the butchery. The temptation was to rush forward to attack my next opponent, but I knew better than to break up the shield-wall. I wiped the blood from my sword on the shirt of a body and stood there and waited for my next victim. How arrogant I was, but that is the privilege of youth!

As men fell, other men came forward and it was apparent to all that our shield-wall was holding and resisting everything the Normans were throwing against us. A huge man came toward me and I quaked a little at the sheer size of the giant. He smiled as he saw me in the front row; naught but a boy to him. He trod on bodies as he waded through the bloodbath toward me. He raised his huge sword and I could see the gleam in his eyes. As he raised his weapon, I ducked down, put my shield over my head, as if to retreat from the blow, but I thrust my sword at his leg. I heard the crack of bone and the leg bent at a strange angle. Now I thrust up with my shield and hit him with the boss. He fell backward into a comrade and the two men sprawled in the dirt and blood. I could have leapt forward and finished him, but didn't. He stared down at the twisted limb, in shock and disbelief. Another soldier hauled him backward and deposited him on the field to nurse his wound. He might survive, but he would not fight again today, and probably not in the near future.

William could now see that our shield-wall was holding, despite the best efforts of his men, and we were greatly heartened by it. I glanced across and saw my father, his chest heaving from the effort he had just put in. His face spattered with the blood of Norman and Englishman alike. He grimaced at me and signalled that I should fall back and allow an older man to fill the gap. Of course, I didn't. I was a warrior, a sword-Saxon!

But now, William changed his tactics. He knew that it was not going to his plan – the plan he had been sure would work to swiftly despatch the Saxons. Now came the cavalry! It was sooner than he had planned, but it was unavoidable if he was to break us down, and he knew it.

The horsemen lined up, horses whickering and jerking upon their bridles. Norman soldiers pulled on their helmets, with nose-guards dividing their faces in two. Forward came the spears and out came the long swords. They stilled their mounts and waited for the signal from their commanders. A cry went up and the men spurred their horses forward. Up the hill they came at a gallop. We watched as they bore upon us. We stirred, not knowing what would happen. Would the horses crash through the shield-wall? Would we be trampled into the dust?

Our men began to beat swords on shields, setting up a terrible din. As the horses approached, their eyes wide and drooling from the corners of their mouths, they began to shy away from the wall of noise before them. They were well-bred warhorses, but this was too much for them. No training on Earth could prepare them for what they now saw and heard before them. The cavalry charge faltered and stopped and most men retreated to their lines. Some came forward but were either thrown from their horses and quickly jumped upon and killed, or simply cut down from the saddle as soon as they were within reach.

And so the fighting continued. Charge and resistance. Charge and resistance. After more than an hour of fighting, the Bretons on the Norman left wavered, their lines broke and they made a hasty retreat down the hill. They had suffered horrific casualties and knew that we would soon outflank them. The Normans and Flemish fled along with the Breton mercenaries.

And that is where we made our fatal error. Some of our men were unable to resist the urge to take advantage of the Norman retreat, many of our number – both fyrdmen and Leofwyne and Gyrthe Godwinson, Harold's own brothers, charged downward to chase the fleeing troops. My heart sank. They should have held the line! Now the fighting was more chaotic. We watched as William's horse fell dead beneath him and the great Norman count tumbled to the ground. A roar went up from our ranks and disconcerted looks spread across the faces of the Normans. Was their leader dead? What was to be done? The Norman troops shrank back further and an even greater bloodbath began. But it was not to last. The Norman leader stood and rose to his greatest height. He cast off his helmet and shouted to his troops to rally them to the cause!

Now William gathered together a number of his knights and they dashed toward us in a counter-attack. But we had broken and were not protected by the shield-wall. And now we were cut down like wheat stalks in a field. Many of the fyrdmen did not realise what was happening until it was much too late. The professional soldiers tried to drag us back and some did manage to scramble back in retreat to the safety of the housecarls on the ridge.

But it was not so lucky for the brothers of Harold. They died in the retreat, cut down by Norman warriors. Of course, their deaths would mean that, if Harold fell, we would be without recognised leaders from the house of Godwin.

At length, the two armies formed up into lines and faced each other again. A strange stillness fell over both sides of combatants. The silence was eerie after the din of battle. We stood, staring, our chests heaving for breath.

The stench of blood was almost unbearable, and it caught in our noses and throats. Sweat ran down my face and into my eyes, stinging and making them water uncontrollably. I wiped my brow with a filthy sleeve and rubbed my eyes to rid them of the irritation.

The battle had turned to the advantage of William and his troops. We had lost our formation and were now largely unprotected by what was left of the shield-wall. Without that efficient structure, we were easy targets for our opponents. Now it was that William hurled his troops at the previously strong Saxon positions and we suffered terrible losses amongst fyrdmen and housecarls alike.

Our front ranks were now manned by fyrdmen rather than the professional troops Harold kept for our defence and the shield-wall, previously so disciplined by the housecarls began to waver. This was William's opportunity, and he took it. Previously, his archers had had scant success as their arrows hit, largely without harm, into our shields. Many on the front rank still had shields and many men at the rear passed theirs forward, but that left men at the rear unprotected. Now it was that William ordered his archers to fire their arrows over the front ranks and into the rear of our lines. And what a successful strategy it was!

It was now, as we looked across the line to see how our men were faring after the archers' assault, that we saw our king fall.

Harold had looked to the sky – whether to see the projectiles winging their way toward us or to pray to the Lord for assistance we shall never know – and an arrow struck him in the eye. He made a grab at it, but it was too late. I imagine that Harold must have been dead before his body hit the ground, though others said that he had raised himself to his knees.

Oh, but we were a weary and dispirited group! William

immediately ordered his troops into action again and, with much further bloodshed, they managed to pierce the shield-wall in a number of places in the line. This they utilized to get amongst us, and we began to fall to pieces as a force.

William was a canny general, and understood the situation. He rallied his troops and broke through the wall and, it is said, that this was the point of Harold's demise. They told us later that William and his men had found our king and struck Harold terribly, so that he would never rise from the ground again.

Without leaders and with many of Harold's nobles lying dead upon the field, hundreds fled the field of battle and made for the forest behind us. I am not ashamed to say that I was amongst that number. Harold's housecarls, however, no doubt spurred on by their oath of loyalty to the king, stood their ground and fought bravely until not a man amongst them stood on the battlefield.

But the battle was not over for us. Norman soldiers, both cavalry and infantry pursued us to the forest, murdering any man they could capture. You could not say that this was still battle – it *was* simply murder. We fled to whatever cover we could find and lay low to avoid the rampant Norman warriors, now baying for Saxon blood.

A few of us found refuge in a deep ditch to the north of the battlefield and hid in the undergrowth until dusk began to fall. We lay there gasping and clutching at wounds to try to stem the blood. Some of us tore strips from our clothing and bound the wounds of our compatriots. I sat there in the shadows and sucked at a cut on my left hand, hoping that I could suck out any poison that might have entered my body from the blood and filth of the battleground. Tears ran down my cheeks.

As the darkness began to fall, we were aware that the

forest was still crawling with bloodthirsty Normans, all hoping to kill us off and finish the task their master had set them of cowing the English.

We suddenly became aware of a troop of men heading toward us on the steep ground of the gill in the oak-wood. We peered through the bushes and saw that it was only a handful of soldiers. Hereric, the man who had assumed our leadership pointed at our weapons and directed us to places in the bushes where we would not be seen by the advancing patrol. We lay flat upon the ground and peered around the bases of tree trunks. When people scour forests, they often look at body height for human prey, but rarely at ground height.

Just as the patrol was passing, our leader sprang from the bushes in front of them, waving his sword in the air. The Normans were startled by his sudden appearance and their horses shied and reared. It was then that we leapt out and dragged the men from their saddles. Hands grabbed mouths to stifle cries, should another patrol be near enough to hear it, and swords and knives flashed in the half-light and throats were slashed as the Normans went to meet the Lord. We grabbed the terrified horses and led them into a sheltered clearing where we would spend the night. The bodies we stripped of anything valuable and they were then dumped into the deepest part of the ditch and covered with brushwood.

The horses might be useful in our flight from this carnage. I equipped myself with a new sword and a mail coat that was rather too big, but was better than that in which I currently was clad. One of the men wore a different helmet to the others. It shone brightly – obviously lovingly polished by its previous owner – and had a raven's head at its crest. It looked more Danish than Norman. I took it from his head and tried it on. Again it was big, but would be good stuffed with grass. One of the other men saw the helmet and made his way with obvious intent to rob me of my prize. I drew my new sword from its fleece-lined scabbard and faced him. Boy or not, he obviously thought better of it and turned away.

That night, as I lay there in the forest, I reproached myself. I had not seen my father and had fled the battlefield without him. How could I abandon him in that manner? Had he abandoned me? Terrible thoughts whirled in my mind and I resolved to find my father on the following day, no matter what the dangers. I knew that, even as a boy, the Normans would probably not spare me were they to find me.

On the following morn, we made our way slowly and carefully to the edge of the woodland. We were always aware that Norman patrols were combing the forest to mop up the last resistance. We wormed our way on stomachs to the woodland edge and peered between the twigs of bushes. The field was largely empty of living people, but was covered by the dead. I had seen battlefields before, but nothing like the slaughter that now lay in front of me. My eyes filled with tears and my stomach heaved. A handful of Norman soldiers stood at the bottom of the hill, watching a number of local peasants looting the bodies for whatever they could find. The Normans laughed at each other's jokes but showed no desire to chase the looters. This was our opportunity. We stripped off our weapons and emerged from the bushes nonchalantly and began to pore over the bodies, as if we too were looters. In reality, we were all searching for friends and loved ones. It was a risk but it worked. The Normans glanced at us but turned their heads and ignored us.

As we moved from body to body, we disturbed the crows and ravens picking out the eyes and stripping skulls of their flesh. It was a sight that I should never have seen; indeed no one should ever see. It would be with me forever and haunt my nightmares. It does still.

As I turned to scan the field, I glanced behind me and my heart stopped. A man lay there on his face, his yellow hair blowing in the breeze. I stood, not knowing what to do. But I knew that I had to look at the corpse to see if it was the man who had given me life. I moved to the man's side and gently eased him over onto his back. And there, staring at me with lifeless eyes, was my father. His woollen shirt was caked with his dried blood, a gaping wound in his upper chest.

Now I broke down. I laid my head on his chest and wept until I had no tears left. I thought my heart would burst. All strength left my limbs and I had no desire to live a moment longer.

Hereric, our 'leader' strode over to me and placed a hand upon my shoulder. Gently, he hauled me to my feet and wrapped great arms around me. "We shall bury him well, Lad," he told me. And so we did. We carried my father back to the edge of the forest and, with swords and tools, sharpened as weapons, we dug beneath the roots until we had a hollow large enough for a man's body. I had taken the rough cross from around my father's neck and hung it around my own. I wrapped my father's body in cloaks taken from the other corpses, and placed his sword in his hands. He would be buried as a warrior. We laid him to rest and I said a short prayer over him that I had learnt from the monks. I could not back-fill the earth and wandered off to fashion a rough cross from branches, tied with beaten bramble stalks, whilst Hereric shovelled the earth onto my father.

Upon my return, Hereric sat upon a log, staring at the grave before him. He looked up as I approached and stood as I screwed the cross into the ground at my father's head. I stood a while and the tears flowed again. Hereric fidgeted, unsure what to do to comfort me. At length, I turned and strode away, back to the clearing where we had left the horses. Nothing was said until we reached our place of safety.

"What will you do now, young John?" Hereric asked.

"I must return to my family," I replied. "I am responsible for them now. I am the man of the home." I paused. "But I am also a warrior now. My name is John Aelricson. I will avenge my father! I will kill Normans whenever and wherever I can!"

He looked at me in astonishment. "John, you are but a boy," he soothed.

"I am a warrior, and I will grow into a bigger, stronger, more powerful warrior," I said. "I have found no other man from my village, so I must travel alone." He nodded, knowing that my mind was set and any further argument would be futile.

"Travel north-east," he told me, "until you reach the sea. There you might be able to get a place on a trading ship sailing north. It will save you a long journey and a good deal of time before you return to your family." He wrapped me in his arms again and we wished each other well.

On the following morning, with nothing but a handful of water in my belly, I pulled on my leathers and mail, buckled on my sword and seax, hung my helmet from a saddle and took a large white Norman stallion from the tethered horses and left the south of England for my home in the north.

# CHAPTER TWENTY

During the following two weeks, William kept his army at Hastings. Here he waited for the English nobles to come to him and bow the knee. This proved very useful to me, as I was able to slip away across country north-east to the coast. I was heading to a place known as 'The Wash' in the earldom of East Anglia. I had never seen the sea before and Hereric told me that it was a sight I would never forget. He said that you can look out over the sea and see no other land in the distance. I couldn't imagine such a thing.

Having still found no sign of Cerdic and the other men from my village, I made my way alone through the weald, all the while watching, watching, listening for the sight or sound of outlaws who inhabited such places. It was my luck, I suppose, that no one seemed interested in me. This came as a great relief to me, as I had thought that many of the brigands of the forest would have welcomed the chance to rob a young lad of the weapons, mail and helmet I carried. (Though I was by now, becoming quite large for my age, and thought myself very ferocious.) Perhaps, I thought, the fact that I did carry such arms was enough to persuade them that it might be a risk not worth taking.

At first it was north and slightly west I travelled, around some of the thicker parts of the forest. I stopped off in villages I visited to ask for food and drink and to tell the inhabitants of the happenings near Hastings. I laugh now as I recall the look on the faces of the villagers when a boy of eleven, as I was now, rode into their villages dressed as a warrior! All wanted to hear the story of the battle, but most were now very alarmed by what they heard. Women pulled aprons to their mouths and their eyes were full with tears at the thought of what might be the fate of their families. I always avoided speaking too honestly in front of the children. At that moment, they didn't need to know the gory details. Men listened sombrely, shaking their heads and looking one to the other. Fear was etched upon their faces.

Most villages were happy to give me shelter and food for the night, and to give me advice as to where to ride the following morning.

And so I travelled on until I came to a small village beside some large ponds at the far end of a large stretch of forest. Here, at last, was a clear view to the east and I decided to make my way as rapidly as I could toward the coast.

Eventually, I came to a river called the Thames where I found a ferry crossing. Coot and Moorhen splashed in the reeds and swans and ducks glided effortlessly across the water. I thought of home and our river. I rode toward the hut upon the riverbank, where the ferryman was busily coiling ropes. He looked up at the sound of my horse's hooves beating upon the earth of the track, and stood, his hands upon his hips, watching my progress.

As I approached, his eyes widened as he realised exactly what he was watching. He looked unsure. Was I really a boy in warrior garb or just a very small warrior? I reined in my horse and looked down at him. "Can you take me across the river?" I asked him.

He paused, still weighing me up and trying to decide exactly who or what I was. "I can, Lord," he replied. "It will cost two pennies."

I pulled off the great helmet with its raven head crest and the ferryman's eyes widened even further at the boy who was addressing him. I became conscious of a woman watching me from the doorway. I turned to her and smiled. She smiled in return.

Still the ferryman stared at me. "Where would you be heading, Sir?" he asked.

"I travel to the coast – to The Wash," I replied. "I shall take a boat from there and travel back to the north."

"From where do you come?" he continued to question me.

"I have come up from South Wessex. I fought with Harold against the Norman invaders."

He started at this. "It is true then? They have come to our land? Did Harold win?"

I shook my head. "They are here," I confirmed, "and Harold is dead."

The ferryman shook his head sadly. "What is to happen to our land?" he asked.

I dismounted my horse and tied him to a rail. "For a meal and a jug of ale I can tell you the story," I said. He glanced at the woman and he waved me into the shack, where his wife busied herself bringing cold meat pie, cheese and a brown jug filled with foaming ale. I ate ravenously, as it was the first food I'd had that day, and I quenched my thirst on the ale. The ferryman and his wife waited patiently until I was more satisfied and began to eat more slowly. Now I sat there and told them the story I had told so many times before in the villages I had passed through.

As I was telling the tale, I noticed another figure sitting in the corner of the room. He was a boy of around sixteen, long and spindly of frame, with a mop of red hair. He stared at me and I at him. The ferryman's wife saw me looking and said, "My son, Scirlocc." The ferryman grunted at the mention of the boy. An appropriate name, I thought, as Scirlocc means 'bright hair'. I nodded and continued.

When I was finished telling my news, the ferryman insisted that it was far too late to ferry me across the river that night and far too late for a lad like me to be riding further alone, and so I should stay with them until the morning. I tried to offer them a few coins from my purse, but they would hear none of it. And so I settled myself in a spare corner and wrapped myself in my cloak. Scirlocc grinned at me as he passed to go to his bed and I tried to smile at him. He was a strange lad, I thought. He had not spoken a word all evening.

I lay in my corner, on a bed of hay, and thought about the following day. Once I crossed the river, the ferryman had told me that I should continue to the north-east and that I would certainly reach the coast soon. My eyelids began to droop and I began to drift off to sleep when I became conscious of a movement. I heard the soft pad of careful footsteps on the rushes on the earthen floor. I opened one eye and could see by the light of the moon coming in through one window space, a figure. I waited and held my breath. The figure was coming closer, closer, closer. Then I saw an arm come up and a fist enveloping a knife. I had made a point of keeping my seax with me and I threw open my cloak and swept it upward toward the hand.

I flashed the seax and it caught the wrist of the figure and a great howl came from its lips. Blood spattered down upon me, splashing onto my face and cloak. I tried to rub it from my eyes. Now two other figures leapt from their beds – the ferryman and his wife. Quickly, a rush-light was lit and kindling thrown onto the fire to light the hut. The couple stood like statues, gaping at the scene before them, whilst the boy, Scirlocc, held his wrist in his hand to try to stem the blood from the wound.

Now I leapt from my corner and pointed the seax at the family. I looked from one to another and them at me, unsure of what to do next. The ferryman grabbed Scirlocc and flung him at his mother. "See to him!" he growled. She bustled to her son and led him away to care for his wound. "My lord," he said. (He still insisted on calling me 'lord' though I was but a lad myself. I guessed that it was due to my weapons and clothing. I had not bothered to tell him that I was but the son of a churl.) "My lord, forgive us. Scirlocc knows not what he does. He meant no real harm."

"He tried to kill me," I snarled.

The ferryman dropped his head to his chest and I saw a tear run down his cheek in the firelight. "He is not ... as other boys," he said. "He never was. We knew when he was but a small child that he was ... lacking in the mind. He speaks only a little. He helps me with the ferry, but can never care for himself. I know not what his fate will be when my wife and I are gone from this earth." Now the ferryman wept bitter tears, though he tried to mask them and rubbed his eyes with his sleeve. His wife stood listening in the corner as she stemmed the flow of blood from her son's wrist.

"I am sorry," I said, "I didn't know." I paused. "But he did try to stab me with a knife."

"Aye," he said, "He did. It would be the glitter of your mail, swords and helmet. He would wish if for his own, to play at soldiers."

I sat a while, thinking about what had happened. "I hope he is not too badly hurt," I said.

"He will live," muttered the ferryman.

At length, the ferryman's wife stemmed the blood and bound Scirlocc's wrist in a length of clean boiled cloth. She pushed him forward until he stood before me. I looked at him and him at me. His face looked troubled and his eyes darted around him, at me and at his parents, and, I thought, toward the door.

"I sorry," he muttered. His head hung down now. He was obviously aware that he was in deep trouble.

I turned to reach for my saddle bags, which were in the corner with me. His eyes followed me. Did he think I was going to pull another weapon on him? I reached into one of the large saddle bags, in which I had stored various pieces of small weaponry and equipment that I had foraged from the battleground. I pulled out a spare jacket of mail that I'd collected and I thought would fit Scirlocc. I held it out to him. "This should fit a warrior like you," I said. He looked from me to his parents and then back to me. He reached out and took the mail jacket and held it in his hands lovingly. A huge smile crept across his lips and he held the coat to him.

"You are too kind, lord," his father said, "but no weapons, perhaps." He looked at me knowingly and we smiled at each other.

"No weapons," I replied.

The following morning was bright and a few white clouds scudded across an otherwise pale blue sky. I rose and dressed quickly, putting on my leathers and mail and buckling on my sword and seax. The ferryman's wife ushered me to the rough table and I ate ravenously of her bread, cheese, apple chutney and honey-cakes. They were as delicious as my mother's! My mother! What must she be thinking? As I washed it all down with a pot of ale, the door burst open and in strode Scirlocc, resplendent in his new mail jacket. His eyes gleamed and he stood there for our admiration. In his hand was a wooden sword his father had made for him.

"Why, who is this warrior?" I asked, and he giggled.

His father followed him in. "He will never want to take it off," he chuckled. "I have the ferry ready for you, Sir, whenever you are ready to go." I thanked the ferryman and his wife for their hospitality and offered a few coins again. Again, they refused, though I left them anyway, beneath the wooden board I had eaten from. We went outside and I untied my horse and led him onto the large raft that comprised the ferry. Scirlocc approached me and enveloped me in his skinny arms. He grinned from ear to ear and I smiled at him.

And now the ferryman began to haul on the rope that dragged the ferry from one bank to another. In what seemed just minutes, he had landed me safely on the other bank and given me directions for my journey. I thanked him again and waved as I rode off toward the sea. It would be another three days of travel before I was to reach the coast. And what a sight it was! I had ridden along the bank of a river which I understood from the local people was named the Great Ouse. It led me to the coastline and a great empty expanse of sand and mud, stretching out into the distance to where I could see the sea. I marvelled at the sight and knew that I had to make my way down to the sands to see it for myself at close quarters.

Well, I can tell you, I was astonished. There, upon the sand lay some of the strangest plants I had ever clapped my eyes upon! And the smell of them! I travelled along the stretch of sand, avoiding the muddy parts, and gazed at it. In some places there were rocky stretches wherein there were small pools. And in those pools were some of the most amazing *animals* I had ever seen! One was the texture of cow-heel jelly and was the most wonderful colour of blue. I had never seen a sky as blue as that!

Along the sea's banks I travelled, stopping every so often just to look at the view. I was intrigued by some of the large white birds that seemed to float over the seascape without effort. Their raucous cries rent the air as they wheeled above my head. At length, I stopped the horse, who I was still to name, and sat upon a grassy sea-mound of sand to eat a little of the food I had managed to buy from an old woman in a small village that morning. As I watched, the sea began to creep toward me and I sat, entranced, watching its progress. Soon it had come close to me and I watched the waves of water crashing upon the rocks and sand. What drove them, I wondered? The wind perhaps? And yet the wind was light.

As evening approached, I rode into a small town – a large village really – where boats had been dragged up onto the sand. In the air was the smell of smoke and fish and my mouth began to water. I recalled the trout my mother smoked for us from our river.

Within the centre of the settlement was a tavern and I turned the horse's steps toward it. I tied him to a post and stepped inside. The interior was dark and smoky and smelled damp. The tavern keeper greeted me kindly, though with some suspicion, I thought. "And what can I do for you today, Sir?" he asked.

"I would have some food, drink and shelter for the night, Sir," I replied, "for myself and my horse."

The tavern keeper looked through the open door at my horse. "Take him around the back and put him in the stable. There's feed there for him. You *can* pay, of course, Sir?"

"I can pay a little," I replied. He 'humphed' and nodded.

A short while later, I was enjoying smoked fish, bread and ale. And very good it was too! It was different, somehow, to the fish I had eaten before.

After the meal was done, I asked the landlord if he knew where I might join a boat that was sailing north. He turned and pointed to an old man sitting in the corner. He had a jug of ale before him and was staring into the flames of the log fire that burned in centre of the tavern. "Ask old Adam. He has a boat goes up and down the coast. He should be heading north soon." I approached the old man. He sat there in dirty breeches and a shirt that somehow smelled of the sea. A pair of long boots came up high upon his legs. He looked up as I approached.

"Sir," I began, "the tavern-keeper says that you might know of a boat that is going north within the next few days."

"I might," he replied. I just looked at him, unsure as to what to say next. "How far north are you wanting to go?"

"To the River Wear or Tyne," I replied.

He looked at me again, up and down. "And how would you pay for such a long journey?"

"I have some coins in my purse," I replied.

"Have you now?" His eyes brightened. "It will cost you twelve pennies if you help with the rowing. Twenty if you don't."

I said I was happy to help out with anything that might need doing, and he seemed satisfied with that. He told me to be at the beach early the following morning. I was there, bags and horse in hand.

"You didn't say anything about a nag!" he cried. "That will cost extra!"

"I have little more than twenty pennies left, Sir," I said,

crestfallen as the thought of either leaving my horse or riding the whole way home.

"Hmmm," he mused. "Twenty pennies it must be then, but I hope you can row!"

I boarded the boat and settled the horse into the bilge, which was full of sacks of grain, barrels of fish and wooden boxes. I had no idea what he was carrying in the boxes and cared even less. In the boat were the rest of the crew and they looked me over curiously. The sea was high now and we pushed the boat out into the channel and the crew began to row out toward the open sea. Old Adam manned the steering oar. I was not asked to join the rowers at this point and I watched in awe as we ploughed out through the waves and I saw the land behind us slowly disappear from sight.

# CHAPTER TWENTY-ONE

Gradually, our little craft nosed her way along the channels between mud and sand banks. Old Adam, our captain, at the steering oar, seemed to know exactly where his craft needed to be to avoid grounding. The crew too seemed to know exactly when to pull hard and when to dip the oars gently to manoeuvre the craft.

As white clouds scudded across the sky from north to south, we made our way out to the open sea. As we emerged from the more sheltered waters of the Wash into the open ocean, the conditions became harsher. Now the wind blew strongly and our boat began to dip and roll on the waves until I became quite dizzy with it all. My horse snickered in the bilges. He, of course, had already travelled by sea, having come across from Normandy with William. I had never been to sea! Indeed, until the last few days, I had never seen the sea! How, I wondered, would we ever manage to make our way north when the wind was against us? Would we need to row all the way? *Could* we row all the way?

But now the rowers stopped and two men climbed up

and unfurled the sail. How could a northerly wind be used to carry us north? I thought to myself. Surely, we would be blown south!

"Row out, ye dogs!" bawled Adam, and the rowers bent their backs to the task of rowing further out to sea. Presently, Adam steered us to a course that pointed our bows north-easterly and the boat began to glide on the wind. The rowers stopped, pulled in their oars and stuffed the oar-holes. Adam let the boat take its head for a few miles and then he changed tack and the boat turned again, this time to a north-westerly direction. And so we continued to zigzag back and forth; all the while moving north, against the wind.

"How is that possible?" I asked one crew member who, like me, sat in the stern of the boat.

"We must tack across the wind," he replied. "If we do that, we can make progress that we couldn't make by trying to sail directly against the wind. That would be impossible."

I marvelled at the process and racked my brain in wonder as to how it worked. My compatriot could not explain it further either, save to say that it did work.

After a few hours of sailing back and forth up the coast, dark clouds began to gather and I thought the wind was becoming stronger. I was still not used to the movement of the boat yet, so I was alarmed as we began to buck and sway much more violently. Adam barked another order and two crewmen leapt up and furled the sail and took down the mast. Now the crew began to unplug the oar holes and push out the long oars to row us on our way.

"Give the lad an oar!" shouted Adam, over the gale, pointing at me in my stern seat.

The crewman I'd spoken to beckoned me to a seat and pulled a long oar from the bilges. He fitted it into the hole and bade me sit upon the bench. "Now, you must pull in time with the rest of the crew," he said, "lest we crash oars and one becomes broken. We shall feel Adam's wrath if that happens!" I sat there and listened to the call of the crew to tell me when to pull. Oh, but it was hard work, and soon my body began to feel the strain. I suppose that I was lucky, in that I had helped farm the land all my life, and so was quite fit and strong, but the repetitive strain of rowing was very different to anything I had so far experienced. My muscles soon began to ache.

Oh, how we strained every sinew to pull the boat forward in the water! It was difficult to time the strokes, as the ship was being tossed upward and then downward by the roiling water. The pounding of the sudden falls into the trough of the waves was bruising to my body, and my bones seemed to shake as if in a bag!

And gradually it seemed to be becoming even worse! Lightning flashed above us and thunder rolled across the swell. Hard rain hammered down upon us, pooling in the bilges. We hauled on the oars and Adam pushed and pulled the steering oar to try to keep us on course. But now he made a decision. "Haul hard to land!" he yelled. "We must try for shore before we are swamped!"

The crewman behind me patted my arm. "We must pull hard whilst the other side do not. We must try to turn the boat to the shore." And so we pulled and the crew on the other side held their oars still above the water, until we could feel the boat begin to turn. But now we were side on to the wind and the boat rocked even more. I leaned to one side and deposited my morning meal into the bottom of the boat. My horse was terrified now; his eyes wide and froth streaming from the corners of his mouth. I wondered whether I would ever see my family and homeland again, or whether I would suffer a watery grave, out in the open sea, where no one would ever find me!

Gradually, we began to pull to shore and suddenly, through the veil of pounding rain, Adam spied the coastline. "Shallows ahead!" he called over the terrible noise. We all pulled harder now, the lure of dry land encouraging us onward. After what still seemed an eternity, there came a grinding sound as the ship's keel hit the pebbles of the shore. Again we heaved on the oars to push the vessel as far up the beach as possible. Then the crew withdrew their oars quickly and stuffed the oar holes. I copied them.

We leapt from the ship and Adam threw ropes over the bows. I was in the water now, which came up to my chest. A great, foaming wave hit me and I toppled over into the surf. Water and sand filled my mouth and I swallowed a good quantity of it. The surf sang in my ears and I could feel the drag of the undertow pulling me back into the deeper sea. I held my breath and my lungs burned within my chest. I struggled to find the surface, but was being dragged back and forth by every wave. Was I to die now, so close to safety?

A great hand pierced the water and grabbed a fistful of my shirt-front and dragged me back to the surface. I spluttered and spat out the salty contents of my mouth. My crewman friend grinned at me. "No time for a swim!" he said. I nodded my thanks and grabbed the rope. Now we hauled as the waves came in until we had pulled the boat far enough out of the breakers, with only the stern end still in the water, so that it would not be washed back. "The tide should be going out," my seaman friend said, "so she'll be safe for now."

We staggered up the beach and I collapsed into the sand and pebbles, too exhausted for much else. At length, we made our way off the beach and sought shelter under a rim of trees. Though, by now the shelter actually made little difference to our condition. We were soaked through, cold and hungry, and I was thoroughly miserable. I heard my horse whinny and I leapt to my feet. The large hand grabbed me again. "Leave him, lad. He's safe there for now. You'll never get him out without injury." I sat back down and curled up to try to find some warmth.

I must have fallen asleep eventually, as I woke to see a brighter scene. A weak sun was peeping between banks of clouds, but the rain had stopped and the wind had died down to a gentle breeze. I looked around me and saw that the crew had brought some food and drink from the boat and were sitting around breaking their fast. I rose to my feet and stumbled toward them, still a little weak from my ordeal. I sat upon the soft sand and my friend passed me a wooden bowl of small fish. They had been gutted and smoked until they were yellow. I took a fish and crammed it into my mouth. Oh, the taste! I ate three more of the fish with a little hard bread and washed it down with a few mouthfuls of ale. I had washed the salty taste of the sea from my mouth and I finally began to feel alive again.

I turned to my friend. "You saved my life," I said, "and yet I still do not know your name."

"Nay, lad," he said. "I just hauled you from the waves. You would have lived by your own efforts, I'm sure. My name is Joseph. My mother named me for Christ's earthly father."

I smiled at him. "My name is John Aelricson," I said, "and I still think you saved me." He chuckled and shook his head.

"What do we do now?" I asked.

"We get back to sea!" old Adam growled. "Raise yourselves! We have a boat to get back to its journey." The men grumbled, but we set ourselves to hauling the boat back to the water. It took us less time than I had thought and we were soon rowing our way back to a much calmer open sea.

I had found my horse shivering in the bilges and I had rubbed him and whispered to him to settle him again.

The wind was from the west now and very light and the waves were smooth, curved and gentle. We had to row to make any real progress, though we did raise the sail to help us on our way. The task was much easier now, and I began to enjoy watching the seabirds and the shoreline to our port side.

As we pulled our oars, I gazed out across the ocean. I glanced at something in the water, passed over it and then glanced back. It looked like a great fish fin, but was solid black. I looked again and a huge hump rose from the water. I called to Joseph. "What can that be?" and I nodded in the direction of the fin.

"It is one of the ocean's great beasts," he replied. "We often see them in groups and they hunt the seals that live along the coast. They are savage beasts, they do say. I would not like to be overboard with them!"

I looked back to where the beast had been and shivered at the thought that only wooden planking lay between myself and it. Then the beast suddenly rose from the water, such as I have never seen a fish do before in our river. It was blue-black and had white patches. It seemed to look at us and opened its great jaws to show a row of huge, sharp teeth. I gawped at it and shivered even more violently. Then the beast slipped slowly back beneath the waves, back to its watery world. As I looked out after it, I could see three of the large fins now disappearing into the distance. I was more than happy to think that it had lost interest in us!

Joseph and I conversed on many subjects as we travelled north. I told him of the battles I had taken part in, and he was amazed that a lad of my age had survived. He told me of the lands he had visited and some of the things he had seen. I never tired of hearing his tales and prompted him constantly to tell me more. "You have a great curiosity, John," he told me. "You should take up a life of travel." I day-dreamed about all of the places I would visit, as we sat and rowed and ate and rested.

My horse stirred in the bilge. He was happier now that the sea was not as violent, but I am sure he was as keen to feel dry land beneath his feet again as I was. "What is the name of your mount?" Joseph asked me.

"He has no name," I replied, "I just call him 'horse'."

"Then he must have a proper name!" Joseph cried. "What shall it be?"

I mused for a while, but could come up with nothing that seemed right for him.

"His colour is like the crashing foam atop the waves," Joseph declared, "when the wind whips them into a fury."

I looked up and smiled at him. "Wind-Wave!" I exclaimed. "That is what I shall call him!"

"Wind-Wave it is then," Joseph chuckled. "After what he has been through on the high seas, I think it will suit him well."

We made good progress over the next few days. At times, we were able to let the wind carry us forward, whilst at others we rowed. I was slowly becoming more used to the exercise and I thought I could feel my muscles becoming the stronger for it.

One morning, Adam looked to the west and began to pull on the steering oar to take us into land. I could see the mouth of a river opening its wide gape. "Hard to land," Adam called to us, and we began to turn the boat into the river mouth. We rowed a little way up the river until a village could be spied on the northern bank. Adam steered us toward it and we came up alongside a wharf. The crew quickly tied up the boat to the wooden pilings.

"This is the mouth of the River Tees," Adam informed me. "You can leave us here if you wish. We shall be here for some days. If we can sell all of our goods here, we will venture no further north."

I thanked him and dipped into my purse to find the twenty pennies I was to pay him. He had insisted that I should not pay him in advance, but only when he had delivered me safely. (Though he had insisted on seeing the colour of my money before I embarked!)

As I collected my belongings and the men began to unload the cargo, a crewman approached me. "I have been wondering what it is you carry in those great bags of yours," he said. "Maybe we should have a look." I immediately froze. I knew exactly what he meant and had no way to dissuade him from taking my belongings as my sword and seax were still in the boat.

But I plucked up what courage I had – for he was a large and muscular man – and faced him. "What I carry is my business alone," I said.

"Oh," he replied, "you make it sound as if it is something of great value! Perhaps too much value for a young lad to be carrying around with him." He strode toward me with a determined expression and something of a smirk on his face at the thought that I might defy him.

As he came within touching distance, he put out a huge arm, made powerful by years at sea, and pushed me aside. He bent to pick up a saddle-bag. As he did so, a voice behind him said, "Pick up the bag and I will break the arm that lifts it!" The man froze and slowly rose to his full height. He turned on his heel to face Joseph, who stood with a look of steely determination in his eyes. The two looked at each other. "The lad's property is his own affair and none of yours." The man turned as if to walk away but suddenly drew a knife from his belt and turned upon Joseph. The knife flashed a hair's breadth from my friend's face and he leapt back in surprise.

Now Joseph pulled out his own knife and the two circled one another, crouching, gliding until one could see an advantage. Suddenly, the man leapt at Joseph and lunged at his neck. But Joseph was nimble upon his feet and feinted to one side. As the man's arm passed his shoulder, Joseph grabbed it and turned. The force threw the crewman to the ground, but he was quickly upon his feet and circling again.

A crowd of seamen had gathered to watch the spectacle, goading the men to attack one another.

Now the crewman leapt in and kicked Joseph's leg, making him stumble. He saw his chance and lunged again dropping Joseph to the ground. The man leapt upon him and tried to bring down his knife but Joseph grabbed his arm and forced it back. Now he tried to bring his own knife into play in an attempt to force the big man off him. A kind of stalemate arose, with each man's arms quivering from the effort. Sweat ran from their faces, despite the cold day, and the effort showed on each face.

Just as the crewman seemed to be forcing his hand and its knife down toward Joseph's throat, I stepped in. "Touch him with the knife and I'll slit you open and gut you like a fish," I snarled. Then I prodded his back with the seax I had retrieved from the boat. Its point pierced his woollen shirt and drew a little blood that seeped in a small patch into the fibres. The man stopped struggling and slowly raised his arms. Slowly, very slowly, he got to his feet. I stood there, with my seax still pointing at him. He slipped his knife back into his belt and scowled at me. He placed a hand on his back, where my seax had nicked him, and looked at the blood on his fingers. Without a word, he strode off.

The other crew and the locals laughed at the thought of what had happened, and one or two slapped me on the back. Joseph rose from the ground and walked across to me. "Thank you," he said. "Now you've probably saved my life."

"You were protecting me," I reminded him.

I packed the rest of my belongings onto Wind-Wave and said my goodbyes. I came to Joseph last. I put out my hand and he clasped it. "Take care, young John," he told me.

"I will, and you," I replied. I mounted Wind-Wave and rode off north, to reach my home.

I made steady progress north. I was not entirely sure how to get home, but I knew that if I travelled north, I would, eventually, come to landmarks I knew.

As I rode north, trying to follow the old Roman road, I passed several villages, where I asked for directions, told them the story of the battle and begged a little food and drink. At length, I came to a small settlement, built on the edge of an escarpment that fell steeply to a river. I sat Wind-Wave and gazed down to the valley floor below. The river meandered around a great curve and a wooded hillside rose steeply to the east of the curve. I could see some sort of settlement on that hillside too, mainly from the smoke that rose lazily into the sky. It seemed to me to be a pleasant spot, with gentle farmland and woodland.

An old man was climbing slowly up the hill before me, carrying a great load of firewood on his bent back. He straightened as he reached the brow of the hill and looked at me cautiously. "What settlement is this?" I asked him, "And what is the river below?"

"This place is called Alclyt," he replied, "and the river is the Wear." The Wear! I was almost home.

"And the settlement on the hill yonder?" I asked.

"Vinovium," he replied. "It was a Roman fort, but is now in ruins. A few churls live there, farming the land."

"Could I cross the river there?" I asked. "I am travelling north, to Brockford."

"Aye, you could" he replied. "You've not much further to travel. But you'd be better to turn to the west from here." And with that, he continued on his way with his load and I coaxed Wind-Wave along the edge of the steep slope, with the river beneath me.

I turned toward the late afternoon sun, now dipping toward the horizon, which had been to my left and headed off toward the northern hills in the distance.

I rode on through the night, picking my way slowly and cautiously in the darkness, and giving Wind-Wave short breaks to nibble grass and drink from streams. As the sun rose upon my back, I began to recognise the landforms around me.

At length, I rode into a valley I knew to be home. I cantered up along the riverbank until I saw Brockford as I rounded a bend in the river. I trotted up to the village, and villagers began to notice me. One yelled toward the village and my family suddenly burst through the gateway and ran to greet me. I leapt down from Wind-Wave and ran toward them. Oh, how we held each other. Tears fell like autumn rain as we stood there, sobbing in each other's arms.

My mother looked me in the eye. "Did he die well?" she asked. "I know your father is dead." And more tears fell.

After a moment to compose myself, I said, "He died

well – a hero, in battle. I gave him a Christian burial. He was a warrior."

My mother fell at my feet and I gently lifted her again. "Thank you," she said, and we walked back to Brockford, arm in arm. Wind-Wave followed dutifully behind me.

# CHAPTER TWENTY-TWO

During the November of 1066, we were spared some of the terrible ravages of William's army when a serious attack of dysentery reduced his forces to a fraction of their former power. The illness spread like wildfire in the close confines of the camps that William had set up to house his men. Indeed, William himself was struck down with it, and was so gravely ill that his commanders wondered if he would ever make the sort of recovery he would need to lead them in the conquest of the kingdom.

A leading noble entered William's tent on a cold, dull and drizzly morning, to find his master once more noisily evacuating his bowels and his face as grey as the sky. With a hand over his nose and mouth to try to mask the smell, he enquired after William's health, though such an enquiry was for little more than courtesy – William's health was laid bare for all to see!

"My Lord, how does your recovery fare?"

"I should have thought your own senses would have answered that question for you," William growled. He left the commode in the corner of the tent for a servant to reluctantly empty. "What news of the rest of my forces? Is this accursed affliction showing any signs of retreat?"

"I fear not, my Lord," the noble replied. "My men have dug a pit in the woodland, but if fills rapidly and the stink is ..." He broke off, considering his words as William glowered at him. "I have sent your message back to Normandy, outlining our situation and asking for further reinforcements. I await a reply. Understandably, the weather and the fear of the illness are deterring a rapid response, though I am sure we will have the necessary reinforcements before the worst of the winter sets in."

And so it was that William eventually received the reinforcements he needed to continue to wage war upon the people of this land. And oh, how the people of this fair land suffered!

Meanwhile, in the city of London, events were happening apace! The country had still been shocked by the arrival of the Norman army, even though it had been expected for some time. The last remnants of what passed for an English government assembled there to decide which path to take to counter the looming Norman threat. It was a fraught and tense meeting of nobles who were panicking like hens with a fox in the coop!

"I say we elect Edgar Atheling as our new monarch." Murmurs of approval. (Edgar was the son of Edward Atheling.)

"Edgar is not Harold! He is a weak man! What use do we have of a weak man at our helm?" Further murmurs.

"The Godwinsons are dead! They are the past! We cannot live in the past. Edgar is the only other candidate who would be acceptable to all within the country. What other choice do we have?"

"I still say that Edgar is too inexperienced and weak and could never rule this country, even without the threat of Normandy. He'd mess his breeches if William came within a mile of him!"

"A weak king is better than no king at all! With no king, we have no leader, even if that leader is little but a figurehead."

And so the argument went back and forth between the assembled nobility. At length a vote was called and Edgar was indeed given the backing of the earls and thegns. Now I think of it, we never did hear if Edgar had ever been crowned, but, it seems to me, it would have been a prudent step to have him formally crowned king of the realm, so that he was not simply the monarch-elect, but the rightfully chosen monarch of the Witan.

A short while later, on a dark and misty night, a group of men made their way through the streets of London. They were on their way to a secret meeting, which was held, away from other prying eyes from the Witan, between the northern earls, Morcar and Edwin. The two earls would be accompanied by their leading commanders.

A knock sounded on a stout oak door and a man-at-arms opened it and asked who might seek admittance. "It is the lord Morcar," muttered a noble, and the door swung open on creaking hinges to admit the visitors to a large timber hall. Rush lights flickered in the breeze from the open door and torches blazed around the walls. A table was set with food and ale. There, seated, and in deep conversation with his followers was Edwin. He looked up as the group entered and a smile spread across his craggy face.

My Lord, Morcar," Edwin greeted his fellow earl, "Welcome. Please, advance upon our table and partake of the repast before us. There is a goodly ale." Morcar and his men slowly took out their weapons and laid them upon the ground before a steward, as was the polite custom. The earl seated himself at the table and chose a leg of fowl and soft bread. "I feel we must discuss between us what further action we will take in the matter of William. I feel that it must firstly be action to protect our own northern earldoms," began Edwin.

"I thought that was probably the reason for this meeting. But what of the rest of the country?" Morcar asked. "Should we not throw the weight of our forces behind the king? If England is to repel these Norman invaders, he will need every help he can muster?"

"Aye, he will," replied Edwin, reaching for an apple, "And he will still lose." Edwin wiped the apple on his tunic and gazed at it before taking a bite from the firm flesh and savouring its sweetness. "Edgar has no more chance than a lamb against a wolf of defeating William and his forces. We must accept that and plan for a future under Norman rule."

Morcar sat and pondered the words of his fellow earl, a look of great concern etched across his face. He glanced around at his commanders and advisors for support or inspiration. What should he do? "And what of the other earls? If we scuttle back to our own earldoms and leave the country short of troops at such a critical time, what then will men say?"

"I am reliably informed," said Edwin, guardedly, "that we would not be the only parties to be retreating north to await developments. I hear that others of our number, and even the king's own sisters, Cristina and Margaret, are making their way to Chester with their entourages to a place of safety. Do we not owe it to our own people to negotiate a peace, protect them and ensure that the horrors that have befallen South Wessex are not visited upon them?

If we fight William, our own people will be shown no mercy when the conquest spreads, as it surely will!"

"What you say is true," Morcar acknowledged, and took a large sup of ale. "England is in a parlous position and the odds are greatly stacked against us. And yet ..."

"And yet we would all wish that it was untrue," said Edwin. "To what purpose should we commit our troops to fight, losing many good men but inflicting only wounds upon William? I plan to return to the north and consolidate my position. If it comes to it, I will endeavour to make my own peace with William, as I have said. I suggest that you do likewise." Edwin knew that if Morcar followed his lead, then it strengthened his own position within the realm and his reputation amongst England's nobles. Reputation was important to a man such as him. He must be seen to be strong, but also prudent and realistic. Not always an easy combination to achieve.

Morcar nodded slowly and scanned the faces of his commanders. Each gave a short nod to show that they too felt that the battle might continue, but the war was effectively over.

"You are right," Morcar concurred, with a deep sigh. "This fight was always a dispute between William and the Godwinsons. I too will withdraw north to my own earldom. We shall await the outcome there. And may God help us in what is to come!"

In the following days and weeks, William continued his progress across Kent. He sacked the settlements of Romney, leaving only blood and destruction in his wake. Whole villages destroyed. Bodies, horribly slain and mutilated littered the land along the south coast.

Upon reaching Dover, in October, William expected that resistance would be strong. He waited and watched the town. He sent in spies to gauge the feelings of the people. Men slunk through alleys and loitered on street corners, listening and watching. They huddled into taverns, taking note of conversations. Then they slunk back to William and reported what they had seen.

William finally decided to move against the town. His troops were deployed so that one force was sent in a wide sweep around the town, to approach from the east, another was deployed to the north and the third troop would come from the west. Only the open sea lay to the south, and the Saxons knew that William would not have left that possible exit unguarded.

But it was all to no purpose, for, with the arrival of so many armed men, the people of Dover submitted the town without a whimper, and also its all-important castle. This was indeed a simple coup that William and his supporters had not expected. On a cold but bright day, William, dressed in leathers, a mail coat and a red cloak, pinned at his chest, marched his men into Dover to an almost silent throng of townspeople who bowed their heads as he passed. The uncertainty of the people was palpable in the atmosphere. The men stood like beaten dogs, a sullen look upon their faces. Women held their children close to them, fear obvious on every face. Smaller children cried, terrified of the heavily armed men. Many would be recalling the terrible happenings in the town, when the Norman drinkers were murdered. Would the episode come back to haunt them?

The procession continued through the narrow, winding streets until, from nowhere, an arrow flashed just inches from the face of William. Had it been loosed a few moments later and caught him, it would have entered one cheek and exited the other. William's head flashed around to see from where the arrow had come. Immediately, mounted nobles and men-at-arms drew weapons and a melee of people churned around a small square. William's men charged down alleyways to apprehend the bowman. They shoved people aside and pushed doors open, investigating every nook and cranny. No stone was left unturned, and yet none could find the mystery assailant.

At that point, unbeknown to Normans and Saxons alike, a young man, dressed in a brown tunic and green breeches, lay wrapped in a dirty brown cloak, upon beams within a thatched roof above a shop selling fish.

William sat his horse and his household bodyguards milled around him, waiting to see if his troops could bring before him the man who had attempted to assassinate him. Time passed and the men regrouped a few at a time in the small square between rows of wattle and daub hovels. None brought the quarry William sought. After a while, with the eyes of the people of Dover upon him, William pulled the nose of his horse around and continued on his way. As he passed by another winding alley, a young man stepped out and passed in front of his horse. He was dressed in a brown tunic and green breeches, and was wrapped up against the cold in a dirty brown cloak. He bowed low as the Count of Normandy passed on.

As William neared Dover Castle, the men-at-arms who still guarded it laid down their arms at their feet and stepped back a couple of paces. William entered and immediately set his own guard upon the castle and sent his men into the town to patrol and to ensure that the people were in no doubt as to who now controlled the area. It would not do for any kind of insurrection to gain a foothold and any momentum.

William enjoyed a meal in the castle, as he made plans

with his advisers as to his next move. "I will stay here for a number of days. We must send messengers to the major towns and cities, demanding their submission. It will be better that way than entering a fight and losing good men. And besides, conquering every town and village would take a lifetime."

"And what if the towns and cities do not submit as easily as the faint-hearted inhabitants of Dover?" a noble asked. "We cannot be certain that every centre of population will simply roll over like pups as they did today."

"I know it, but we will give them the chance to think it through and come to a sensible decision. If they do not, then we will fight. But it would be better to conserve and protect the troops we have. Compared to all of the people of England, we are but a small force; albeit a powerful one."

It was not long before a delegation arrived from the city of Canterbury. William sat in a large chair in the main hall of the castle and watched as the Saxon delegation approached. It was obvious that they were somewhat nervous by the very way they carried themselves. They had been relieved of any weapons before entering, and were surrounded by well-armed men-at-arms. They glanced from side to side as they neared William's chair. William smiled to himself at how cowed the English people were, now that he was here in their land – his land, now! But, of course, he kept the stern look upon his face as the men approached and bowed their heads to him.

"My L-lord," one man stammered, "we bring greetings from the people of Canterbury. The council has met and a decision has been taken to welcome you to our country, and to assure you that we have no desire for conflict."

William mused upon his visitors. It would not do to be seen to be too congenial. He was, after all, to be their lord and master. "Gentlemen, I am pleased that we seem to be of one mind in the matter. I too would regret the need for violent conflict. It would only lead to a great loss of life, and yet the outcome would be in no doubt."

The men looked from one to another. William certainly seemed confident that his forces could win in any conflict with the Saxon armies. The leading man stepped forward, bowed low and presented William with a parchment roll confirming his city's surrender to the Norman. William unrolled it and read it, glancing up from time to time at the messengers, who shifted their feet uneasily and tried to ignore the beads of sweat running down their faces.

William finally laid down the parchment and gazed at the messengers. "I would ask that you take my best wishes back to your council, and say that I look forward to meeting them to make certain 'agreements' in the near future." He then stood, turned and paced out of the room, leaving the delegation in no doubt that they were dismissed.

William had also sent messengers to the recently-widowed Queen Edith in Winchester. From there, his men returned with the submission of that city. "So the widow poses no threat to our plans," William observed. "I wonder whether she is simply level-headed, or whether she is, perhaps, grateful to us for ridding her of her Saxon lord?"

William's men guffawed at his witticism. "Who knows, he might be grateful to us for sending him to a better place, away from her?"

A short while later, William travelled to Canterbury and made no bones about the treaty he would enforce upon his subjected people. There could be no doubt that the people were less than happy with the situation, but they were also realistic enough to know that they had little choice.

From there, William trudged his forces toward London. He approached the settlement of Southwark where he intended to cross London Bridge and enter the city. South-wark had been built as a suburb south of the River Thames. It was the lowest crossing point of the river. The Roman roads of Watling Street and Stane Street met there, in a major communication junction. It was abandoned and fell into ruins after the Roman armies left Britain to defend their homelands. But in Saxon times, Southwark had grown again and flourished into an important settlement on the river.

As William's men hove within sight of Southwark on a bright, cold afternoon, he held up his gloved hand and brought his men to a halt. He sat awhile, studying the land-scape before him. It was obvious to all that this might not be as easy as the conquest of Canterbury and Winchester had been. The people had closed their great gates against him and there was much activity along the defences.

William moved on and brought his men to within striking distance of the bridge and gates. Here, he paused again, dismounted his men and bade them make a tempo-rary camp. As his men bustled around, he turned to one of his earls. "Send messengers to the Saxons. Tell them that I would cross their bridge and make my way peacefully to London. Leave them in no doubt that I *do* intend to enter London."

Minutes later, three heavily-armed nobles set off against the glow of a slowly descending autumn sun, toward the defences, approaching slowly so that there was no doubt that they came in peace. The walls bristled with spears. When the trio came within hailing distance they halted and called to the Saxons. "We would speak to you on behalf of William, Duke of Normandy; King of England."

After a short while, the great wooden gates opened and a similar contingent of the Saxon leaders rode across the open land before them. The Saxons stopped just a few yards from the Normans, and each eyed the others for signs of treachery. Hands strayed unconsciously to sword hilts as they sat their horses.

The Normans opened the dialogue. "My lord William would request that our forces be allowed to cross the river without hindrance, to enter the city of London. No harm will come to your people, should you allow our passage. But be in no doubt that we do intend to enter the city, one way or another. You must decide how it will be."

The Saxon in the centre of the group sneered. "We will never allow William the Bastard to cross the river or enter our city. We will defend it with our very lives. This is no village of churls, armed only with farm tools! Go back from where you have come. You and your master are not welcome in our land."

"Your attitude will lead to much blood-shed that is neither necessary nor desirable. Why should men die when it can be avoided?" the Norman asked.

"You have heard us! Go home! The people of London support the kingship of Edgar Atheling as our rightful monarch," was the reply.

With a final malevolent stare, the Normans wheeled their horses and rode back to William to give him the news of the intransigence of the Saxons of London. His face clouded and, with a snarl, he turned to his commanders, "Organise your troops for an attack in the morning."

"My lord, is it worth a frontal attack on a well-defended crossing? Should we not move upriver and find a simple crossing point? That way we could tread a similar path to that of Dover."

William nodded. "We will see what the morrow brings." All that night, the Norman leader brooded on his humiliation by the people of London. How dare they refuse him entry? Did they not know the strength of his forces? Would they choose death over life? But his advisors were probably right. The bridge was a tight front on which to fight. His men would be like rats in a trap, and many would die. But would the Saxons crumble if they saw an advancing force?

On the defences, flaming torches and lanterns burned into the night, ensuring that the Normans could not mount a surprise attack under cover of darkness. Guards paced up and down, peering into the darkness, all the while hoping not to see anything untoward. There was no doubt that William's reputation went before him and many a man debated with himself the wisdom of remaining with the Saxon forces defending the city or leaving and moving north, as many had already done. In the distance, the people could see the campfires of William's troops flickering in the gloom. They could imagine the troops eating and resting, and wondered what the morning would bring. The good people of Southwark were the more anxious. They had not the protection of the defences of London, and sat there, vulnerable to the will and might of William of Normandy. Many had packed what few possessions they had and moved off to hide where they felt safer; some moving to forested land to hide in woodland glades, whilst others fled to the marshes and islands of the Thames estuary.

The Normans, for their part, could see the glint of the flaming torches flashing from sharpened spear heads and polished mail and helmets. Would tomorrow be the day they marched into London or their last day on Earth?

On the following morning, a weak sun still shone and a brisk wind blew across the land. Again, riders from the Norman camp rode out, but this time they were followed by a troop of the household guard. They approached the London Bridge, as they had the previous day. William intended to give the people of London one last chance.

They might have held debate that night and come to their senses. Who could tell? But it soon became obvious that this was not the case!

As the troop neared the wall, there was no opening of the gate this time. There was no delegation from the defences to talk terms. This time, the walls were crowded and they were subjected to a sudden barrage of arrows which left them in no doubt as to the decision taken by the people of London. It would not be a peaceful entry. The soldiers raised the great pointed shields above their heads to deflect the path of the death that winged its way toward them. Arrows thumped into wooden shields and horses whinnied and bridled. Some of the horses took direct hits from the missiles and reared in pain and panic, leaving their riders struggling to hold on and defend themselves at the same time.

As it became obvious that the intent of the Londoners was defiance, the troops wheeled their mounts and rode back to the Norman lines. William stood, stony-faced, gazing at the defences, his brows knitted by thought. "So, the people of London defy me!" he murmured. "So be it!"

William quickly gathered his council around him. Each man commanded a troop of men, all professional warriors; not the fyrd of the Saxons, armed with their farming implements and little else. William spoke briefly and pointed this way and that. Finally, he dismissed his men and mounted his great horse to watch what happened next. And oh, what a terrible sight it was!

Mounted men and foot-soldiers began to move out from the camp. One troop moved east and north. Another travelled west and north, and the third north, straight toward the settlement of Southwark. Its remaining inhabitants watched in terror, the warriors approaching them. Many ran, clutching children to them and made for any woodland or boats moored on the river. Some of the stubborn even emerged from houses with an odd collection of old weapons and sharpened tools, in the misguided belief that they could repulse an attack. Some just stood and wailed, not knowing what else to do.

Oh, the horror! William's men gained pace and, with a great howl, descended on Southwark. A few brave men stood their ground but soon fell under the vastly overwhelming force. Sword clashed against old sword. Sharp spear thrust against hoe and scythe. Blood flowed and mingled with the mud of the settlement's streets. A large man roared his defiance and dashed forward to attack a rider. The Norman saw the attack just in time to wheel his horse and flash his sword. The large man's head rolled into a clump of grass and a woman behind him wailed as his lifeless body slumped to the ground before her.

Within a minute, the woman herself was lying prone in the dirt, a bloodstain spreading over the back of her dress where a spear had pierced her body and split open her heart.

A dog ran out, barking and snapping at the invaders. It howled as a Norman sword caught it across the side of the head, and it fell to the ground, tongue lolling, panting and mewing until it breathed no more.

And so the slaughter continued. Now men strode the settlement with burning brands. They set them to thatch and wattle until smoke and flames rose from every building. From some buildings, terrified residents fled, only into the weapons of the Norman soldiers. Many were cut down before they had made but a few strides from their burning homes. Norman soldiers laughed as they forced Saxons back into the flames of their homes with their spears. The screams of the burning could be heard over the noise of battle, and the smell of roasting flesh permeated the air.

Upon the defences of London, the people stood and watched, transfixed, at the scene that was playing out before them. Surely this was a nightmare from which they would wake? But all knew that it was not. Was this the fate that was yet to come for them? Would reinforcements come to relieve them? What price their defiance now?

As the flames began to burn themselves out and the smell of burning thatch and charred flesh began to give way to the acrid stink of smoking embers, William's men retreated to their lines. His camp was now packed up and, within an hour, began to move off to the west. The defenders watched it leave, incredulous that William had not continued his attack, but also worried and wondering what the Norman's next move would be.

# CHAPTER TWENTY-THREE

During the following days, William led his forces along the long stretch of the river, watching wildfowl and herons rise from the water as they passed by, until they found a crossing point. His scouts, including more than one Saxon who saw a chance to save his own skin, found a shallow spot at a small place called Wallingford. Norman horses, men and wagons of supplies waded out into the stream and gingerly felt their way to the farther shore. There were a few slips, and horses and men tumbled clumsily into the stream, to the great amusement of their fellows, who laughed and slapped their thighs in mirth at the site of soldiers wading, soaked, to the bank, but eventually, the force regrouped on the opposite bank of the Thames. A wagon had broken a spoke on the river stones, and carpenters were quickly at work fashioning a new one from an ash bough.

All the while, as William's men travelled, the landscape behind them was ravaged and burnt. People were thrown from their homes and butchered, whilst their hovels were set alight and everything that was of any use was taken.

The bloodied bodies of men, women and children littered the ground of small villages and settlements, where crows gathered to peck out eyes and pull at bloated bodies and putrefying flesh. Farm animals too were taken – some alive and some slaughtered to feed the Norman invaders. The land to the south and west of London was gradually laid waste! No doubt, the defenders of London would be kept informed of the carnage taking place, and it would prey upon their minds. But then, that was the intention.

In late November, with a deep mist upon the land, William and his forces reached Berkhamstead. Here they set up a wet and miserable camp once again and went about the daily round of chores and tasks that befall an invading army. Fires were built and meat roasted on spits above it. Men sat down with jugs of ale they had stolen from the villages they had pillaged. They cleaned off the dried blood, sharpened weapons and ran running repairs to boots and clothing. They rested.

William was not quick to send out messengers again. He knew that the people of London would know by now that he had crossed the river. They would know what he had left in his wake. The Saxons had their spies, just as he did. He knew that the people of London would be terrified and wondering what his next move would be. He would let them wait and stew for a while.

Eventually, in early December, as hard frosts gripped the land and men flapped their arms about them and blew their nails, and when he felt that the people of London had stewed for long enough, William sent out another delegation of messengers, protected by fifty troops – he didn't feel that a greater force was necessary. Again, they left London William's declaration of intent and his price for peace. Surely, after watching the demise of Southwark and the lands along the valley of the river, the people would recognise the futility of resistance. But the negotiators had to ride back, equipped only with further proposals for the Norman leader to consider.

William, now incredulous, though, secretly, also somewhat impressed by the courage of the Saxon people he would shortly rule, issued one final ultimatum.

"Take this to London," he said to his hand-picked messengers. He fixed his seal, rolled up a parchment and tied it securely. He turned to his council of advisors. "As we agreed, I have guaranteed that London will be spared the carnage we have inflicted upon the surrounding area if Edgar abdicates and I am recognised as the rightful king." The advisors nodded and chorused their agreement. Still, many wondered if the people of London would ever agree to this, or whether further blood must be spilled to achieve their aim.

At length, on a bitterly cold day, a group of Saxon messengers and a small patrol of troops were led into the Norman camp. William had been alerted to their imminent arrival and pushed aside the opening flaps of his tent, striding out onto the crisp, frost-rimmed grass beneath his feet. He stood there, wrapped in a cloak of black bear fur and a beaver fur hood. Strapped to his sides were a sword and seax. His bodyguards crowded behind him as the delegation approached. The horses were stopped and the riders dismounted. They were quickly relieved of their arms. The troop of Saxon soldiers was quickly surrounded by Norman troops, and they eyed each other warily. Norman hands touched sword hilts. Saxon hands couldn't.

The messengers approached William and were halted by spear-wielding guards when they were but a few paces distant. The men dropped politely to one knee and then rose again. "My lord," one man began, "we bring an answer to your latest ultimatum."

"My *last* ultimatum," William replied.

"Eh, quite so, my lord. The Witan Council have asked that you make your way to London. They will meet with you in a great field before the city, where they will discuss your ultimatum."

"What is to discuss?" challenged the Norman. "I have made it quite clear that this is my final ultimatum. Anything else will lead to military action and blood will be spilt. Most will be Saxon!" He glowered at the messengers.

The Saxons visibly wilted under the hot breath of the Count of Normandy. They cowered, shaking with fear. "My lord, I am sure that all areas of your ultimatum will be acceptable to the Witan."

"Acceptable? How many times must I explain the situation to you Saxons?" He sat back into a chair that a servant had quickly placed behind him. He fumed. He glared again at the Saxon messengers before him, who, I am quite certain, would rather have been anywhere than where they were. "I will be at the gates of London tomorrow ... along with my troops! I will meet your Witan and then I will *tell* them what is to happen. Should they disagree with one word of what I have to say, I will unleash my forces upon London. I am quite sure that you all witnessed what happened to your settlement on the south side of the river. I cannot believe that you would want the same to happen again." His words were slow and deliberate. The meaning could not be misinterpreted. A murmur of approval ran around the Norman watchers.

The Saxons bowed their heads and their leader simpered. "I assure you, lord, that all will be well by the morrow."

"Hm. I wonder if my message would be more forceful if you returned to London butchered like a stag at the hunt and tied to the back of your horses?"

"Lord, I beg you. Allow us to return and emphasise your determination to reach a peaceful agreement."

"Take them away!" And the men were bundled back onto their horses, whose rumps were slapped so that they sprang into a gallop, followed by the raucous laughter of the Norman soldiers.

On the following morning, after another cold and frosty dawn, the Norman soldiers packed up their camp and prepared themselves for the short journey to London. Their horses trotted across the frozen ground, their hooves sounding hollow on the frost. The Normans could not drive them faster, as a horse that slipped on the hardened mud threatened not only to injure itself, but to injure or even kill its rider.

They soon rounded a bend and could see before them the tents erected by the Saxon Witan for their 'meeting'. As soon as the Normans appeared, the camp burst into a hustle and bustle of life, as servants and men-at-arms rushed to do their appointed tasks and to be in their appointed positions. William paused momentarily, before waving a hand casually to lead his troops forward.

As they approached, commanders began to bark orders and the Norman soldiers began to deploy around the periphery of the area. Here they would sit until they knew for certain what the outcome of the meeting would be. Each man knew exactly what to do in any situation. Many hoped in their hearts that the Saxons would not submit to their master, for then the bloodletting could continue. Their bloodlust was up and they wanted to kill again!

William and his advisors and bodyguard approached the largest tent and stood their horses. The tent was red and yellow, with small yellow flags flying from its twin peaks. No doubt it was meant to look grand, but if William was impressed, he certainly didn't show it.

A heartbeat later, the tent flaps opened and members of the Witan spilled forth. The leading member was Ansgar, the Sheriff of Middlesex. He nodded his head to William and addressed him. "Count William. I am honoured to meet you. Will you do us the honour of dismounting and joining us in our tent for refreshment?"

William looked at the assembled throng of Saxon nobles, each man dressed in his winter best of furs and thick wool. Chains hung around necks and glittering brooches fastened heavy cloaks around the shoulders. Furs topped heads in an attempt to keep their owners warm in the chill air. One young man caught William's eye. He was young and fresh-faced and seemed dispirited – perhaps more dispirited than the other Saxon nobles. He looked up at William from beneath hooded brows and his mouth seemed to pout in something of a sulk.

The Norman Count nodded and dismounted, followed by his advisors and commanders, who had waited to see their leader make the first move.

A small group of stewards came forward to collect the weapons of the Norman guests, as was the custom. William flashed one look of contempt and the stewards shrank back. The snub did not go unnoticed by the members of the Witan. And swords remained in Norman scabbards.

The men disappeared into the tent. Inside, tables had been spread with a sumptuous feast and servants scurried around to bring food and drink to the assembly, as they took their seats.

Ansgar rose from his seat and addressed the assembled antagonists. "My lords of Normandy, may I introduce the members of the Witan." He waved a hand at each man, who nodded as he was introduced. "The Archbishop of Canterbury. The Archbishop of York." Further nobles were introduced, but William was not listening. Ansgar's voice was but background noise. His attention was, again, fixed upon the young man on Ansgar's right hand. The young man looked at the table before him, hardly raising his eyes from the board. How nervous he seemed. "And on my right hand," Ansgar continued, "I have pleasure in introducing my lords to Lord Edgar, ... our chosen leader," he continued, not knowing quite how that introduction would go with his dangerous visitors.

William's eyebrows leapt. So he was right! This was indeed the Atheling who had usurped the throne – his throne. This callow youth was the choice of the Saxon Witan to lead them against his forces.

Ansgar continued. "My lords, the Witan has assembled to discuss the situation in which we all find ourselves. We had indeed elected Edgar to be our king, following the unfortunate death of King Harold." The assembly shuffled uneasily. Norman hands strayed toward sword hilts, but William sat as still as stone and his supporters relaxed.

"Lord Edgar," Ansgar continued again, "has come to the decision that it would be to the benefit of all if he was to abdicate his throne and accept your lordship as the rightful successor to Harold and Edward before him."

Ansgar sat and all eyes fell upon the young man. He rose from his seat and spoke for the first time. William thought that the speech was forced, and could understand the reason why. "My lord, Count William, it is as my lord Ansgar has outlined for you. It is my decision," and at that he paused and looked around at the Witan, who, to a man, avoided his eyes. "It is my decision," he repeated, "that I will indeed stand aside and abdicate my throne in favour of your claim. I hope that our people will be able to live in peace and harmony, and that the senseless slaughter will cease." Norman hands strayed again to sword hilts and men leaned forward. William stiffened and then relaxed again, as the young Edgar rounded the table and knelt at his feet. The Norman held out his hand and Edgar took it and kissed it. Now the other members of the Witan followed, all looking relieved that the ordeal was over and that bloodshed had been avoided.

William sat, relaxed now, and looked around him. Finally, he spoke. "My lords, I am delighted that we could come to an agreement upon the succession to the throne of England. It is, after all, what the good Edward wanted and what he promised to me before his death.

"I can make a promise, this day, to rule the land well and fairly, with mercy and justice. I intend to move my forces to a place called Romford, where I hear that there is appropriate land and fresh water to accommodate us. From there, we will take stock and decide on our next movements in settling this fair land to peace and tranquillity."

"I will, however, require you to provide a number of appropriate hostages, who will be well treated but kept with us. That will ensure that no man in the land will try to renege on the agreements made today and attack myself or my warriors."

The Saxon earls and important people assembled gasped. "My lord," began Ansgar, "why would you need hostages? We have all agreed on what is to happen in the future. I can assure you that no man here would break the oaths we have pledged today!"

"*You* might assure me, Ansgar, but there are many men in this land who have not made an oath today. They are not bound by your oath. And therefore, it will be as I have said. Edgar will be amongst the hostages."

The Witan looked from one to another. This was unexpected. William had accepted their agreement and oaths, as they had expected, but hostages? This was another matter. They had hoped that William would be a benevolent king, but now they were less sure.

William was duly crowned on Christmas day, 1066, at Westminster Abbey. And what a change was to come to the country of England!

But it was not all to end happily for my people, for during the coronation, many people in the abbey began to shout their acceptance and allegiance to William. However, the troops stationed outside the abbey began to be nervous at all the roaring from within, and thought that a rebellion had broken out. They feared for their leader's life.

"Drive back this mob!" cried a senior commander of the Saxons crowding the precincts of the abbey to catch a glimpse of their new Norman ruler. The soldiers pushed and the crowd slowly but resentfully moved back to the narrow surrounding streets.

Now, becoming more afraid of an outbreak of violence from their new subjects, new orders were barked out. "Raise the area! Burn down the houses! We must cow this Saxon mob!" And so it was that the troops began to lay waste to the area. Many of the Saxon leaders tried to speak to the Norman commanders, but most could not understand the language of the other, and so carnage was the sad result.

And what of the legacy of the battle and its consequences? Well, all was recorded in a great tapestry, made at Bayeux, I understand. Its story is, of course, from the Norman point of view. History is always written by the victors.

It is said that, after the battle was over and bodies lay scattered across Senlac Hill, Harold's mother, Gyrtha, begged William to return to her his body for proper burial. She had even offered Harold's own weight in gold for the body. But the victorious William refused the old woman's request. The stories are confused and I have heard many versions. Some say that the Saxon king's body was thrown into the waves to be devoured by the fishes. Others say that he was buried on the beach at Pevensey Bay. Others still that he was buried at Waltham Abbey. We shall never know the truth of it.

Although he ascended the throne in London, William still maintained Winchester as the capital of the land.

The Battle of Hastings also had a great influence on other areas of English life. Many new words entered the English language from the French-speaking Normans.

William's conquest of England placed yet another foreign king on the English throne, and that changed the society from a Scandinavian one to a more central European one. Much was to change! More terror was to come!

This was the last successful invasion of my land.

# CHAPTER TWENTY-FOUR

I was home. Back in the bosom of my family. It was but a few short days to Christmas, and the preparations were in full swing for the festival.

But the home-coming and the season were not as joyous an occasion as they normally were. This year, my father would no longer be there to lead the family celebration, and the role would fall to me. I was now the man of the house; my grandfather too old and frail now to assume the responsibility. I thought I detected a decline in his health and strength since we had all left, no doubt made worse by the loss of his son.

My mother, too, was not herself at this time. Christmas is always a busy time for the women, as they try to make something special from the food we have, but this time she seemed to lack the energy she normally had for the tasks to be done. Of course, my sisters and aunt helped around the house, and that took some of the burden from her shoulders. How my siblings seemed to have grown since I had been away! I suppose they, too, saw a change in me, their older brother. I looked at the members of my family and thought of the changes to all of our lives now. What would happen to us? Would we be able to survive as we had, without my father? I simply didn't know.

There was little that could be done on the land now, as winter held it in its icy grip. Cold winds swirled from the north, bringing rain, stinging hail and finally, a covering of snow. The animals still had to be fed and watered and I rose to the task with my siblings, wrapped against the chill in thick woollen clothes of my mother and aunt's making. How cold it was on those dark, grey mornings, as the sun struggled harder and harder to crawl above the horizon and short days submitted to long bitter nights.

Many of the birds had fled now – to where, I know not. But others had arrived to take their place. Geese and swans had honked their way to our rivers and lakes and nibbled at the short grasses where they could. The mice worked hard to counter the protection we had given to our grain stores. The leaves were long-gone from most of the trees, except those that remain green all year long. My grandfather told me that this was where the spirits hid and lived through the winter. The world around us seemed to have fallen into a deep slumber, from which it would only awake when spring came and the sun warmed it and prodded it back into life.

Twelve days of 'holiday' were approaching, and that would be a bitter-sweet time for my family. Some of the other families had lost men too, so we all understood how each felt. I am certain that the families whose kin had returned safely also understood and, I thought, treated us more gently, as if not quite knowing exactly what to say and do.

But now was not the time to sit and brood. There were still jobs to do. It was Christmas Eve, and all of the men, now including myself, were up in the woodland, dragging home the yule logs that would burn in the great festival fires. My sisters had been out in the wood with my aunt, gathering the holly, ivy, yew and mistletoe that would decorate our home. Here, the spirits of the forest would reside during the cold months, until they were freed again when the spring sunshine warmed the land.

The holly and ivy represented fertility symbols in the old Pagan religions that once dominated our land.

But the holly meant more to us than just a fertility symbol. Holly can be eaten by livestock, despite the sharp thorns, and we used it during the winter as a fodder. The hay and grains would often run short in our area, and without the holly, we would need to slaughter more animals than we needed to.

The mistletoe is also a potent symbol at Christmas time. Mistletoe is a plant which often grows on other trees; in our area in the oak and apple trees. There are many old legends about mistletoe. One, as everyone knows, is that a kiss under the mistletoe would lead us to marry the girl kissed. Of course, we boys avoided it at all costs!

In times gone by, the ancient Druids thought that the mistletoe plant brought health and good luck. It was used to treat some illnesses, though my grandmother had told us that the berries were poisonous and we should be very careful when we handled them. We also believed that the mistletoe would help to ensure a good crop in the next season's harvest.

The yew trees seem to be always putting our new stems from the old trunk. They can live to a very great age. This joining of the old wood and new young shoots symbolises reincarnation and immortality.

Once the work was done, we would all settle into the comfort of home and enjoy a meal cooked by my mother. She would always save a particularly plump bird for Christmas Eve, and this would be followed by honey cakes and ale. How we all enjoyed it, though it seemed a strange meal this year. Everyone tried to be happy and we forced smiles onto our faces. I know that I found it difficult, and I was sure the rest of the family felt the same. I was pleased that my mother had managed to make the festival season as normal as possible, particularly for my younger brothers and sisters, but I still felt that it was strange, not having my father there. Surely, he would walk through the door soon. But, of course, he never did.

Just before midnight, Brother Matthew rang the church bell and we all filed out into the inky blackness and made our chilly way toward the church for Midnight Mass. I looked up at the clear starry sky above us and wondered if my father was looking down upon us.

As we entered the church we blinked in the light from a myriad of candles that burned in the windows and around the walls. The church was decorated in much the same way as our home, (which I always thought was odd, as many of our traditional decorations harked back to Pagan times.) At the rear of the church was a model, carved from wood, of the stable at Bethlehem. In it were the manger with the baby Jesus and the cattle, sheep and donkey, along with figures of Joseph, Mary, an angel and the shepherds.

Brother Matthew welcomed us all and we enjoyed the service, singing carols and listening to the story that we had heard so many times before. But somehow, we never seemed to tire of it. I liked to imagine how scared the shepherds would be when an angel appeared to them from nowhere. And to think of the kings on their camels – it all seemed so exotic to us.

This year, though, Brother Matthew broke off from the service for a short moment to ask us to remember those who could not be with us at this time, and it was at this point that my mother broke down into sobs. I held her to me and my siblings crowded around us. Others in the small congregation were also weeping and those who had not lost loved ones looked on sadly. What could they say or do to make it any better?

On Christmas morning we arose early and dressed again in our clean clothes. The bell rang out again and we repeated our journey to church. The church was brightly lit, with weak sunlight streaming through the windows, and looked well, I thought, in its finery of holly, ivy, mistletoe and yew.

Brother Matthew led the service again, but this time there was no mention of absent friends. We sang and said prayers and listened as the Brother preached his Christmas sermon, reminding us all why we were there.

Once the sermon was over, some of the village folk entertained us with a Christmas play. The 'angels' appeared, singing "Glory to God in the Highest'" and the characters assembled at the chancel step. I enjoyed the spectacle, especially when Martha forgot her lines and stood, mute, staring out at us, until Brother Matthew prompted her with the whispered words, "Behold the Christ Child." People smiled, not wanting to appear rude, though some of the children giggled, getting a look of annoyance from Martha in return!

After the religious duties of the day were over, we returned home briefly before setting off for Cerdic's hall. We all trooped into the brightly lit hall, each with our own wooden plate and a piece of cloth to protect our laps from spills and to wipe chins clean. In the centre of the hall, a great fire was blazing and torches around the walls also contributed to the warmth and cosiness.

Soon, one of Cerdic's chief servants blew on a horn as a signal to the assembled throng to take their seats at the long tables and benches. My mother fussed around my younger siblings, seating them carefully and tucking their cloths into the necks of their tunics.

The tables were laid with flat bread, which some used as plates, and salt cellars, along with huge jugs of ale, almost too heavy for me to lift.

Once everyone was settled, Cerdic and his family greeted us all and took their places at the top table. A couple of Cerdic's men began a wail on the bagpipes and this heralded a slow procession from Cerdic's kitchen. The servants appeared at the tables, carrying great bowls of hot, steaming food. There was venison and hare, roasted chickens and geese, (I always enjoyed the greasy meat!), and there were great platters of beef and pork.

Once the main meal was finished and cleared away by the servants, fruit, jellies and sweet cakes arrived for our pleasure. How we feasted. Our stomachs were full to bursting and one of my sisters began to look a little pale, after the fourth honey cake. My mother would not let her eat more. Some of the men, and not just one or two of the ladies were decidedly merry by this time, having supped Cerdic's ale in copious amounts.

Once the feasting was over, the tables were quickly cleared to the sides and space made for the music, dancing and games that were to follow. A great game of blind-man's-bluff was played, and Luke chased the children around the hall – eyes covered and arms outstretched, accompanied by much laughter and merriment when he tripped over a bench. Some of the servants took up their instruments to play for us. One man had a harp. Another had a fiddle. Two more had a drum and pipe. They struck up some of the old tunes we all knew and everyone joined in as they sung ballads about bold deeds and battles that had been fought and were famous in our history. I have to say that this brought back to me the memories of the battles that I had been involved in at such a young age, and about finding my father lying dead on Senlac Hill. My mind flashed back to events of those terrible days. Would they ever leave my memory, or was I damned to remember them forever?

Soon, people began to dance to the beautiful sound of the instruments. There were circular dances, where people sang, and dances in long lines too. I had never been fond of dancing, but one of the local girls dragged me up and made me join in with a line dance. I could feel my face becoming hot and the redness spreading through my cheeks. My brothers and sisters giggled and pointed, much enjoying my discomfort! Mother just smiled as she watched my clumsy attempts at line-dancing. I wondered if, in her heart, she was remembering how it had been with my father, and how they too would have been on the floor by now, twisting and twirling to the rhythm.

All at once, there was the noise of people shouting outside and a heavy rap at the door. We all stopped dancing and looked to the great doors. We knew what was to happen now – it was the same each year. The great door was opened and in came the strangest creatures you have ever seen, to great cheers and laughter. It was the village mummers. Of course, everyone pretended not to know who they were. They wore strange head-masks. There were goats, rabbits, deer and donkeys. There was a great bird of prey and a sheep. They proceeded to the centre of the floor, as we tried to look puzzled and asked who these 'strange creatures' might be. The children, of course, were spell-bound.

The mummers laid down long sticks and performed a dance over them. Then they cleared the floor and a play ensued. It was about old St. George.

Well, the fun and games went on until quite late and my younger siblings were, by now, lying at the side of the hall in slumber. At last, we all began to collect our things and went to thank Cerdic for his hospitality. (He really was a kindly then!) Then we gently awoke the older children and carried the little ones back to our home, where we laid them softly to sleep again. What a day it had been!

And was it all to end there? No, of course not! Could the good people of this land have hoped for peace and tranquillity, given what had happened? I suppose not.

But I am tired now, and must end my tale and take my rest. I am an old man, but the memories of those days linger in my mind like a disease and trouble me in the dark hours when sleep refuses to come.

You must wait for tomorrow to hear the rest of this sorry tale!

End

# NOTES

- William of Normandy was attracted to England as it was a 'rich' island. This was what had also attracted the Romans, Saxons, Norse and Danes, over the centuries.
- William had around 6000 men at Hastings. Many were mercenaries who were dismissed in 1070, when William finally felt that the north was defeated.
- William won at Hastings because his army was more specialised for war than the English, who still fought mainly on foot, using battle-axes. The Normans also had mounted troops, who fought with the sword and lance.
- Some of the English warriors travelled to Scotland to serve Malcolm.
- After the conquest, all land belonged to the king. Everyone else was a tenant of William. They held their land in return for service to the king. This was new to English thought.
- The Normans built castles in every county town.

Many houses were demolished to make way for them. A Constable commanded each castle. Other castles were built as they were needed, at the king's expense, though rich lords built their own private castles to defend the land they oversaw. The general plan and layout of all castles was much the same.

- Robes were worn to keep out the draughts. Masters and knights could afford squirrel fur. Lesser men wore rabbit skins.

- The central point of life was the hall, where meals were served and the public life of the household took place. A steward would look after the pantries, whilst the master butler took care of the cellars. The safest place in the castle was the bedroom, where personal treasures would be kept.

- William held three feasts per year. At Easter, he would be at Winchester. He spent Whitsuntide at Westminster, and Christmas at Gloucester. These were great social occasions, and were used by the greater men of the realm to discuss matters.

- For most English, life continued as normal. Life was simple - everything was scarce! Hunting was important, if the lord wanted enough meat for two meals a day. (Some meat had to be salted down for the winter.) Peasants would eat little meat. On occasions, they would eat game and fowl. Salt was expensive, even though it is a necessity of life. Salt pans were built along the coasts to produce it. Salters would bring it inland in carts. (Have you ever noticed roads in our towns called 'Saltergate' or something similar?)

Pepper and spices were also very expensive. (To pay a 'peppercorn rent' – a very low rent, paid for in pepper.)

- Fish that was eaten included pike, roach, bream, dace, eels and lamprey, as well as trout and salmon.
- Fruit and vegetables were seasonal and generally poor quality, compared to our food today. Honey was used for sweetening. Sugar was available, but only to the rich. It came from sugar beet.

# ABOUT THE AUTHOR

Graham Temby was born and grew up in County Durham, where he still lives in the town of Bishop Auckland with his wife. He has two grown children and two grandchildren.

Graham spent over thirty years as a primary school teacher in Lancashire and Darlington, where he spent most of his years teaching Year 6.

In his spare time, he is the Education Officer for Durham County Badger Group. http://durhambadgers.org.uk, where he has written an extensive Education section, containing much that a teacher could need in most primary subjects. (Not everything is to do with badgers, but badgers are often used as a 'vehicle' for learning.) The site also contains fun activities for children and is FREE to use.

In 2014, Graham became a police volunteer, and travelled around the county to primary schools, where he spoke to children about wildlife crime.

Graham also volunteers for archaeological excavations.

Aclyt is Bishop Auckland, Graham's hometown.

Lightning Source UK Ltd.
Milton Keynes UK
UKHW022240010622
403825UK00007B/368

9 781739 875107